LEAVES UPON THE RIVER

LEAVES UPON THE RIVER

A Novel By ROBERT K. WEN

iUniverse, Inc.
New York Lincoln Shanghai

LEAVES UPON THE RIVER

iUniverse, Inc.

For information address:
iUniverse, Inc.
2021 Pine Lake Road, Suite 100
Lincoln, NE 68512
www.iuniverse.com

ISBN: 0-595-27709-8

Printed in the United States of America

This book is dedicated to the author's mother, Wen Luo Shenghua; his father, Wen Keli; his brother Wen Guoyu; and his teacher, Grace Brady.

Acknowledgement

The author wishes to thank Marshall Chao, Jacquie Foss, Mabelle Hsueh, and Patricia Wen for their generosity of spirit and of time in their careful review of the first draft of the book. He also wishes to thank the iUniverse reviewers for their conscientious work, which has been very helpful for the revision. He is indebted to Linda Ames for her comments on the poems in this volume. Appreciation is due Judy Wen, and Robert Ullmann for their helpful comments.

CHAPTER 1

❁

At the Taipei crematorium, as Jing Guoda watched, his older brother Rende made arrangement to have their mother's ashes stored there temporarily. They returned to the apartment. Fuli, their father, seemed to be in a more relaxed mood, which they also shared after all the activities and emotions of the past few days. After dinner, Rende dozed off on the sofa. Fuli said to Guoda, "Why the hurry that you have to go back so soon?"

"My classes begin next Monday. Leaving tomorrow, I'd be home by Friday afternoon."

"You said this is your last year of teaching."

"Yes. After that I'd be a consultant to the university for one year. Then, I'll be officially retired."

"Do you get paid as a consultant?"

"Of course, I'd still be a full-time faculty member."

"Why would you retire? You are still energetic."

"Didn't I write you and Mama about that? I'd like to do something else other than academic engineering while I still have some energy left. I wouldn't like to follow a colleague, who had his last breath behind a stack of ungraded papers."

"Are you being forced to retire?"

"No. Because I would like to use some of my time left to write," Guoda said. He has not been listening to me.

"The short story you sent me is pretty good, certainly better than the pages you wrote in Hong Kong as I remembered."

"Thank you. I had forgotten all about those scribbles. That was so far back...so childish, rubbishy."

"Can you sell this short story?"

"I don't believe so. I am still learning."

"You wouldn't make much money this way."

"It'll probably cost me some. I hope I could afford it. I have worked for financial security all my life up to this point. Barring out of control inflation, my pension should suffice; my needs are relatively simple."

"Good enough!" Fuli said. "But if I were you, I would try to write for publication, say, in magazines like *Harper's* and *The Atlantic.*"

"You are putting pressure on me again!"

"Why would I pressure you now? Whatever I did when you were young, I did for your own good," Fuli said.

"But you are being unrealistic, and unfair." Guoda would like to tell his father why not apply his standards to himself, like getting published in *The Atlantic.* "Yaya (father), I used to try to please you. With you I could never use age as a talking point. Nevertheless, now having passed sixty myself, I think it is about time that I please myself first. From now on, I am going to do whatever I please."

"You have been doing that for some time now. Haven't you?"

Guoda paused for a second, "You are probably right."

A year and half later. Mrs. Ju, his father's part-time housekeeper, called: "For two days in a row the old gentleman had gotten up at 5 o'clock to join a mountain climbing group. Now he is sick in the hospital…." Guoda at once saw a long flight ahead of him. He had been enjoying his first summer after retirement—the three R's: reading, writing and racquet. It took some 17 hours to cross America and the Pacific and land in Tao Yuan Airport, Taiwan, on a Friday night in mid-July.

He had only a carryon—a retirement gift from the Department of Civil Engineering at Wisconsin Technical University (WTU). Together with two other travelers, he got in a taxi. All the way the driver chattered animatedly like a comedian about Taiwan politics—Election Day tomorrow—whisky and aphrodisiacs.

Guoda was let off at Banjiao Hospital around eleven. The place was impressive; well lighted, it looked modern and clean, and felt cool and dry in contrast with the cloying humid warmth outside. He identified himself and his purpose to the security person behind a desk. After casting a glance at the carryon on wheels, the man looked up a list and sent him to the 7th floor. The lobby and hallway were eerily quiet in bright bluish light—like some hospital scene in a

Friday night suspense movie—except for the echoing, low grinding of the wheels.

The door was open. In fluorescent light a bed by the window was empty. Against the inside wall was another bed. On it lay an old man, almost bald, his eyes closed. Guoda called lightly, "Yaya!" Fuli opened his eyes, focused, and croaked, "Guoda, you have come." The son bent over and gave the father a partial hug.

"Where is Rende?" Fuli asked.

"He is at his home in California. He has been in poor health recently, and as you probably know, Sister-in-law just had an operation for her colon cancer. After her first post-operation check up, he would come if needed. How do you feel?" Guoda asked.

"Tired. I had overexerted myself."

Someone came in the room. A fortyish woman, in a dark shirt and trousers, not a nurse, rather like a local shopkeeper. "I am Mrs. Wu. I've been helping to take care of Mr. Jing. You are—"

"I am his second son."

"You must have just come from America?" She noticed the carryon. "You must be tired. Should rest soon then."

"Guoda," Fuli said, his eyes closed, "sleep on the other bed."

Guoda wasn't particularly keen on being inside a hospital, let alone sleeping in it, and he didn't appreciate Fuli's commanding tone of voice. But it was late, and he was relieved seeing now that his father was not in as bad a condition as he had feared. After the woman left, fatigue caught up with him and he soon fell asleep on the other bed.

Next morning, he was awakened by muffled fusillades of firecrackers and rhythmic shouts. Out the window, down on the street a truck moved slowly with droves of people following. Fuli chatted a little about Taiwan politics and the electioneering before returning to his health. He confirmed Mrs. Ju's account of his mountaineering and it as the probable cause of his problems.

Guoda went to the nurses' station. The nurse on duty, after looking at the records, said that there was water in the patient's lungs and more tests were needed, but they couldn't be done today; it being Election Day, a holiday, no doctor would come to work.

In the afternoon Fuli handed Guoda a ring of keys for his apartment and desk. "Go over everything in the desk," he said.

Guoda slept in the apartment from that night on. It had two bedrooms, one and a half baths, a living room, a kitchen and a veranda in the front and another at the back, both protected by metal gratings. He slept in his father's room; it had a 3/4 ton air conditioner that would also cool the living room some when the door between the two rooms was left open.

In Fuli's desk he found old resident certificates, passports, employee identifications, bank statements, commendations, receipts, and letters from friends and relatives, etc. There was also another small sheaf of letters, separately clipped together. He had some qualms about reading them, but curiosity won, aided by his father's words, "Go over everything." The letters were all from a woman. Apparently she was a schoolteacher, married, living with her husband and two children in a small town south of Taipei. All the letters appeared innocent enough, almost identical in substance, thanking Fuli for writing to her and apologizing for not replying sooner. One letter welcomed his proposed visit. The next thanked him for the visit and the box of chocolate he had brought her, which she shared with some of her colleagues, her husband and her two "small dogs" (old-fashioned Chinese reference, affecting modesty, to one's young sons).

Each letter, addressing him as Mr. Jing, had some words of solicitude like "You should take care of yourself in your old age...." Only one appeared to reflect a somewhat deeper feeling, seemingly more on his part than hers: "...Today riding onto the hill, I saw a hauler on the road, about 50 or 60 years old, carrying two big bulging cloth bags, the contents of which I couldn't guess. Anyway, the man seemed at ease, treaded along lightly and at a good pace. A while later, nearing the gate of the school, I came on a white-haired, old woman bearing a load of produce on her shoulder—to the market, I suppose. Initially I felt some pity for her. But seeing the expression on her face, showing life's joy, I realized that my sympathy was not needed. Instead, I saw that everyone has their individual life pattern. Life grows in that stream of industry and efforts. One must accept one's own life, and enjoy the happiness it offers. I hope you, living alone, would recognize and enjoy your own life...."

Guoda couldn't help feeling a little sorry for his father's loneliness as well as respect for the schoolteacher for her good heart and good philosophy.

In addition to jet lag and things on his mind, the loud frogs in the bamboo grove behind the row house kept him awake much of the night. The next morning, he chewed a piece of ginseng from a bunch that he had brought with him, hoping it would help to keep his energy level up.

In the hospital still no doctor came because it was Sunday. He stayed in the room to keep his father company. Two young women nurses breezed in, greeting the patient in a singsong, took readings of his vital signs and waltzed out. Just you wait, thirty years in a wink! Guoda warned them in his head. Mrs. Wu stopped by, bringing Fuli's washed clothes and left. Guoda had learned from a nurse that Mrs. Wu was hired by the family of a final stage Alzheimer patient as a full-time (24 hours) caregiver, and that she was a devout Buddhist. (Professional caregivers were hired outside the hospital services.) Since the comatose patient's room was just down the hall, she was able to spend some time to help Fuli. She would cook for him and change his bed sheets, generally supplementing whatever the nurses couldn't or wouldn't do.

Guoda finally got a chance to talk to his father's physician, who told him that Fuli's problem might be tuberculosis or simple infection. Monday morning, over 1000 cc of fluid was drained from the patient's chest and sent to a pathology laboratory in the city (Taipei). After that, Fuli seemed weaker, having a slight temperature, wouldn't eat much and complained of discomfort in the abdomen. In the late afternoon a Mrs. Chen, recommended by Mrs. Wu, came to be his full-time caregiver as requested by Fuli.

With Mrs. Chen's care the patient seemed more settled; his abdomen felt better after an enema. But then he complained to Guoda that she was too "strict and severe." Guoda saw no sign of impropriety and thought that perhaps a caregiver needed a certain amount of firmness in doing her job, so he did nothing.

There wasn't much to do except waiting for the report from the pathology laboratory. Guoda went to the hospital every morning, taking his daily little stick of ginseng, and returned before supper. In-between he talked desultorily with Fuli, when the father felt like talking. Much of the time Guoda would read or listen to mostly Mozart, on a Walkman, while Fuli slept.

This day, Guoda decided to go into the city to pay his respects to the few elder close relatives and friends who had remained on the island. There used to be more; practically all had come from the Mainland. Most of them had left now—gone to Australia, Canada, or the United States.

First he visited his Uncle Xian, a relative on his mother's side and a retired colonel of the Army. In the early 1950s, when Guoda was waiting in Taiwan for his visa to America, the army pay was so low that Major Xian then was nearly destitute. It was rumored that his wife had died of malnutrition. Now he had remarried, and the dramatic upturn of the Taiwan economy had enabled the army to handsomely reward its loyal members. His pension afforded him a comfortable living. A dozen years or so younger than Fuli, he had generously helped him around the apartment, when a younger hand was needed. Fuli was appreciative of that, but in the past he had complained to his sons of Xuan's boasting of his youthful appearance, of his full head of black hair at past seventy, and of his sexual prowess with prostitutes.

In his airy and well-appointed apartment, 11 floors up, Xian slowly shuffled out, helped by his wife, spoke haltingly and in a largely unintelligible jumble, stopped and then sobbed. He had suffered a stroke. Guoda stayed for a while, talking mainly with his Aunt Xian, presented them with a box of ginseng, and left.

Then he called on his Uncle and Aunt Han, longtime family friends, no relations. Also recovering from a stroke, Uncle Han, once China's minister to France during WWII, came into the living room aided by a helper. Aunt Han shook conspicuously from Parkinson's disease. They visited, updating one another. Before he left, he presented the couple with a box of pears.

After seeing another aunt, who was widowed and also infirm, he went back to the hospital, a little depressed. When Fuli saw him back in the room, he closed his eyes and said, "What kind of shenanigans are you pulling off now, disappearing all day!" Guoda remembered the tone of voice; it wasn't that different from that of decades ago, when he came home, if only minutes late, from high school. Odd enough, the reproof, offensive as it was, seemed to him now to have a beneficent aspect—it signified that he still had a living parent, and that fact could be a sort of shield against the pounding of time. He gave his father a brief report of the visits, which was ignored.

The next morning, the attending physician came in and told them that the pathology laboratory report had come; it indicated that the patient had TB of the lung. A standard treatment would now follow the firm diagnosis.

To seek a second opinion, Guoda took the report and went to see the Chief Physician of the Chest and Heart Division of the Central Clinic in the city, one of the best medical centers on the island. The doctor agreed with his colleague at Banjiao Hospital. The treatment would consist of 10 tablets of antibiotics a day for 6 to 9 months. However, it would take only two weeks after the start of the treatment that the patient would be considered no longer a transmitter and released from the hospital. Then what?

CHAPTER 2

Guoda had been in touch with Rende since his arrival. They had agreed that their father should not live by himself in the apartment after he was discharged from the hospital. A nursing home seemed the most practical. (Fuli had talked about living in a Buddhist monastery. Guoda understood old age's readiness to concede the world for peace and religiosity; nevertheless, the monastery idea was a fancy.)

Guoda spent the next few days visiting nursing homes, some mentioned by friends or relatives, but mostly from a list that a friend's secretary had compiled for him. None of the places appealed—hot, humid, odorous air, old folks in wheelchairs, heads drooping to one side, a few tufts of hair clinging like beach grass on sands, eyes either closed or staring blankly into nothing, or at the visitors, eagerly, as if pleading for a word or two. Managers talked of games, TV sessions and changing diapers. Is this to be my final shelter on this earth too? Guoda thought. More than likely? if I live that long.

Guan En Nursing Home, located in the north suburb of the city, appeared relatively suitable. It was up on a hillside, thus cooler. The rooms seemed clean, spacious and well aired. The manager, a thirtyish woman, sounded knowledgeable and professional. The charges were reasonable.

He knew his father would not like to live in a nursing home. To broach the subject, he watched Fuli's mood. On a couple of occasions, when he brought up the subject of continuing convalescence after leaving the hospital, Fuli would say, "I am tired," and close his eyes. Guoda would then desist.

He needed to find someone to be Fuli's local guardian after he left Taiwan. There was no relative or friend close and young enough to be considered for such a responsibility. The idea of setting up a trust suggested itself. He spent almost a whole day in visiting a number of financial institutions. None offered such services. The trip earned him just a cold and cough from alternations of sweat and air-conditioning. Fortunately, it lasted only a few days.

The treatment for Fuli started. Each morning, Mrs. Chen patiently coaxed and negotiated with him over the rest time between each intake of oatmeal and two of the 10 antibiotic pills. Today, after they finished, he sat in his chair by the bed, looking contented. She took a break and went down the hall to visit with Mrs. Wu.

Judging his father in a fair mood, Guoda told him about the results of his investigations of the nursing homes and futile efforts in finding a trust service. Fuli listened, his expression indifferent. Guoda went on to suggest that Fuli still handle his own money while his part-time housekeeper Mrs. Ju would act as an agent for Guoda and Rende. "I would make all the arrangements to bring this about before I return to America," he told his father.

"When would that be?" Fuli seemed quite alert now.

"In about a week…" He thought he would give a reason, but decided not to. After a moment of silence, Fuli said "I am tired."

The next morning, a Sunday, the hospital was quiet. They talked disjointedly about the weather and Chinese literati for a while. At a pause, Guoda asked, "Have you given some thought to our discussion yesterday?"

"What are you talking about?"

"Your care after I return to America."

"Oh…Would you hand me the pillow. Or better yet, just put it behind my back."

Guoda did as told, and waited.

"I am tired," Fuli closed his eyes, seemingly resting. Suddenly, he said, in a clear voice, "I would like you to send me eight hundred American dollars every month, beginning next month."

Guoda was surprised. "I won't do that. There is no need. You have your own money. I'll send you the usual amount; I'll support you when you need it. I assure you." His midsection tightened as he said this, his conscience was unsure with itself. He had begun sending money to his parents since he was a graduate assistant at the University of Illinois, at US$30 a month. The amount had been steadily increased to $300 a month. Extra amounts were remitted on such occasions as birthdays and illnesses.

He braced for some kind of a confrontation. There was none. Fuli was calm. In a while, he said, "Would you find out for me whether the Bank of America would handle trust?"

Guoda had heard from Rende before that their father would not trust his children with his money. Guoda himself had thought too that sometimes Fuli sounded suspicious and cynical. It is natural for old people to feel insecure on account of their declining faculties and confidence to fend for themselves. Fuli had mentioned to him some horror stories he had heard or read of trusting parents who, after having handed all their savings over to their children, would later be utterly mistreated by them. Therefore, Guoda thought he ought not to have been surprised that his father wanted to continue the trust search. Yet he was.

That evening Guoda went to a dinner hosted by the Hans. Back at the apartment, probably because of the food was too salty, he felt anxious and a little lightheaded—a sign for him of high blood pressure, which normally his daily medication had kept under control. He slept fitfully. Otherwise, nothing untoward happened.

The next morning, he went downtown and found out that the Bank of America wouldn't handle trust cases either. He returned to the hospital. Fuli had a haircut and bath earlier, looking refreshed and rather spirited. He gave no response to Guoda's report on the trust matter. Instead, he asked, "How come your grandparents' tomb looked so messy?"

Guoda had to quickly switch circuits to realize that Fuli was referring to the snapshots of his grandparents' tombs he had taken several years ago when he visited Changsha, Hunan, their native town on the Mainland. "I don't know. Apparently no one had regularly taken care of them. Even just to find them wasn't that easy."

"Why were the tombs moved?" Fuli asked.

"I don't know they had or hadn't been moved," Guoda said, thinking what a strange question. More than I, he should know. This is just his habit and knack of putting pressure on whomever he is dealing with—get the other person on the defensive.

However, Guoda remembered how in years past every summer in mid-July, Fuli would lead his sons in a ceremony at home to honor their ancestors and deceased relatives.

The main preparation for the annual ritual consisted of making a number of paper packages, containing imitation monies, gold and silver ingots (all made of paper). Each package was addressed to a departed relative; its contents varied with the closeness of the relationship. For very close ones, more than one package would be offered. Each was about the size of a pillow. In Guoda's childhood, dozens were made every year.

On the day of the ceremony, the departed relatives would be "invited" into the home with an incantation. Descendants, took turns according to seniority to kowtow to welcome them. Paper money would be burned to pay the servants, who had accompanied them on the trip. They were served with such refreshments as fruits, cakes, and tea. At the head of the dining table stood a tablet—between red candles and behind incense sticks—on which was inscribed: "The Ancestors of the Jing Family through the Generations."

A sumptuous dinner would be served. At the start, Fuli would with all gravitas, like a mandarin before the throne, lead the kowtow sessions. Only male descendants took part in the ceremony, although females did most of the preparations.

Since college, Guoda had gotten away with substituting bowing for kowtowing, claiming as reason his Christian belief. He did it less for the formality of the faith than as a sly protest against the use, or misuse, of ancestral remembrances to strengthen a feudalistic kind of paternal power.

After the (imaginary) dinner and another kowtow session, the guests would take leave; paper money would again be burnt for their attendants. Afterwards, the living would partake of the food. Late in the afternoon, the climax of the whole ritual would take place in the burning of all the prepared packages. The entire ceremony was called *sou bao* (burning packages)—as remittances to the departed relatives. Through the years of changes in physical and economic environment, as well as social norms, the list of addressed departed relatives had been pared down, and so was the number of packages. The practice ceased for the Jing family altogether after Guoda's mother died.

Now Guoda asked his father, feigning innocence, "Did you do anything for the tombs in the years you were in Changsha?" He had a pretty good idea about the truth.

Fuli didn't answer. Instead, he asked, "Do you visit your mother's grave often?"

"Whenever I went to visit Brother." After their mother's body was cremated, Rende had brought the ashes to California and buried them in the Rose Hill Memorial Park in Whittier.

In a while, Fuli said, "I think I should be able to live to 90."

Guoda didn't know right away how to respond to that. "There is no reason why not beyond. On this sort of matter, it's not for us to decide," he tried. Already 88, he isn't asking too much, Guoda thought.

After a silent moment, "Do you believe in religion?" Fuli asked.

Guoda understood that the question referred to not just nominal affiliation to a man-established religion but the existence of some being that governs the universe. "Basically, yes."

They were quiet again for a moment. Then Fuli put his hand on top of Guoda's, which was resting on the arm of a chair next to his, and said, "You are a good son."

Guoda had an impulse to put his other hand over his father's, which felt quite warm. But he didn't. When the moment passed—his father had returned the hand to his own lap—Guoda regretted that he had missed the opportunity. He said, "Brother is a better son than I; in fact he is a better person than I," thinking of all the years Rende, and his wife, Aili, had taken care of their parents in Taiwan, while he had the good life in America.

"I wouldn't say that. He has his good qualities. Loyal, quite capable.... His problem is that he doesn't like books," Fuli said.

"It only affected himself," Guoda said. "Besides, there are lots of successful people who do not like books, and he's been successful."

That afternoon a friend of Guoda's came to the hospital to pay his respects and presented Fuli with a box of peaches. After he left, Fuli gave Mrs. Chen one and proudly told her that the visitor was President of National Central University. He was not that, but only the chairman of one of its departments. Seeing his father in a good mood, Guoda told him of the scenario as he saw it. After another week or so, Fuli would be considered a non-transmitter (of TB) and be released by the hospital. Guan En Nursing Home would send their ambulance to receive him. Mrs. Ju would be his nominal guardian. She would be in regular contact with the brothers in America, and they would make all consequential decisions. Whenever the nursing home called her, she'd call one of them. Fuli listened but had no comment.

Next morning Guoda called the airline to put his name on the waiting list for the Saturday flight (it was a busy time of tourists and Taiwan students going to the United States). He was surprised to hear that, owing to a cancellation, a seat was available on the Thursday flight. He took it, a bit uneasy that Fuli didn't know it yet.

CHAPTER 3

He had hoped that Fuli would say something about the plan he had suggested the day before. Fuli did not. Guoda wrote it out on a sheet of paper and showed it to him and told him that he was leaving in two days. Fuli read it calmly and gave his consent.

At the Bank of Taiwan, with some persistence Guoda convinced the reluctant assistant manager to have Fuli's signature on record, in addition to his chop, as authorization for withdrawal of money. The banker had maintained previously that the chop imprint was enough—a practice that Guoda questioned because the chop could be lost or stolen.

In the evening, he brought back to the apartment a box of fast food. Before he started on it, Mrs. Ju came to the apartment with a thin, lanky man in his mid-forties. "He is the old gentleman's second son," she introduced Guoda to her husband. She had told Guoda before that due to some physical injury her man, a factory foreman, had stopped working, and had been just smoking and drinking, and when he felt like it, would beat her up. Guoda thought it strange why she would put up with that. Besides, it would appear that in a straight physical contest, she should have a pretty good chance to prevail. Perhaps, it was the Taiwan culture.

Guoda showed them the agreement he had drafted, in which she would be the guarantor to the nursing home for Fuli's payment. He explained to the couple that her role would be nominal only, as all significant decisions would be made in America. His initial offer for her trouble was NT$1200 per month, and of course, all actual expenses, such as for telephone and transportation, would be reimbursed to her additionally.

She read it first and handed it to her husband, who, with a cigarette dangling from his mouth and legs knocking, glanced over it quickly and nodded to her. She then told Guoda that the draft was all right. He then said that he'd make copies for them to sign tomorrow.

After they left, he felt a big stone had been lifted from his mind. As he was halfway into his meal, the phone rang. She called to renege, saying that both her mother and an older brother, who, she said, was a branch office manager of some local bank, had told her it was unwise to take on responsibilities of this kind.

Guoda lost his appetite. After pondering the problem for a while, he called to ask her to come to the apartment again. (She lived only a block away.) She did. He asked her to reconsider.

"It's just too much responsibility," she said, sounding resolute.

"How could it be?" he was flustered. "The agreement specifically states that all the decisions and responsibilities are ours, my brother's and mine."

"I can't do it, Mr. Jing. I like to help you and the venerable old gentleman. But I can't."

Perhaps, he thought, it *is* that she wants to be paid more, but face is in the way of asking. "Is this not a matter of money, Mrs. Ju? Suppose I offered you ten million dollars, you'd do it and tell your mother and brother to go away! Right?" She blinked her eyes and studied her black plastic slippers. "How much do I need to offer you for your help?" he asked softly.

After a pause, she said lightly, "I think I would do it for NT$4000 a month, just for you and your family. I wouldn't do this for any other."

He accepted this, affecting a bit of hesitation, not to betray his gladness. This time he asked her to sign the appropriately corrected agreement, copies of which would be made the next day. She obliged him.

The next morning, it was drizzling and gusting. Picking his way in the streets, he made three copies of the agreement in a scribe's office. Back to the hospital, he updated Fuli about the arrangements he had made. "How much are you paying her for it?"

"Initially, I offered her NT$1200 a month—"

"That's ridiculous. You are such a cheapskate!" Fuli interjected.

Guoda quickly added, "I don't know the market of such things. Anyway, we agreed on NT$4000 a month."

"That's better," Fuli said.

Guoda then asked him how to deal with the apartment keys and his bank papers. "You are such a square. Just won't listen," he said.

The remark was a non sequitur; Guoda thought Fuli was simply unhappy. "I only wanted to know what to do with the keys and the bankbook. I don't think that I should take them with me to America."

"Let Uncle Huang take care of them."

Guoda had never met this "Uncle Huang" before. He got his full name and went back to the apartment, found his phone number and called. The man did not decline the request outright, but said, "I am 82 and recently have not been feeling that great myself."

Guoda called Fuli, asking whether he should deliver the bankbook and keys to Huang. Fuli said, "He has already called me. Forget about him. Listen, whatever you decide and do is all right with me." Guoda hung up the phone, feeling a little pricking. The gust and the rain swept into the veranda and darkened its wall. A typhoon advisory was in effect.

He went out and bought a boxed supper and a large vinyl cover envelope, into which he put Fuli's papers: 1. Citizen I.D.; 2. Medical Insurance; 3. Bankbook; 4. Withdrawal forms and a filled out sample; 5. Phone number and address of the manager of Guan En Nursing Home; 6. Phone number of Mrs. Ju; 7. NT$1000 cash; 8. A detailed explanation of how to pay people, and 9. A list of the contents in the envelope.

He ate the food while the wind whistled crisply outside. When he took Fuli's umbrella and went out, it was already dark. The streets seemed deserted. In the hospital, he explained the contents of the vinyl envelope to his father and sat with him for another hour. Neither said much; what was said was about minor matters, like how often would Mrs. Chen wash Fuli's clothes. Although Fuli's eyes were closed most of the time, Guoda knew he was awake, unhappy, probably sad too. Maybe not so sad, for surely he'd know that the separation was inevitable. Guoda was silently wrought-up with the prospect of leaving the place and with guilt. He went to the room a couple doors down the hall and presented a small red envelope containing a gratuity for Mrs. Wu as a token of appreciation for her help. She refused at first, saying that her help was based on her Buddhist faith, but accepted it only after Guoda insisted. When he returned, Fuli complained that he had been out too long. The wind was screaming shrilly through a narrow opening of the window. Guoda went over to shut it tight.

Afraid that he might be stranded in the hospital, he said he had to go. Fuli nodded. Guoda bent over, placing his cheek over his father's. "Yaya, please take care. I'll call you. Rende should be here shortly."

Fuli said, "So long!"

He went out to get Mrs. Chen in Mrs. Wu's room and said good-bye to the women in the soft gaze of a Buddha behind burning candles. He returned to get his jacket. Fuli's eyes were closed, the big envelope beside the almost bald head. Guoda left the room for the last time.

The street was dim. A few cars and motorcycles passed by. The umbrella nearly buckled inside out in the wind. Letting it open halfway, in the shape of a cone, Guoda walked to the left side of the street to intercept a taxi. Several drove past, ignoring him. Finally he reached a major street and got one.

In the apartment, he called to ask Mrs. Ju to come. He paid her the money, including that for her service to the apartment during his stay. She would keep the apartment keys and look in every now and then, on the condition that she wouldn't be held responsible for any loss of property in the apartment besides reporting it to the police. He readily agreed. After she left, he packed, took a sleeping pill and went to bed.

Next noon, in the plane heading for Chicago, he closed his eyes to rest. The thought of Fuli's bald head on the pillow troubled him some; but he tried to assuage the uneasiness by the big envelope he had placed beside it. Gradually, anticipation of seeing his own children and grandchildren in a family reunion in Cape Cod planned a year ago loomed more distinctly than the hospital scene.

CHAPTER 4

Not that long ago Fuli was someone else's grandchild.

Early 20th century, when China was still under imperial rule, in the village of Malin Qiao (Bridge of Mottled Woods) northeast of Changsha, capital of Hunan province, lived the Jings, a small clan. Their ancestors had come from northern China in the 5th century, when the horseback riding "barbarians" of the Asian steppes subjugated the farming Chinese much of the time. Immigration registers at the Yanmen Pass (Wildgoose Gate, which was a checkpoint along the Inner Great Wall in northern Shanxi province) had shown entries with the surname Jing.

By stages, they moved further southward to flee from the marauding nomads and to seek an easier life in a land with more fertile soil and clement climate. By the 14th century, they had settled in Ji'an in Jiangxi province, almost 1000 miles south from the Pass. Half a millenium later, when the country was governed yet by another erstwhile nomadic people from the north—the Manchus—the Jing clan moved again. This time to escape from the spillage of bloody battles between the government troops and the Taiping revolutionary forces, they trekked several hundred miles to the west and settled in the basin of the Xiang River, that part of Hunan often referred to as a "land of fish and rice" (of plenty).

Jing Fuli's grandfather was a farmer. Fuli's father started out as an apprentice in a "money shop"—a proto-bank, performing the rudimentary services of a modern bank—and eventually rose to become a partner. He married late and retired early, in his mid-forties, with a fair-sized fortune. His only son, Fuli, was born in 1908. Later, he adopted a daughter, whom he had intended to be his future daughter-in-law. The plan was subsequently dropped when the marriageable Fuli wouldn't agree to it.

Pampered since childhood, Fuli liked the good life. Besides several tracts of farmland, the family also owned a "sauce shop" (where customers went for cooking needs and delicatessen items), which a relative managed for them. For cash Fuli would go to the shop and demand the money from the manager. A small stack of silver dollars would be handed over to him. When he deemed them not enough, he would simply fling them to the "money bench"—an elongated box along a wall, with its top formed by two boards sloping like a V with a slit at the valley, so that coins from sales tossed over there would slide and fall into the box. Each time he would usually leave with ten silver dollars or so.

He was of average height—the Jing clan was not noted for their stature. But he was handsome, with fair complexion, large, deep-set eyes, thin lips, and a straight, high-ridged nose. His schoolmates and friends called him "ocean man," (i.e., a Caucasian, ocean signified foreign) a nickname that would stick with him even among his relatives. He was not offended, if not pleased, by it. China was at another nadir in her cycles of national fortune. Foreign influence had extended from the coastal areas into parts of the interior. National confidence and self-esteem were low. Almost anything associated with "ocean" was deemed of a better quality than that with the "land," or native, version. Changsha, an inland city, did not have as many foreign ties as some coastal cities, such as Shanghai or Guangzhou. Nevertheless, it had some. The city's Yali Academy that Fuli went to was connected with the Yale Mission of the United States.

Fuli barely got by in his school work except English, in which he did well. In spite of his scholastic mediocrity, he was popular at school because of his outgoing personality, energy and generosity (quick to pick up the tab). In his senior year of high school, he visited his classmate Su Qizhi at his home. The Su family was presided over by its patriarch, Qizhi's grandfather. The patriarch's father had been a governor of Guizhou province and had been posthumously honored with the title "Baron of Martial Perseverance" for his contribution to the suppressing of the Taiping rebels. The patriarch himself had acquired (rumored as purchased) the degree of *Ju Ran* or the third degree in the imperial examination system (highest being the fourth).

At that visit Fuli's appearance impressed Qizhi's father. With additional commendation from his son, he thought the young man would make a good husband for his elder daughter, two years younger than Qizhi. A matchmaker was engaged, photographs were exchanged, and before long Jing Fuli, 18, and Su Qisheng, 16, were married. They had their first look at each other on their wedding night, and both were pleased. In a year, their first son, Rende, was born, followed two years later by a second son, Guoda. A daughter was born a year after Guoda, and a third son, another year later.

Both of Fuli's parents had died of a stroke in their fifties before their son's wedding. Fuli lived his life largely free of restraint, not that his father had imposed much of it either when he was alive. In fact, he had taken Fuli to his first visit to a brothel. His theory was that since it was a virtual certainty that his son would be there some day, it might as well be he who could properly show him the ropes and how to avoid serious pitfalls.

Although married, Fuli continued his life of partying. He loved his wife, but not enough to shun philandering. He compartmentalized his extracurricular activities as a man's due, separate from his familial duties. A Beijing opera aficionado, he played the fiddle and was good at it.

After high school, many of his classmates went on to universities, mostly in Beijing and Shanghai, where his brother-in-law Qizhi enrolled in Quang Hua University. Fuli found himself a job instead, with the Texas Oil Company as an inspector. At the time the main Euro-American business in China's interior was to sell kerosene and tobacco. His main responsibility was to accompany a Caucasian inspector to pay surprise visits to the godowns (warehouses) of their native agents to count kerosene cans. The company consigned cans of five-gallon kerosene to its retail agents around the province. (For much of the population, kerosene was used for lighting at night.) Some agents would delay reporting sales to the company in order to keep the money for the interest it would earn. The company representatives would tally the reported sales with the inventory in the warehouse (the sum should be equal to the total amount consigned). Fuli enjoyed working alongside of his Caucasian colleague, his equal in title but boss in fact. Conversation in English with a Caucasian was the real thing, not practices in school, where even the teacher had a strong Hunan accent when pronouncing English words. Many of the Caucasians sent over to do trade in China's interior were not particularly refined. From them Fuli would pick up cursing in English—language one would not learn in a classroom, but robust-sounding and awe-inspiring. At home, when he became cross, which was not infrequent, he would shout in English at his servants or whoever he considered his inferior, "God damn it!" or "God damn you!"

The Jing family lived in a one-story house with a courtyard behind the gate. The floor of the rooms was of compacted clay. The main room was the sitting room that one would enter from the courtyard over an almost one foot high threshold. A square table stood against the inside wall. Darkly lacquered chairs and tea stands sat along the side walls. In the two corners at the front, hidden in the shade, were two urns that contained pickled peppers. People would eat them as refreshments. The Hunan palate favors hotness, which supposedly also characterizes their temperament.

For transportation the family owned a rickshaw. Like other privately owned rickshaws, it differed from the ones for public hire in its better build and cleaner appearance, even with a touch of luxury, featuring a pair of lanterns with their brass edgings and tops polished to a mirror shine.

Jing Su Qisheng, mistress of the house, was relatively tall. The combination of her shiny eyes, a well-shaped mouth and white, regular teeth would produce a most winning smile. But she very rarely showed that. Her smiles, which appeared often enough, were usually restrained, seldom revealing her teeth, and her demeanor was generally reserved. At the time of her marriage, she had barely completed the second year in Fuxiang Middle School for Girls. Although the school was also affiliated with the Yale mission of America, her outlook was essentially "traditional Chinese": the "Three Compliances and Four Virtues." (The compliances consist of that to father, before marriage; to husband, after marriage; and to the eldest son, if widowed. The virtues include chastity in "morality "; proper diction in "speech"; gentleness in "bearing"; and weaving in "merit.") For years, she would address her husband as "Young Master." It was later changed to "Fuli," when social norms became more modern, i.e., Westernized, her social circles enlarged, and she gained greater maturity and confidence.

She learned her responsibilities quickly. She was soft-spoken, never raised her voice to anyone, but ran the household with effectiveness, assisted by two maids to do the cooking, laundry and cleaning. There was a rickshaw puller, plus one or more wet nurses, one for each child until it reached three. Each morning she would discuss with the cook the menu for the day and go over the expenses of the preceding one.

The children spent more time with the servants than with their parents. Yet between the two parents there were major differences. Father meant sternness, and fear, and mother kindness, and trust. Particularly at night, the children liked how one by one she would gently push the face toward the basin and run the warm, dripping wash cloth cover it, dry it, and then roll up the sleeves, soap the wrists and wash that too. She'd apply a dab of a slightly fragrant cream on each face and send them to bed.

Each fall, it was her job to go down to the village, assisted by a couple of relatives, to collect the grains that the tenant farmers owed the family. She would restrain her assistants from knocking the measuring bucket to compact the contents, saying that it wouldn't be fair to the peasants. The grain collected would be sold for cash.

She would tolerate her husband's philandering and some unwholesome behavior such as gambling—so long they were play—but not behavior that she considered threatening to family security. On one occasion she heard that he was trying out opium smoking while on assignment in a town some sixty mile away; she rushed over there and put a stop to that. From then on, when he had to leave town for any extended length of time, she would accompany him, staying in a hotel or some rented dwelling. The children would be left home in Changsha cared for by a long-time senior maid.

On one such occasion, the second boy, Guoda, complained of discomfort with one of his eyes. The maid noticed a black spot in it. A neighbor told her that if the spot moved to the iris, the eye could go blind. So she took the boy to a Taoist priest. He wrote some symbols on a yellow slip, burned it in a saucer, doused the curling charred paper, and told the boy to open his eyes wide. He sucked the mix into his mouth and, like a cobra, spit it at the boy's eye in question. The kid would not complain about the eye again. After Qisheng learned of the episode, she would put her children in the care of their maternal grandmother when she was going out of town with her husband.

The Su house had several units all fronting a wide, stone-paved yard. The first unit consisted of the kitchen and the servants quarters behind it, the next housed the patriarch, his wife and a widowed daughter. The patriarch's only son had now died. His widowed wife—Qisheng's mother—and three sons and another daughter lived in the third and largest unit. In the year when Guoda was born, his maternal grandfather, a plump man, had fled Changsha to Hankou ahead of the Red Army. (Mao Zedong was one of its leaders. It was also the year when the American stock market crash precipitated the Great Depression.) It was reported that the rebels would kill any fat person on the spot, on the presumption that corpulence was proof of idleness, living off others' labor. Indeed, the grandfather did not work that much, spending a great deal of his time on the family's collection of gold fish, including a rare breed called "heaven-facing dragon," with large bug eyes at the top of the head. The fish were kept in the front yard in a row of large earthenware vats, where the Jing children would first rush over when they came visiting.

Once, when the boy's parents, returning from an out-of-town sojourn, came to pick up their children, their Aunt Qijin, Qisheng's younger sister, jovially remarked, "Your little Chacha could really eat." Chacha was Guoda's pet name (Cha means tea, because his mother had an unusual liking for the drink while pregnant with him). That afternoon, Fuli took the boy, who was five then, to the streets, telling him that he could have anything he wanted to eat. After at a street stand he had two deep fried sticky rice balls, in a delicatessen Fuli asked him whether he would like to have a big piece of fat barbecued pork. He said yes and he had that. Then they went to a noodle shop, and Fuli asked the boy whether he would like a bowl of noodle. He said yes, and a big bowl of noodle was ordered. Now he could not quite finish that. Fuli insisted that he did. Only after he tried a couple more times and couldn't, his father let him off.

Fuli proudly told his cousins-in-law of the lesson he had taught the boy. The story was relayed to their grandfather. The patriarch called Fuli to his room and admonished him not to be so rash and willful in bringing up the young. Fuli listened respectfully, but the word went in one ear and out the other.

CHAPTER 5

In the mid-1930s, the world was generally at peace; so was the young, growing Jing family. It was not to last. Within a year, the family lost the two youngest members. First, their daughter died of meningitis. Shortly afterwards, the youngest boy succumbed to tuberculosis.

The funeral rites, formalities and customary exchanges with relatives and friends kept Qisheng occupied. People said that she handled herself with uncommon grace during that sorrowful period. But once in a long while, on the order of years, she would say something like, "If Number Three Lass were alive, she would be as tall as…" or, "The girl did have a temper, you know…." At times, about the lost son, she would say, "He was such a beautiful boy…." A dark shadow would move past her blank face, like that of a cloud crossing a pond. Such remarks would also make the surviving brothers sad, not only for the loss of the siblings but also for their mother's grief.

The tragedies jolted Fuli to pay more attention to the surviving brothers. Noting that Guoda had a large mole, the size of a small coin behind his left ear, he insisted that it be surgically removed, even though his grandfather-in-law thought it unnecessary to "knife a mole." Rather enlightened for the times—in some respects at least—Fuli also had the boy circumcised. When the stitches were being taken out, it took two nurses to hold the lad down. In fear, pain and anger, he lashed out at them, "Look at the rouge on your faces; they are like monkeys' bottoms!" That hurtful experience associated with the aseptic smell in the hospital room impressed on the boy's mind for years.

Fuli also ordered the brothers to take pure cod liver oil—which had such a strong unpleasant fishy smell that they had to hold their noses to do it—supposedly to strengthen the lungs and prevent tuberculosis. Daily, after getting up from a mandatory afternoon nap, they were commanded to ingest soup of pork liver and spinach as a tonic.

The brothers had mixed feelings about the new attention coming from their father—gladness of his care balanced by a wariness of his severity. However, before long the balance was decisively tipped. On one of those hot Changsha nights in July, the parents were out attending some social occasion, which normally would end near midnight. After supper and bath, the brothers lay on a couple of bamboo couches in the yard, listening to the crickets singing in the crevices at the foot of the wall and watching the lightning bugs drift in the air. The family's two maidservants also came out, each with a small low stool, lighted a mosquito-repellent incense coil and sat beside their young masters to rest. The older one, who had been with the family since Rende was a baby, asked him, "Big Young Master, would you like your back scratched?"

"Sure," Rende turned to lie on his stomach. The other maid and Guoda followed suit. The rough fingers drew slowly up and down the young backs. Humming village ditties intermittently, the women lazily rocked and chatted about how the sky was full of stars, and it'd be another sunny, hot one tomorrow, and how the year's fresh jasmine flower had this year come on the market earlier than usual.

The boys' eyes closed, they could smell the fragrance of the white tubular flower that were pinned on the maids' shirts. The heavenly state lasted well into the night, and the boys were half-asleep. They heard the gate open. The fingers stopped moving.

"What is this!" their father exclaimed.

They quickly sat up. The maids took their stools and headed inside. "How absurd! You two runts enjoying life so! Eh! So young yet! You'd grow up to be useless softies! Tell me! Who's idea was it?" Their father was towering over them, his big eyes glaring in the starlight. Their mother, standing behind him, mumbled something like, "You two should be sleeping in bed at this time."

"All right, go inside and kneel down!" their father commanded. Their midsummer night's dream turning into a midsummer nightmare, the boys went in and knelt, facing the wall by the chairs, thighs vertical. After the parents went into their room, they relaxed, sat on their heels—which actually was not allowed—and waited for their release, periodically slapping the mosquitoes off and the ears following their father's movements inside. The waiting seemed to last forever. The coughs that usually accompanied his mouth washing told them that freedom was at hand. Hearing his footsteps, they quickly plumbed up their thighs. "Get up and go to bed!"

Some punishment would descend on them even more like a fall from the sky than that night's nightmare. The late summer, Fuli had bought a new radio with short wave that could get programs broadcast from Hankuo, and on a clear day, maybe even the Beijing opera from Shanghai. One evening, he discovered that the tuning needle was stuck at one end of the dial. He figured it must be the doing of one of the brothers. "Tell me who'd played with this and damaged it," he asked the boys angrily. Both denied responsibility. "I'll find out soon enough." He took a bamboo ruler and told them, "Five slaps each to start."

When comparing taking the bamboo ruler with kneeling, the good news was that the extent of the punishment—the number of strokes, in each session—was announced ahead of time, while in kneeling, the duration was uncertain. The bad news was that the pain was sharper. The hand was to be still for each hit. Any downward movement of the outstretched hand at mitigation, instinctive or otherwise, that resulted in a less than a square strike giving off a rich clap of bamboo on flesh, would void that count. Sometimes, it would be administered to the buttocks, with pants down.

After each got the five slaps, there was no admission. "Now ten slaps, five on each hand. "Rende! The other hand!" After administered the strokes to both boys, Fuli said, "Who did it?" The boys looked away from the ruler, closed their hands and kneaded the palm with the fingers, their faces morose and mouths remained shut.

"Still not talking, eh! Speak up! And you won't get more of this…. It's going to fifteen now. Rende, that hand."

"I did it…" Guoda admitted.

"You! Why?"

"I don't know."

"All right. Ten, right hand."

"I was playing with it…trying to find a new station."

"Anyway, ten more. You'll know to leave it alone."

Guoda's almost numb hands got the last ten.

When they were alone, Rende asked his brother, "What station were you trying to find?"

"No station! I didn't do it. Did you?"

"What!…Of course not! I would have said so if I did? Why would you say you did if you did not?"

"You want to keep getting the beating?" Guoda said. He believed that Rende didn't do it, but wondered what really happened?

During the sessions of the beating, the young new maid was busy in the kitchen, washing the dishes over twice, shaking imperceptibly.

CHAPTER 6

Fuli found a new job, which paid better than the old one, with the Yingmei (British-American) Tobacco Company. Working for foreigners had its advantages but also irritations. He discovered that fundamentally his Caucasian colleagues did not treat him any differently from the rest of his countrymen. He was a Chinaman in their eyes, although his friends called him "ocean man." In the meantime, somewhat ironically he developed a genuine liking for the English language. He quit his job and went to Shanghai to study English.

He enrolled in Guang Hua University. There he also assisted a professor of English in editing an English magazine. However, he needed to take other courses besides English. His habits and life style could not cope with the rigor and the discipline required of college studies, such as taking examinations at regular intervals. He tried, but it was too burdensome for him. Frustrated, he quit.

Back in Changsha, encouraged by his experience with the magazine in Shanghai, he started an English biweekly himself. Shortly it was reported that the national government was going to appoint a non-Hunanese to replace the current Hunanese governor. He daringly criticized the change in an editorial of the magazine. When the new governor came to office, Fuli heard that retribution for his outspokenness might be in the offing. As he was weighing the pros and cons of leaving Hunan, history settled it for him.

In August that year, 1937, Japan openly began executing its plan of total conquest of China, having in previous years already taken Taiwan and Manchuria and established footholds in northern China. The army with the flag of the rising sun marched south. The Chinese, sensing that their nationhood was facing a coup de grace, decided to unite and resist. The national government moved from Nanjing westward to Chongqing in Sichuan province, up the forbidding Three Gorges of the Yangzi River, hoping that natural terrain would help to hold off the invaders.

Apprehensive that the Japanese might bomb the city of Changsha, Qisheng took her two sons to stay in the country—in the Fans' Farm which the family owned. To the boys, the fields, the pond, and the farmer's kid, who attended the buffalo, were all a vacation. Shortly Fuli decided to move the family to Chongqing too. The Jings were joined by Qisheng's two younger brothers and a younger sister.

They went by rail from Changsha to Hankou with baggage consisting of suitcases, bedrolls—with their quarter widths folded in and rolled lengthwise, enveloping not only bedding but also clothing—and "net-baskets," lidless rattan baskets with a handle across the top, securable by a net of cords. On the train they had fried rice with eggs and green onions. For a bit of luxury, one could order a bowl of abalone soup with its deep rich scent. In the Jing family, Fuli alone experienced its taste.

From Hankou, they boarded a steamship, owned by the Min Sheng Industrial Company. Headquartered in Chongqing, it was China's second largest shipping company, next only to the China Merchants' Navigation Company. Su Qizhi by then had graduated, first in his class at Guang Hua University, worked for the Ming Sheng Company, and risen steadily in the organization to be the controller of its Shanghai office. His position had enabled his relatives to book their passages on the ship crowded with refugees. The Jing brothers joined their uncles in the general cabin, making beds on the floor with their bedrolls, while their parents had a semi-private cabin, which their young Aunt Qijing also shared.

There was a small dining room aboard the ship that served Western-styled food, generally regarded as exotic by the populace. Its customers were mainly first class passengers. However, anyone willing and able to pay the price would be served also. One morning, Fuli announced that he was going to try the place out. That noon, the boys skulked up the third deck and found their way to the door of the dining room and peeked. Their father was sitting alone at a table covered with white damask, on which ranged all kinds of shiny knives and other silverware. Head lowered, he was gazing into a bowl while stirring it with a spoon. As he lifted the spoon to his mouth, he raised his head, and his large eyes looked—straight at two darkened hemispheres sticking out from behind the door. The boys were hypnotized, like deer in headlights, then startled, and ran off like two frightened animals. Later, contrary to their apprehension, they shared a buttered slice of bread that their father gave them, saying with much condescension: "This is real 'ocean food.'"

At the port of Yichang, the family waited on board for another vessel with more horsepower in order to go up the Three Gorges. It was an early fall night and the moon was bright. By the wharf, hundreds of conscripts, with nothing on them but tatters, many of them emaciated, shivered around a bonfire. They were to be trained to fight the well-supplied and -trained Japanese Imperial Army. The Jings rested at the stern. Qisheng, wearing a coat, sat on a bench, averted her eyes from the shore scene and looked at the moon. Guoda laid his head in her lap. A breeze blew from the waters. She drew up her coat to cover the boy's chest.

The transshipping vessel was still not powerful enough. As it struggled its way upstream, at some spots it had to be aided by the combined muscle power of a team of laborers on whose bare backs ropes, stretching to the ship, tightened and pulled, their toes curling for purchase over the slippery banks. In unison they chanted: "Oh-You-He!...Oh-You-He!..." as they pulled, against the Yangzi waters roaring eastward to the Pacific, the passengers westward to safety.

After a journey of some 1,400 miles from the Mid-south to the Mid-west of China, the Jings and the Sus arrived in Chongqing. Qizhi not only helped his brothers find employment, but also got his brother-in-law an interview with the Ming Sheng Company. They asked Fuli about his work experience. He replied "in the area of oil," thinking of his experience with the Texas Oil Company. He was first assigned to work in the company's Fuel Division. Subsequently, the General Manager, being informed of the new employee's proficiency in English, made him his English secretary.

The family was assigned two rooms in one of the company's crowded housing units. That summer the boys contracted amebic dysentery. After they appeared to have recovered, Guoda suffered relapses. Qisheng put him on a strict diet of only thin porridge cooked from singed rice with a pinch of salt. Qisheng enforced the regimen for months after he was apparently cured and complained of hunger. It was only when his grandmother joined them from Hunan, that he was released from the debilitating diet. She had come to Chongqing, accompanied by her second son, who had been back to Changsha as Fuli's agent to sell a tract of his farmland. The old lady reproved her daughter for risking stunting the growth of her grandson. It was one of the very few instances that Guoda was not on his mother's side.

After weeks of warning from the government, the Japanese planes did come to drop bombs—"lay their eggs," as some undaunted would say. Air-raid shelters were dug all over the city. Inside, the widely spaced bald light bulbs illuminated only the reddish walls of water-oozing clay; the floor was muddy, strewn with puddles, and the air damp, chilly and stuffy. The air-raid sirens would sound in stages. A series of wails warned of enemy planes approaching. Rapid short hoots of alarm confirmed that attack was imminent. When the danger was past, the siren uttered a lengthy cry of relief.

Once the Ming Sheng compound was hit. A couple of three-story houses were torn into two one-and-a-half-story of jagged ruins. Shards of bricks and mortars strewed around the grounds. Thanks to the shelters, no one in the compound was hurt. The Jing boys felt more excitement than fear. But their father knew better.

Fuli moved the family to a hamlet in the countryside. There were rock caves nearby. These natural shelters, relatively dry and spacious, were a lot more friendly then man-made ones. Refugees once again, the boys had no school to go to. As their father, having to commute to work, wasn't around much, they would loiter and explore the rural surroundings. Their favorite hangout was a high outcrop, from which they could have a good look down at the beach of the Jialing River that flows from the north into the Yangzi. Further away they could see an airfield with a few forlorn planes of their country's air force.

On this bright spring day, when they were playing on the outcrop, they heard the siren whine from the city. They watched the Chinese planes rise up from the airfield, fly on and disappear to the right. In a moment, from the left came the Japanese planes, in triangular configurations. Three planes formed a basic triangular unit. Three such units in a triangular pattern made nine planes. A total of 27, configured in a similar manner, approached ominously. Balls of white cloud popped under them, and muffled flack was heard. The invading planes did not appear bothered at all. The brothers couldn't see the eggs being laid but their effects. Red flames and black smoke rose over the city. Expanding and mounting, the flames glowed luridly in the smoke.

The next day the attack was even more intense. The Japanese bombers arrived in waves, keeping the city in flames and smolder. More people moved to the countryside. Files of people trekked past their neighborhood, many with loaded baskets hung from both ends of a pole over their shoulders, some injured, in bandages or slings, some feeble and/or old, and women holding the very young, treading wearily or slumping in sedan chairs carried by bare-backed laborers. Chongqing no longer seemed that safe.

CHAPTER 7

Fuli resigned his job and led his family, including his mother-in-law, to move to Shanghai, where residents inside either the International Settlement, administered mainly by the British, or the French Settlement would be safe from the Japanese. Because of the war, they traveled a circuitous route. By bus they reached Kumming, where they boarded a train that took them to the port of Haiphong, Vietnam. A ship brought them to Shanghai via Hong Kong. After a journey of some 5,000 miles, they found a new haven.

Qizhi assisted Fuli to find and rent the third floor of a lane house in the French Settlement. The space included a main room with its attached bathroom, and half a floor down, a "pavilion room" with its lavatory. The main room served as the master bedroom, the living and dining room as well. The boys shared the smaller pavilion room with their grandmother.

Life inside the settlements appeared normal—normal for Shanghai, including its bacchic aspects. One wouldn't think that the nation of China was in the throes of struggling for her life. Fuli did not work at first. He tried his hand at playing the stocks, via a telephone in the second floor vestibule. He bought a small English automobile, gallivanted among nightclubs and dance halls, and also visited casinos, like the famous Six Nations Hotel. He would drink some. But his capacity for alcohol was quite limited. One late night, his family found him slumping over the steering wheel of the parked Austin. Apparently, after he had managed to get close enough home, he had allowed himself to vomit and pass out.

Qisheng in appreciation of his recent efforts in taking care of the family, her mother in particular, let him have his fun. Now in her late 20s, she had matured into a fairly stout woman, no longer the tall slender girl when she first

- 31 -

married. Before the family left Chongqing, Fuli had sold two tracts of farmland in Hunan. She told her sons worrisomely that the tracts were the family's last. Although she had quarrels with her husband before, they were neither that frequent nor serious. Now they became fights, more about his girlfriends at the dancing halls than about his prodigality.

Late summer, she fell ill with stomach problems, recovered, but had lost much weight and the stoutness. One morning she had a major fight with Fuli over some lipstick stains on his shirt, and ingested an amount of potassium permanganate, which was kept in the apartment as a disinfectant for such use as sanitizing fresh fruits. Her purple lips alarmed Fuli; help was called. She was treated and sent to a sanatorium to rest for a week. The event made Fuli to stay home more.

The brothers took the entrance examinations at a neighborhood primary school. Rende had the appropriate marks to continue on his regular schedule—the fifth grade. When Fuli noticed that Guoda had essentially the same marks as his older brother, he insisted that his younger son be also admitted to the fifth grade, which resulted in Guoda's skipping the fourth grade.

One night, after supper, Guoda was studying in the pavilion room. His grandmother, looking out of the window, said wearily, "The moon is bright again tonight." From past experience, he knew she was worried. Worried of the bright moon. Her youngest son was now bursar on a Ming Shen Company ship navigating on the upper stretches of the Yangzi. The ship would usually sail at night to avoid possible Japanese air strikes. She was concerned that moonlight would make the ship (hundreds of miles away) a clearer target.

She came from an old, well-known Hunan family. The family had been declining, however. She had learned to be extremely frugal, to the extent that she would make her own letter envelope from a sheet of plain paper rather than use a regular manufactured one. Once Fuli and Qisheng took her to a dance hall. Seeing man and woman holding each other in public, she immediately demanded to be taken home. She would usually stay in the pavilion room unless her son-in-law went out. Then she'd go up to be with her daughter, and return to the pavilion room when he came back. The in-laws spoke very little to each other, but he was correct toward her. Apparently she felt contented with the arrangement. Since her arrival in Shanghai, she had chosen to live with her daughter instead of her son, over Qizhi's mild protest.

That night, Fuli came into the pavilion room. (He rarely did this in deference to his mother-in-law.) In a low voice he said something to her. She left with him to go upstairs. A while later, she returned and said to Guoda, "You go up there and talk to your mother. She has been laughing. Neither your yaya nor I could make her stop. Maybe she'll listen to you. Go up there, go!"

Guoda went. His mother was alone, sitting on the bed and laughing, not a loud kind, nor a giggle, but more like a series of amused chuckles. "You have come too," she said.

"Mama, what are you laughing about?" Guoda said.

"Nothing. They think I have lost my wits, Chacha."

"I don't…. Why don't you stop. You are making us concerned."

"You are concerned. Aren't you?" She looked at her son, fanning herself with a small towel. She was sweating some.

"Of course. But I think you are all right." He did feel that there was nothing seriously wrong about her. He moved closer to the bed and sat down.

She held his hand and stopped laughing. "Don't worry. I am all right…. I've been just thinking about whether this household will be all right…. Now pat my back for me." When she was sick, he would sometimes pat her back to help relieve her discomfort. He made soft fists and drummed lightly.

His grandmother stole into the room. "You all right now?"

"I have been all right all along," Qisheng said.

The episode passed. The family never talked about it afterwards. She would stay in bed most of the time. None of the physicians of Western medicine or Chinese medicine consulted would diagnose her condition more specifically than "general feebleness." She would take several kinds of vitamins. A nurse visited her regularly to administer shots of liver extracts. She had even arranged blood transfusions for Qisheng at home. The donor would be lying on a cot from whom the nurse would draw blood and, turning around, inject it into Qisheng's veins. Fuli, who usually watched his money fairly carefully, especially when it was not spent on himself, never quibbled about his wife's medical expenses.

Now he began to think more seriously about finding a job. He consulted his eldest brother-in-law. Qizhi, medium height, had a face with rather delicate features, which, together with his noted composure, reminded one of a Toaist high priest. Qisheng had observed that the only sign of emotion that her brother would show under any circumstances was just a slight flushing of the face. It seemed an oddity that he and Fuli would be such good friends—perhaps it followed a law of nature that opposites attract—even before they became in-laws.

In spite of his outward seeming detachment, deeds spoke of his warm-heartedness and generosity, even though in the case with Fuli, some would comment that he had to be mindful of the fact that his mother had been living with Fuli's family. However, although now acting manager of the Shanghai office of the Ming Sheng Company, he couldn't render much direct assistance to Fuli. Since the breakout of the Sino-Japanese War, Ming Sheng Company, Shanghai, had been steadily shrinking in operation and staff. Furthermore, the war in Europe had started, there was no justification for a new position. He suggested to Fuli that Ni Zhihan, a high school classmate of theirs, might help.

"I haven't been in touch with him since I invited him to a dinner when he returned to Changsha for a visit. The last time I heard he was assistant manager of their cotton mill," Fuli said.

"Associate manager now," Qizhi said.

"Hum…Of course, a St. John's University diploma is worth a lot."

"In this case, family relations probably counted more, even though his mother was a concubine," Qizhi said.

"Anyway, family background and St. John's, the combination makes life easy for him."

"I heard he has been working with some Japanese businessmen lately. He always has his connections with the English and American ones. By the way, I understand his wife has become a real aficionado of the Beijing opera," Qizhi said.

"Is that so?"

"Perhaps I could arrange a dinner for all of us."

Qizhi proceeded to arrange the dinner, after which Fuli accompanied Zhihan's wife for a couple of arias. Since then, she would have sessions of "Diao Sang Zi" (to stretch the vocal chord) at the Jing's apartment. She usually came alone—becoming a good friend of Qisheng too—while her husband busied himself as an industrial executive. Fuli, still without a job, couldn't help regretting that he did not get a college degree, like Qizhi did, or better, like Zhihan, did—from St. John's University.

CHAPTER 8

❀

At the end of the school year as a fifth grader, Guoda was ranked second in the class. Fuli took his report card and paid a visit to a middle school at Hartung Road. At dinner that night he told Guoda, "You are going to St. John's YMCA Middle School."

Before the son reacted, his mother interjected, "Middle school? Is he going to skip another grade?"

"He should be able to handle it," Fuli said blandly.

"St. John's YMCA...Is it part of the university," she asked. Of course, she had heard of St. John's University before—almost an American school, its graduates have no problem finding jobs, with the Customs, foreign trading firms, government, diplomatic services...and plenty examples of illustrious alumni.

"No. But in a sense, yes, because its graduates can directly enter St. John's High School, which is part of the university," Fuli explained.

Guoda was indifferent to the news. He'd do as told. He did feel some regret for not having a diploma that would come with completing the sixth grade, which he saw hung on the wall of a neighbor teenager's room. He was not particularly concerned about the schoolwork. After all, he had skipped the fourth grade and did well enough in the fifth.

At the middle school, Guoda soon found that he was not at all prepared for the change. The classes in algebra, physics, English...all went over his head. The worst was botany. (He had once in class questioned the instructor regarding the usefulness of the subject, admitting that zoology made more sense because "animals are at least alive.") He was lost and didn't know it. Before long he sensed that the classes were out of his depth. His confidence gone, naïve impudence was replaced by emptiness and dread.

At the end of the academic year, Fuli thrust the school report to his face, "You look at it yourself!" Guoda had flunked 24 out of 27 credits, barely passing English that his father had helped him during the course of the year. He felt shame, fear, and worthlessness.

Fuli went to talk to the principal. The latter agreed that if his son would go to summer school and pass make-up examinations, he would be allowed to join the second year class.

Guoda did both. Before the new school year began, however, he fell ill with paratyphoid. After a couple of weeks, the fever subsided but not completely—a slight temperature would continue to register in the afternoon. X-ray indicated there were a couple of questionable spots in a lung. He was ordered to rest in bed, taking calcium tablets and cod liver oil tablets.

In the meantime, Ni Zhihan came through for Fuli. A small bank needed help in the English language field. Upon Zhihan's recommendation, Fuli not only got the job as an assistant manager, but also an invitation to share in the renting of a house with the manager's family.

It was similar to the one the Jings had lived in before, but of a much higher quality. (The bathroom on each floor even had a bidet, which would puzzle and/or embarrass a number of unwary, curious visitors.) As previously, they occupied the third floor with its pavilion room. Half a story above the third floor, there were an additional small room, which was used as a study, and a glass enclosed roof patio. As before, Guoda and his brother shared the pavilion room with their grandmother.

The house was inside a compound on Albert Road. A tall aging man with a goatee, known as Old Tailor, who lived in a small room by the black iron gate of the compound, kept watch. He would pull the gate open if a car honked or a pedicab-man yelled. Pedestrians would use a wicket, which could also admit a bicycle with some maneuvering. If one rang the bicycle bell loudly enough, Old Tailor would open the gate too, although his face wouldn't show any enjoyment of the work. Later on, having his own bike, Guoda would negotiate the wicket if he was alone, and work the bell hard for a grander entry if he had a friend with him.

The compound was owned by three brothers of a Qiu family in the dye business, which their deceased father had built. It contained three separate three-story houses for regular residence, and a row of smaller, lower buildings on its north side used as offices, storage spaces, and dormitory for the Qiu family employees, including two bookkeepers and several functionaries. The main rooms of the residential houses all fronted south, overlooking a spacious lawn, about the size of half a soccer field. At the ground floor, the sitting rooms opened to terraces with elevated flowerbeds trimmed with white and orange porcelain tiles. Beside the house at the end, a small plot provided for recreational cultivation of such vegetables as potatoes and sweet peas. The Jings shared the first house. One of the Qiu brothers lived in the middle one. The last house, at the compound's end, was rented to a Huang family.

Having gradually regained his health, Guoda waited to rejoin the middle school when the academic year began. Fuli hired an American to tutor him English. The lessons were taught in the small study on the top floor. Before Guoda could get used to the accent and the body odor the Lincolnesque, middle-aged teacher brought into the small room, he was sent to a concentration camp. The United States and Japan had declared war on each other, and the Japanese had taken over both the International and the French settlements. Fuli took over the teaching himself, using the editorials of *The North China Daily News* as teaching material, requiring Guoda to memorize whole editorials on such topics as traffic problems on Nanjing Road.

In the morning, he would be awakened by his father's holler from the staircase landing for him to report to his room. There Guoda was supposed to read aloud the current lesson, over and over again. Just waking up from sleep, he would mumble and muddle through as he watched his father out of the corner of his eye busying himself with his toilet. He knew Fuli was satisfied just by hearing the sound he was voicing. But whenever he noticed that Fuli was starting to listen, as when he was putting on his tie and in the mirror his fingers stopped moving, Guoda would concentrate and enunciate more clearly and louder. It was a relief when his father left the house. Yet, the mnemonic work needed be done anyway to recite the article when he returned.

Sometimes Guoda was told to produce a composition. Once Fuli gave him the subject: "My Family." Guoda wrote about it pretty much factually. His father worked to support it; mother nourished it; brother did a lot of chores, and grandmother added much warmth to it. As for himself, he wrote: "I try my best to do my duties. But my parents sometimes still seem not satisfied." The inclusion of his mother in the complaint was only nominal and diplomatic. Generally, she followed the traditional paradigm—supporting her husband and loving her children, in that order. She was loving enough that her sons were not afraid to complain about their father in her presence. However, although her manners and countenance indicated sympathy, her formal pronouncements would always come down in favor of her husband, saying, for example, "There is no such thing under the sun as a parent in the wrong." The tone was mild, though.

Fuli read the composition. "Uh hum!" he snorted, "Don't try to play the game of pen-and-ink-litigation with me! I used to make a living out of that, you know...." He was referring to the biweekly magazine he had published a few issues, back in Changsha. That was the extent of his reaction. Guoda thought afterwards that he had gotten off easy; he wouldn't be surprised had his grievance brought some retaliation. On the other hand, his complaint didn't reduce his father's demands either.

Becoming busier with his work at the bank, Fuli hired Mr. Popov, a White Russian, who wrote for *the North China Daily News*, to teach Guoda once a week. An urbane young man with curly hair, he was masterly in the language and at teaching too. Once on Guoda's writing of "feeling dream-like in the evening breeze," Mr. Popov said it was "poetic." Guoda didn't quite understand the meaning of the word, but knew his teacher meant it as praise, and felt good.

By common adolescent standards, Guoda's curiosity and interest in girls was slow in developing. It was first kindled by the Huang sisters. Mr. Huang, their father, had a chauffeur-driven automobile that used charcoal and needed hand cranking to start. It was whispered that he was a collaborator with the Japanese and that he smoked opium. Indeed, on several occasions, Guoda did smell a tobacco-like scent, but with a cloying sweetness, emanating from their house. Mr. Huang's older daughter, named Yun Qiu, was Guoda's age, and her sister, Yun Yu, a couple of years younger. Yun Qiu was tall and slender, high-cheekbone and reserved, while her sister, round faced and bright-eyed, was more open, tomboyish and fun. When Guoda was allowed to go out of the house after his recovery, he was young enough to play hopscotch and other children's games with them. Once, while he and Yun Yu were playing the shuttlecock kicking game, they both wanted the shuttlecock and ended up wrestling on the lawn. His grandmother saw them from the third floor window and later lectured him that he was getting too big to be seen doing that.

Getting older, the children were together less. Yun Qiu appeared even more of a cold-fish kind, like upward chin and downcast eyes. During their encounters, getting more infrequent, the interactions were often disjointed both in talk and familiarity. Then the girls became boarders in a Catholic school.

Guoda would now see them only when they were getting in or out of their family car. Their long black school uniforms made them look all the more forbidding.

The following summer, he took more remedial courses, getting ready to advance to the 8th grade. He would often take a walk after supper around the compound to catch some cooler, fresh air. One day at dusk, he came on Yun Qiu in the quiet of the vegetable garden, tinkering with the beanstalks. "Haven't seen you for a long time," he said.

"You go to school too. Don't you?" she retorted.

"How have you been?"

"Why should you care?"

He felt humiliated by the rebuff, had a notion to walk away, but stayed, even though embarrassed. She didn't leave either, picking at the over-ripe yellowish pea pods. Suddenly, she rushed over and thrust something into his hand and hurried off. It was a beaded necklace with a cross pendant. He never had a chance to talk to her again. Many nights that summer this 13 year old lad, lying on a lawn chair on the terrace, looking up into the low, dark blue sky, full of twinkling stars that he thought he could almost reach for, would think of the girl with a perpetual frown.

CHAPTER 9

✿

After the Pearl Harbor attack, with the Japanese controlling all of Shanghai, there was no advantage in security for St. John's YMCA Middle School to be located in the Hartung Road building, which was in the interior of the former International Settlement. It moved back to its original campus. Like St. John's University, it was situated behind Jessfield Park near the west border of the former settlement.

At the end of the eighth grade, Guoda's was ranked 7th out of 35 in the class. Fuli ordered him to take the entrance examination for St. John's High School. If admitted, he would be skipping the ninth grade. His name did not appear on the posted list of successful applicants. Guoda had mixed feelings about that. Glad that he didn't have to skip another grade; guilty because he had thrown part of the examination. Fuli went to the school and asked to see the examination papers. It turned out that his son had passed the examination—apparently Guoda had done only a half-hearted job at throwing the examination. The school explained that an agreement of long standing between it and St. John's YMCA Middle School prohibited class skipping. Fuli remonstrated with them, and Guoda became a high school student.

He was apprehensive at the beginning. But the classes gave him no great difficulty except for a biology course. He was baffled by all the science about the hermaphroditic earthworms.

In 1943, the tide of WWII was definitely turning against the Rome-Berlin-Tokyo Axis. Their troops suffered devastating losses in North Africa and Soviet Union. In Asia, hundreds of thousands of Japanese army were tied down by the tenacious Chinese, whom they were unable to decisively defeat. To help her war efforts, Japan tried to squeeze more resources from the occupied land. She had the puppet Chinese government of Wang Jingwei declare that it would purchase all cotton and cotton cloth within its domain, at a price it would set later, and all warehouses would be sealed off. The owners of the commodities generally interpreted this to mean that the Japanese were going to appropriate the goods, paying only a token price for them.

Fuli was one of such owners. He had invested in the commodities most of his money, including the proceeds of the sale of the delicatessen in Chang-sha—the final piece of his inheritance—and the commissions that Qizhi had helped him to earn when the Ming Seng Company in Shanghai had to sell some of its properties to keep the office afloat.

In gloom he told his sons, "Only yesterday, you were 'xiao kai' (young silk-stockings). But today, you are 'bie san' (poor street urchins)." Although they had never felt that they were young silk-stockings before, they understood what he meant. In time the maid was let go, and Guoda's tutor, Mr. Popov, was terminated. Qisheng and Rende did most of the housework, with grandmother and Guoda helping out. In the family it was understood that time spent study-ing was equivalent to, if not weighing more than time doing chores. Rende, no bibliophile, didn't complain at all.

The business climate deteriorated; Fuli lost his job at the bank. He seemed to have aged fast, losing much hair, and, for what remained, turning peppery; he was only 36 years old. Usually well groomed in one of his tailor-made West-ern suits, he would now dress in the conspicuous austerity of a plain blue cloth Chinese gown. He picked up a new hobby—calligraphy, for which, as for the fiddle, he had considerable natural talent. Connected with that, the brothers noticed in his manner—added to his usual sternness—a certain ascetic style of the old-time Chinese scholars, which was quite a departure from his long-time "ocean man" image.

He turned even more severe with his children. They were supposed to be home at all times except for attending school. In modern American parlance of the young, they were "grounded, like forever." The only time off was two hours on Saturday afternoons.

Once, after school Guoda had stayed on to play soccer for a while. Coming home, he hoped that his father was out. No such luck. Asked why he was late, Guoda said that there was a blockade by the Japanese military police. Such interruptions in traffic would indeed happen every now and then when the feared Japanese military police, with muscle-bound faces, would block off an area for some such purpose as to catch a suspect. The lie was soon confessed to when Fuli threatened to go out to verify it. Guoda was locked up in the roof patio.

It was used mainly as a storage space. He sat on some box, stood up, moved about a bit, chose another box to sit on, and watched the sky and the wave-like roofs. The day waned. Neighborhood lights flickered on. The glimmering became more vivid as the sky grew darker. The air felt cooler. He was hungry. Time passed so slowly. He had no idea when he would be released.

Some noise came from an open side of the patio. He went over and saw his grandmother knocking on the window by the staircase landing. "Your father and mother have gone out." He responded with a mixed feeling of relief and disappointment. It was always a relief when his father was out of the house; now a disappointment because he would also have the key to the patio with him. His grandmother said that Rende would get some food to him. A while later, Rende crawled out of the window, moved gingerly over on the ledge and passed a bowl of rice mixed with sweet potato (a cheaper staple than rice) to Guoda's outstretched hand.

He understood that the punishment was greater because he had lied. However, another time, he was accused of having played with Fuli's fiddle, which he hadn't, and denied it. Now he was charged with impertinence in his denial and was ordered to kneel. Like his brother, he had long been conditioned to be submissive by their father's big fierce eyes and the sudden downward pull of the cheek, and to be contented to have a home for food and shelter. But this time, Guoda felt the experience insufferable. After the punishment, he ran away from home. He left it in the afternoon with no preparation. He walked about in the streets. Night came; his stomach grumbled and legs felt weak. Pedestrians were getting scarce. A crippled beggar tried to grab his feet before he quickly skipped away. Shadows everywhere. He skulked toward home. About a block away from it, Rende found him, their father trailing half a block behind. They returned home without saying anything, as though the incident never happened.

As promised, the puppet government began to pay for the cotton and the cotton cloth it had taken from the owners. Unexpectedly, the recompense was not as trivial as first supposed, although still appreciably below the original market value. That relieved Fuli from the financial strait he had found himself in; he gradually relaxed his recent asceticism—and the stringent constraints on his sons—and returned to his earlier life style.

Through the Ni Zhihan couple, Fuli had come to be friends with Ni Heye, who was the youngest of Zhihan's eleven uncles but only a few years older than the nephew. The Ni family was among the most prominent in China. Heye's maternal grandfather, a preeminent scholar-general of the Qing dynasty, had played a major role in modern Chinese history in defeating the Taiping rebels. Heye's father, once the Imperial Magistrate of the County of Shanghai in the last days of the Qing dynasty, had left the family a large fortune, including a cotton mill in Shanghai and thousands of acres of farmland in Hunan. Heye didn't need to work to lead a comfortable life, even though he had to share the family fortune with eleven siblings. When a young man, he would drive his automobile weaving an S pattern so that no other vehicle could pass him. When he heard how difficult it was to hit a jackpot at a slot machine, he had a servant bring a comfortable chair to one in a store. There he would sit down and crank continuously, until a jackpot rolled up. And in poker games, he had been known to purposely let a bluff take the pot after showing his winning hand to a third party before he mixed his cards into the pile with a sardonic smile.

He had two sons about the same age as the Jing brothers. They lived in a house just two blocks from the Jings. Naturally the boys, like their fathers, became friends. Guoda and Ni Zhiyu, the younger Ni boy, were particularly close.

Heye certainly enjoyed all the power traditional Chinese culture invested in the man of the house. Once he had poured a bowl of noodle soup on top of his wife's head when she displeased him. Toward his children, however, his style tended to be the nonviolent, benign neglect variety. They were allowed broad freedom, which they would not abuse, and thus enjoyed a generally blameless reputation among the elders. Mindful of the contrast of that example with his own children's case, Fuli would have preferred that his sons not associate with the young Nis. But he found it difficult to issue that order, so long as he openly admired and socialized with the senior Ni. More importantly, the Ni boys were, after all, great grandchildren of that famed scholar-general, that dignified lion of Chinese classics and powerful proponent of Confucian virtues, a personage whom Fuli absolutely revered.

Besides the two-hour free time the Jing brothers were allowed on Saturdays, the boys of the two families could still hang out together inside the compound, provided Fuli was not home or was occupied, as with his visiting Beijing opera friends. When the Ni boys came, they would whistle a special trilling tune as a signal of their presence. If feasible, the Jing brothers would come out and join them. If they didn't show after a while, the Ni boys would leave, assuming that their friends were shut away.

It was anxious moments for Guoda when he heard the signal but couldn't get away. One summer night, Fuli fancied to listen to the opera: *The Fourth Son Visits His Mother*; he told Guoda to operate the gramophone. The job included turning the crank to wind up its spring, changing the 78-speed record and replacing the needle for each side of a record. As Fuli listened, he would comment now and then on the performance to his son, whose mind, however, was on the trilling and the night air outside. By the time the opera ended, each of the pile of records having had its turn and returned to its sleeve, and the needles in the tin almost depleted, the night was deep. The only sound was the singing of the insects through the open window.

It was also Guoda's job to make fresh ink for his father to practice calligraphy. He would grind an ink stick slowly on a circular inkstone that contained initially some half an inch of clear water. Round and round his hand holding the stick would follow the elevated edging, like a miniature ox treading around the millstones. Those moments would be made insufferable should the trilling whistles waft in. In time, wearily he would watch the liquid gain in viscosity. The job was completed when the thick fluid parted by the stick's passing would appear to be stationary (like congealed lotus-root powder paste, or the Red Sea parted by Moses). But by then his friends would be long gone.

In that period of forced leisure, Fuli's interest in the Beijing opera also intensified. To improve his skill with the fiddle, he befriended some of the top professionals, including Li Moliang, the fiddlist for the singer Ma Lianliang; Zhao Lama, the left-handed fiddlist for the singer Tang Fuying; and Wang Xiaoqing, the fiddlist for Li Shifang—all established artists of the first rank. Fuli would invite them to the apartment—when they came from Beijing with the singers on engagement—to give him pointers or lessons.

Guoda would watch them inconspicuously, like a fly on the wall. He also played the fiddle, on the sly—often with a mute across the snake skin membrane of the instrument—in particular, never when his father was home. Fuli knew something about it, but did not pay much attention, assuming his son was just dabbling at it, until one day one of his fiddle friends congratulated him on Guoda's performance in a duet number on a radio program.

On Saturdays, Guoda's free time was usually spent in the Ni house. Heye, a major patron of the Shanghai Theatrical Academy, sponsored a sort of Beijing opera singing party at his house every Saturday afternoon. The party took place in the parlor on the first floor. Heye himself was almost never there. He would usually be on the third floor in his bedroom just getting up after the mahjong or poker party in the night before with friends and his in-laws who, like him, had abundant inheritance.

The afternoon party would be for his children and their young relatives and friends. Some afternoons, a few students at the Theatrical Academy would come, among whom was a goddaughter of Heye's, the Academy's number two female student in artistry, and number one in looks. Although she was about the age of the boys there, she would treat them as "little younger brothers." Nevertheless, whenever she agreed to sing, Guoda and Zhiyu would eagerly offer to play the accompaniment. Zhiyu usually played the "jin hu" (capital or first fiddle, made of bamboo); and Guoda the "er hu"(second fiddle, made of wood.) They had accompanied—with great concentration and feeling—her singing the main aria in *The King's Parting From His Concubine*. Then they would follow it with the duet piece *The Night Is Deep*, which accompanies the Concubine's sword dance after the aria. Through a family friend of the Nis, they were invited to play it on a radio program. That was where Fuli's friend saw and heard them.

When Fuli was presented with this fact, he first told Guoda to lay sheets of newspapers over the bathroom's tiled floor and get the cleaver from the kitchen. "How could you indulge yourself so! I know how the hobby could eat up your time and energy if you let it bewitch you." Then he ordered him to split the stem of his fiddle and collect the splinters by rolling up the sheets. However, he did not explicitly order Guoda to cease playing the instrument altogether.

With a "loan" from his mother, Guoda bought another fiddle secretly. Once he was at the fiddle shop to get some resin for the instrument, the man at the shop said to him, "The fiddle been playing O.K.?" "Yes." "I know, the other day I told your father that I was impressed how well it sounded when you were try-ing it out here." Guoda thought, "Uh-oh." But nothing hurtful happened after-wards to his new fiddle or to him physically so far as that was concerned.

CHAPTER 10

Guoda completed his first year at St. John's High School with fairly good grades. Fuli told him that it was time to forge ahead—skip another grade. Surely, the school would not allow it, even if his academic performance were the best, let alone only marginally good. He was sent to take the entrance examination at Pudong High School—a respectable academy—which he passed as a senior class enrollee. Thus he skipped the 11th grade. He failed in two courses in the first term. With Rende's help he intercepted the school report mailed home, bought a small bottle of ink eraser, guided the glass pointer over the failure grades, waited for the spots to dry, and put on passing ones.

With no steady income, Fuli's financial conditions were getting tight again. Qizhi came to the rescue once more. It started when two low-level employees of the Ming Seng Company in Shanghai thought they could take advantage of the mild-mannered acting manager Su Qizhi. In collusion with a couple of flunkies in the puppet government, they tried to blackmail him and the company for the company's apparent connection with its main office in Chongqing. They were either unaware or forgetful of the fact that, although the day-to-day running of the office was Qizhi's responsibility, the Shanghai office was then under the general oversight of a Mr. Zhou, who was on the company's Board of Directors.

Trustee Zhou was one of those personages in the old Chinese politics who seemed to have connections to all circles of power: the Nationalists government in Chongqing, the puppet government in Nanjing, the Japanese and even big-time gangsters. He wanted those blackmailers fired. Qizhi suggested that

Fuli be hired to do the firing. Zhou reluctantly went along, and Fuli was retained, with the title of Acting Assistant Manager.

To carry out the assignment, he had to work closely with Zhou, a peremptory, gruff curmudgeon. Fuli, unused to being on the receiving end of despotism, suffered but stayed. Jobs were hard to come by, let alone Acting Assistant Manager of a well-known company. He would come home with a sullen face, long and grayish, and Qisheng would surmise that he had again a hard time with the cantankerous boss. He would throw his jacket on the bed and say, "The old despot scolded me like a son. I have to eat all that shit."

In those days his two sons were especially careful and wary, like a couple of zebras by an African water hole. They had now nearly grown up. Rende was of medium height, broad shouldered, fair and good looking like his father. Guoda was slightly taller, but thin and a little darker in complexion, featured more like a Su than a Jing. Their temperaments were also different—Rende more Hunan-like (direct and pugnacious) and Guoda more Shanghai like (tactful and diplomatic). However, they got along well. Exceptions were few, such as once when Guoda complained that, without his permission, Rende had ridden the new bike he was given after he had successfully skipped the ninth grade, Rende gave him a solid punch on the chin. He took it and didn't tell anybody. (Fighting Rende would be foolish.) In addition to natural brotherly feelings, they were united by their common fear of their father, like prisoners' shared fear of the warden.

Fuli did the job he was hired to do. The fired employees retaliated by making some kind of report to the Japanese Military Police. Warned by Ni Zhihan about the threat, Fuli disappeared before the police came. The information reached Qizhi too late and he was arrested and jailed for several days before Trustee Zhou worked out his release. The latter also made the firing stick by convincing the Japanese that the Shanghai office of Ming Seng had no political function, and those troublemakers were just revenging their blackmail failure.

Fuli returned from the city of Hangzhou, where he had hid, but was still not confident enough to live at home. He stayed in a hotel a few blocks from home, and admonished the boys not to tell anyone about it. With the cat away, the mouse plays. One afternoon, while Guoda was playing a game of jai alai with the Ni boys in the compound, a friend of Fuli's, the same person who had told Fuli about Guoda's fiddle playing at the radio station, came by and asked "Is your father home?" Guoda's attention occupied by the game, he forgot his previous experience with this busybody. "No, he is in Jiang Sheng Hotel."

Later that evening, Guoda visited his father at the hotel while he was taking a bath. Sitting in the tub, he gave Guoda a good dressing-down, calling him all kinds of names. Guoda wondered why no greater punishment than that had descended on him. Later on, his mother told her sons the good news that Trustee Zhou, pleased with their father's work, had agreed to let him keep the job originally intended to be only temporary. Fuli returned home a couple of days later. All clear.

The Jing and Ni boys had learned to play jai alai. A few blocks from their homes, near Joffre Road was a jai alai arena—a place for betting. The customers, or gamblers, bought tickets picking winners. The boys played the game in the compound yard, throwing the ball against a solid panel of the concrete wall of a storage building. They learned by watching the professionals (practically all Spaniards) in the arena. They did not gamble; they didn't have the money for it, not that gambling exerted no fascination on them. Once it definitely did on Guoda.

It was Chinese New Year. On this occasion, the young would pay homage to their elders by kowtowing or bowing. In return, the elders would give the juniors "hong bao," red paper packets with money inside. For many families, the Jings included, the children were not allowed to keep the monies. Their parents would tell them to have the monies deposited in an "account" with the parents, which, after the holiday, the children knew better than to remember the account had ever existed. The parents would give such packets to the children of those who had given or would give to their children. The circulation enabled the parents to exhibit generosity for free at the expense of the children's feeling of loss. However, the Jing boys were allowed to keep the money their own parents gave them for the occasion.

Rules were relaxed for the holiday. On New Year's Eve the boys were allowed to participate in some gambling games with small stakes. They would be sent away when the elders were ready to play in earnest. The festive atmosphere would last beyond the New Year Day. The office of the landlord Qiu family would be closed for five days. The employees would still spend their time there, not working but gambling. Second class citizens in the compound—the staff of the Qius, the servants of the several households, and the children—could join in. The Jing boys did.

Usually the game was *pai-jiu*, played with 32 tiles that resemble dominos. For the game of *big pai-jiu* one would be dealt four tiles to be arranged into two rows, two tiles a row, employing the best tactics at his command in order to compete with the dealer's two rows. For the game of *small pai-jiu*, one is dealt just two tiles to vie against the dealer's two, no tactics at issue.

Guoda had watched his parents play mahjong, poker, dice, and others play *big pai-jiu*. None of those games could compare with *small pai-jiu* in its simplicity and purity as a gambling medium, with just the right duration of suspense, followed by the explosiveness of its decisive resolution. The greatest excitement—even to the losers—came when a hand called "supreme treasure" appeared—a combination of the one-dot:two-dot tile and the two-dot:four-dot tile. An experienced player needed only to feel the tile with a finger (usually the middle one) to tell the dots. After his first touch told him he had got one of the two "supreme treasure" tiles, he'd keep it, face down. If the finger under the second tile felt the other, he would square himself, puff up his chest, slam both tiles on the table, face up, with a big bang! and shout out, "His mother's! (a swearing phrase) I got it! The supreme treasure!" If he was the dealer he'd sweep clean all the bets on the table to himself, with so much panache like the Emperor Qin Shi Huang vanquishing all the other warring states. The losers would watch in awe. The gusto of such a moment enthralled young Guoda.

The brothers placed their bets gingerly. Lost some, won some. At the end of a session Rende lost a small amount, grumbled a little and left to meet his friends. Guoda had won some and was exhilarated, not so much by the money but by the excitement of the ebb and flow of the game. In those few days, even in daytime the doors of the room would be closed and windows shuttered. Stepping in from the cold outside, he immediately felt the room's warmth. In the cone of yellow light from a lamp hanging low from the ceiling, cigarette smoke whirled with the action. The incessant talking—griping, boasting and bantering—and the mystery of what was on the other side of the shining beige bamboo covers of the ivory tiles formed a cocoon around him to experience an exotic fascination and high. He returned the next morning. He lost some. Then he lost some more, until he lost all the money that was his to lose. He reckoned his bad luck couldn't last all that long. He went back to his room, with hesitation but in the excitement of that moment, he took the tuition he was to pay for the next term to Pudong High School and went back. He kept losing, slowly sinking into an abyss. Then he had no more to lose. My life is over, he thought.

There was no way he could cover up the deed. The punishment came swift and lasted for over a week. The beatings were in two sessions. The second one was to follow the first in a week after the wound healed. The physical pain was considerable but the humiliation was worse. The worst moment was when he had to lower his pants. He was almost sixteen years old.

Fuli paid the tuition for the second time, and Guoda duly graduated from high school. There was no question as to his going to college, nor as to which college. He passed the entrance examination to St. John's University, and was admitted as a freshman for the fall term.

Germany had surrendered in Europe, and the dogs of war were loosed upon the islands of Japan themselves. In Shanghai people began to look forward to the advent of dawn after eight years of darkness. At dinnertime, they opined on the big changes to come. No doubt, Generalissimo Chiang would become the President; Wang Qingwei—President of the puppet government—and his ilk would be shot as traitors. For the first time, Guoda became aware of the significance of another force in China's future as he heard the well-informed Ni Zhihan tell Fuli, "Don't underestimate the third player." He was referring to the Communists. Off and on, the public in Shanghai had heard a bit about the New Fourth Army, which was commanded by the Communists. However, people had the general impression that that army was merely guerrillas (some called them bandits), and that, as a military force, they were certainly not in the same league as the American equipped new Nationalist army.

The American planes were making their appearances in the skies over Shanghai. The brothers watched as they had watched six years ago atop the outcrop outside Chongqing, airplanes in triangular formation. This time they were America's B24's, their silver wings high above, glistening in the sun, bringing great expectations to the people below. Bright puffs exploded harmlessly below the "flying fortresses." Unlike the Japanese planes over Chongqing, no "eggs were laid." The planes seemed only to herald good tidings.

Some of the puffs came from the antiaircraft installations on the roof of the Cathay Building, then the second tallest buildings in the city, a 13-story "skyscraper," only a few blocks to the east of the Qiu compound. Fearing that the Americans might yet retaliate, attack the Building and perhaps miss, the Jings took refuge in Qizhi's apartment on the second floor of a building, which was in a safer area and owned by the Ming Sheng Company. The first floor also served as part of the company's office. After nightfall, not to overcrowd others, the Jing brothers would return to their room in the Qiu compound to sleep. ·

At night the neighborhood was usually quiet. One night in August, while taking his shower, Guoda heard loud noises, sounding like shouting, mixed with singing. It came from the street. Rende ran out first. Quickly Guoda dried himself, put on his pants and rushed to join his brother outside the gate. The Qiu family's employees were already there. Guoda got himself between his brother and Old Taylor, the gatekeeper. A continuous throng was parading through the street. There were some Caucasians singing with the crowd. Leading them, surprise, was Guoda's erstwhile tutor Mr. Popov, the White Russian. "Finally, his mother's, the dawn has come!" Old Taylor said, rubbing the corner of his eyes. Japan had surrendered!

The brothers celebrated with the employees of the Qiu family, babbling long into the night, all were overcome with joy, incredulous of the end of their country's seemingly endless oppressed state. The brothers went to bed late. In the morning, they woke up late and arrived at the Ming Sheng Company building behind the usual allowed time. Fuli demanded to know the reason. Rende said that they had spent much of the night exulting with the neighbors in the good news. Fuli, in the presence of some of his colleagues, gave Rende two quick slaps, forehand on the left cheek and backhand the right, saying, "That's no excuse!" Guoda, who had kept his mouth shut, was spared.

CHAPTER 11

Like the dawn that stirs the quick in repose, the victory brought among the Chinese people at large a burst of activities, including much traveling. Contingencies of armed forces and representatives of branches of the government were deployed to the various key points in the occupied territory to take over control from the Japanese. People who had left their homes because of the war planned to return. The process resembled a reverse run of a movie. Of course there were differences, not the least of which was that everyone was eight years older, and a period of eight years means differently for different age groups. The younger the age, the greater the difference.

For the Min Sheng Company, the first order of business was to resume its shipping line along the Yangzi River. Fuli was sent to Nanjing, the nation's revived capital, as chief of its bureau office—a lower level of representation than "branch company." It would serve as a precursor to the reestablishment of a branch company, to be headed by someone from the main office in Chongqing. Fuli worked hard at the new assignment and opportunity. It earned him a gung-ho and can-do reputation. That and his conversance in English as well as his role in the erstwhile firing of the trouble makers in Ming Sheng's Shanghai office drew the attention of the manager of the Nanjing branch company of the China Merchants Navigation Company. He recruited Fuli as his Assistant Manager.

The vast machinery of the national government, waiting to return to Nanjing, all needed transportation; shipping via the Yangzi was the most popular route. Fuli came to meet a number of high officials. Some of them soon became friends; they evolved from former schoolmates, acquaintances, or simply "tong-xiang" (fellow provincials), i.e., Hunanese. The company remuneration included a good size stand-alone house and a car (with a chauffeur), when cars were quite scarce. After the military, transportation units ranked high in priority in the taking over of enemy materiel. His friends appreciated his help in transportation even within the city, let alone along the Yangzi. All and all, his new position, his English—in communicating with foreigners, especially Americans—and even his Beijing opera, often proved to be a popular socializing medium, allowed him to move among more influential circles than he used to. He was busy and happy.

In Shanghai, his two sons also felt that their fortunes had made a good turn, including a relief from an almost constant pressure in their daily lives. Not particularly interested in schoolwork, Rende found, with the help of his uncle Qizhi, a job as a teller at the Shanghai Commercial Bank. He lived in the bank's dormitory in the Hongkou district, once a Japanese Settlement in Shanghai. The (now un-)settlers stoically took the consequences of their country's defeat. The first dinner the brothers had alone together as more or less grownups were sukiyaki, served for a price (paid by Rende) in a Japanese home by an humble-mannered housewife in geta—an experience they'd have never imagined even a few months ago. Outside on the streets, multitudes of her stony-faced compatriots had much of their possessions—vases, paintings, tea ceremony sets, low tables, Go games etc.—spread out on the sidewalk for sale in preparation for a dispirited return to their home archipelago.

Guoda had moved into the dormitory of St. John's University. He felt like a creature on a new planet with a lower gravity. His steps were lighter, as if there were lift under his arms. The air itself was lighter, sweeter, and the sun shinier. Is there indeed life like this under heaven?

Even when "The sky is high and the emperor far away," he still needed sustenance from the emperor. But he had little problem in getting that. Responses to his requests for money were prompt and simple, no lectures, demanding almost nothing. It was as though getting into St. John's University was the goal. Not quite. His father had earlier discussed a major for him. The understanding was that it ought to prepare him to *make a living* by acquiring a useful skill like medicine or engineering. Guoda had barely mentioned history as a possibility, and Fuli told him, "You can't make a living on that. Most liberal arts graduates are lucky if they can find a job teaching middle school," he dismissed the idea.

On the St. John's campus, at the end of a school day, the medical students, their white gowns flapping, marched as a group, like a flock of angels, back into Mann Hall—then their exclusive dormitory. Guoda did not really want to have anything to do with them. The thought of the aseptic smell in that hospital room where they took out the stitches seemed enough, let alone the fact that he always had a hard time with chemistry and biology in high school.

On the other hand, the new engineering students sauntered between Science Hall—which housed the Engineering College—and their dorms, each carrying a drawing board and T-square that represented on campus a cachet of distinction almost equal to a white gown. Every time Guoda eyed them, enviously, he became more determined to join their ranks.

Because of low scores in mathematics and chemistry in his entrance examinations he couldn't enroll in a technical field. In his first term he declared himself a major in Political Science but signed up for remedial math also.

After the term, having passed all the courses he had taken, he pleaded his case with Professor Lin Yaqi, Dean of Engineering, promising hard work. At first the dean shook his head. Then, casting another glance at Guoda's record, he commented that "You did well in the history course," pointing to the B grade on it. He sounded appreciative, softened and let Guoda join the 1949 Civil Engineering class. It was rumored that the dean's first degree was in history; after he lost his girl friend to a civil engineer, he enrolled in civil engineering—aiming to prove something to somebody. Apparently he did just that by becoming not only a leading academician but a partner in one of the largest engineering/construction companies in China.

In Guoda's second term, by far his toughest course was mechanical drawing. Each assignment was a struggle—the razor blade scrapings of misplaced inked lines, the candle singeing the hair as he bent down his head too close over the work after the dorm lights were out, and the mad dash to the instructor's collection bin to beat the dead line. He survived the course with a C.

He shared a room with Guang Pengxi, an engineering major, and Zhu Daigu, an agriculture major. Both had matriculated directly from St. John's High School. Besides being a top athlete—first string left forward on the varsity soccer team—Pengxi was also a competent violinist. Daigu, a major in agriculture, was equally eminent as an athlete—center forward on the same varsity team, dubbed the "petit general in white gown," striking terror in the opposing team's goalkeeper as the quick feet pushed the ball toward the net. Thus their room was a spot of considerable fame in the dorm. Among the pilgrims was Ting Zhougao, then the sports writer for the school's weekly paper, *The Dial,* and decades later, the movie mogul and zillionaire in Hong Kong and Hollywood. Even though the Beijing opera wasn't nearly as appreciated as

Western music in the school, Guoda's fiddle playing gained for him some notoriety. But that paled against the distinction of his roommates.

That summer he went home by train. Home was in Nanjing now. The cars were very crowded. More stood, like him, than seated. A seated passenger to whom he was the closest left at the Wuxi station. He took the seat as a matter of course. A military officer with blood shot eyes, apparently desiring the seat, said to him, "You get up. You are just a student." He neither answered nor budged, ignoring the officer's fierce eyes with his own frown and clamped mouth to restrain his pounding heart. Nothing happened.

He dozed on the train that was losing more passengers than gaining as it made more stops. When he woke up, he found his head over his folded arms by the windowsill and a breeze tucking his hair. He felt relaxed, but then wondered how it would be like living with his father now, even just for the summer.

He was glad that the house was big enough for him to have a room all to himself, and gladder that his father was out-of-town on business. Qisheng busied herself with instructing the cook about the dinner to welcome not only her son home from college but also her sister-in-law, who was visiting.

A year older than Fuli, and having had only a middle school education, Guoda's aunt was "traditional." During dinner it was the job of a maid, who would stand near the table, to refill the rice bowl of any of the diners who had consumed its contents and wanted more. All one needed to do was to hold the bowl behind his or her ear and the maid would come over to get it. It wasn't necessary to say anything, not even to look at the person. Guoda wouldn't let her do it; he did the refilling himself. Later on when his aunt asked him about it, he said he thought it was demeaning for the maid to be serving in that manner. While Qisheng smiled, his aunt said, "Nowadays, you wonder what they learn at school besides all this so-called progressive stuff."

Fuli returned home shortly. Guoda anticipated instructions from him as to what to do in the summer. Fuli, however, was busy almost all the time—with his work or socializing. Guoda would be told to call the guests Uncle this and Aunt that. Most of them he had not met before, but they were apparently people of status: minister of finance of province A, minister of civil affairs of province B, (or spouse of). He would forget most of them after the introduction. However, he was very much impressed by a former schoolmate of his father, Lu Chongkai, Minister of Mines and Metals of the Central Government, reportedly the youngest cabinet member in the history of the Republic. Tall, stout and whose every movement seemed to end in an elegant pose fit for a portrait, he had a master degree from the famous Columbia University in America and had been the representative there for the largest tungsten company in Hunan.

Guoda would hang around in the living room unobtrusively, watching the big officials, and listening to their anecdotes, such as that about the Generalissimo's command of the English language. At the time, General George Marshall was in Nanjing to mediate the conflict between the Nationalists and the Communists. General Pan, a high school classmate of Fuli and later a graduate of Sandhurst of England, who served as the interpreter between the Generalissimo and Marshall, told the room that once the Generalissimo was trying to give the American envoy a verbal social invitation in English, the only word the envoy could understand was "picnic."

In spite of General Marshall's efforts, the Civil War continued. Most of the public south of the Yangzi River paid little attention to it. The media, under government control, treated it as a minor matter. Brief coverage would appear on the back pages. In fact, many felt a bit perplexed that the Communists had come to matter so much that the venerable American would be here to work on the problem. The Nationalist's military force outnumbered the Communist's 4:1, and was so much better equipped too.

Guoda got no assignment from Fuli in the first week. He thought he was given a time to rest. In the second week he was told just to organize Fuli's book cases. In the meantime, Guoda would amuse himself some with the fiddle. Read a little. *The Romance of the Three Kingdoms*—good stuff, a little long, and repetitious nearing the end—took him two weeks to wade through the almost thousand pages. He read the Bible some. (He was given a copy in his 8th grade English class at St. John's YMCA Middle School.) Couldn't honestly believe the very first chapter, but, jumping to the New Testament, felt much resonance with sections in the Gospel according to St. Matthew. He memorized the Lord's Prayer. "Give us our daily bread" made a lot of sense to him but wondered why "Lead us not into temptation" was so important. On the other hand, his mother found that he wasn't around watching anymore when she was at a mahjong table. Maybe it has to do with being progressive too, she thought.

Rende came home to visit. The brothers sailed on Xuan Wu Lake at night—to avoid the daytime heat. (Nanjing was known as one of the three ovens on the Yangzi River—the other two being Wuhan and Chongqing.) In a tour boat, they drank pop, watching other boats, like theirs, decked with lanterns, glide by in the longing female voice accompanied by a melancholy erhu fiddle. Rende called his brother's attention to a beautiful young woman sitting in their boat with presumably her family. They made the usual appreciative comments. Later, when the ride was over, they were surprised to note that she was crippled. They laughed at themselves and commented under their breath that the girl was a "half Kwan-ying" (half goddess). Seconds later, Guoda was overcome with shame and pang of conscience by that remark.

He passed that summer largely like a person who was hired and waited for his work assignments but glad they never came. He didn't know enough to make use of free time and was contented to while it away, waiting to begin his sophomore year at St. John's.

CHAPTER 12

In his first term as a sophomore, Guoda studied analytical geometry while his classmates were already on integral calculus. In their descriptive geometry class, often while nearly all his classmates had already handed in the assignment and left the drafting room, he would still be struggling. Yet he didn't cut down his extracurricular activities in order to remove his academic deficiencies. For he had other kinds of deficiencies to make up for. He was like an animal that has been let out after a prolonged period in a cage. Initially it would hesitate, move slowly, not quite knowing what to do; gradually it would recognize the new environment and freedom, and start to run tentatively. He was like some organism that has thus far been deprived of some essential nutrient, and is now suddenly immersed in a medium saturated with that nutrient. The university is the medium for him to soak up the joy of youth and freedom.

At mid-morning of every school day, a break of 20 minutes allowed students and faculty to attend a short morning service in the university chapel, attendance of which was not mandatory, and thus low. Some students would rather use the time to lean against the corridor balustrades and talk, to stroll, to muse under the big camphor tree on the South Lawn—a campus landmark, like the chapel itself—or, gather by the steps of the sundial, between S.Y. Hall and the stone Memorial Arch to listen to some larger-than-life campus figure, such as a former air force pilot—so he told his audience, while others whispered that he was just a civilian employee in the force—expounding on the demands of flying a P-38 fighter plane.

Pengxi, however, would occasionally play a violin piece, like Massenet's *Meditation*, at the chapel service. He and Daigu were also members of the Sunday choir of the chapel. At their suggestion, Guoda went to church service one

Sunday. After it ended, Pengxi introduced him to the choir conductor, Miss Helen Yeats, a middle-aged lady from California, stout and kindly. She encouraged him to join the choir. He said he didn't know how to sing. She suggested that he come to their next practice and see. Before he returned, Pengxi taught him rudiments of music reading and interpretation of key signatures for solmization. After he had muddled through at the practice session, Miss Yeats said to him, "Why, you sang so well." He was recruited.

The choir was a place to make beautiful and often inspiring music; it also provided opportunities to meet the opposite sex. Guoda felt little contradiction between the noble and the profane. A trim soprano with a pleasing pumpkinseed-shaped face attracted the interest of the three roommates. Zhong Juan was still a student at St. Mary's Girl School. Her father was a professor of physics, and the family lived in the faculty compound on campus. None of the roommates was audacious enough to claim exclusivity; they proceeded together. They would take walks with her after nightfall. Since there were only two sides beside her, and when she chose to walk close to the bank of the Suzhou Creek—that flowed leisurely round much of the campus—there would be only one side, unless one was willing to swim. So, it took some tactics to get to walk right by her side. After several outings, a pattern evolved, on which Daigu would comment to Pengxi, "When it comes to jockeying for position, I thought you and I, the right forward and the center forward, ought to have an advantage. But Guoda out-maneuvered us both. We ought to get him to try out for the team." Subsequently, the varsity players relinquished their rights and set out for their adventures elsewhere.

Guoda and Juan would generally meet once a week, usually on Saturday nights. They would stroll on campus, choosing less traveled paths and unpopular spots. They would sit on the steps to the door of Professor Throops's house, listening to J.S. Bach's beat inside, or on the bench in front of the Agricultural College, watching the moon over the Suzhou Creek, but never under the famed big camphor tree—too popular a place for rendezvous. The relation lasted many months. The whole thing was low-keyed, almost platonic. They would talk about their daily activities—her piano lessons and softball practices, his homework and the clothes that needed washing. She'd advise him that washing the socks more often would actually prolong their lives. Eventually, they kissed, not much more than little pecks, as if they were obligated to do so. It was not a matter of keeping passion in check; it seemed that there was just not that much inside. Perhaps it was due to culture, or to the wartime meager nourishment in the recent past that had slowed the biological development.

Rarely they would meet in daytime. When they did, it would then be outside the campus, such as in a movie theater or a park. They'd ride the university bus, which was an old open army truck affair with benches installed along two sides. Without help one needed to be a bit of an athlete to get on it, since there were no steps to the deck. Once on it, if one was to remain standing, he would need to flex the body constantly to keep balance when the vehicle was in motion. It ran between the campus and certain key points in the city, including the Bund by the Huangpu River. Guoda and Juan wouldn't sit or stand together; in fact, in the bus they wouldn't even acknowledge that they knew each other, coming together only after reaching the destination.

Other than the weekly rendezvous, life with Guoda appeared thus far quite orderly and appropriate for a college dormitory resident. Then a story was going the rounds in the dorm that one night, on the third floor, which housed the medicine majors, a student woke up and saw a human form shrouded in white, kneeling by his bedside. He gave out a cry and pulled the quilt over his head. Afterwards, his awakened roommates and he found nothing unusual. The word went out that a spirit had returned to haunt some clumsy medical bookworm, who had probably mangled its body in the anatomy laboratory.

The following Sunday night, Pengxi, returning to school from his home in Hongkou met Daigu at the gate. In the evening chill, they talked about the scary story. Once inside Yen Hall, their dorm, Pengxi said, "The breeze felt downright cold. So nice to be inside," his sonorous bass voice resonating down the corridor. "You can say that again!" Daigu echoed, as they sauntered to their room. Pengxi opened the door and saw a form, shrouded in white, kneeling by his bed. With a loud "Ahh!" he turned and ran; Daigu, who had shared a glimpse of the form, chased him. In their dashing down the hall, the varsity soccer players heard rapidly pounding footfalls behind; they turned their heads to look. In the dim corridor light the white form was jouncing toward them. Before they could run much harder, they tripped over each other by the hall's entrance and were caught by the form. The three rolled into a ball, with a white bed sheet ten feet behind on the floor. When Guoda first heard Pengxi's "Ahh," Guoda had thought: "Good, it worked," but then, "It can't be that bad! Something else is here?"

Although Guoda survived the descriptive geometry course with a bare D, he flunked general chemistry II. That didn't give him pause to join his roommates and some others on spring break to vacation in Hangzhou. They hired a boat to sail the West Lake. The young boatman had reneged on his promise to maintain a supply of tea. The college students got him to supply the drink anyway by offering to take a picture of his face, which, they told him sincerely, was extraordinarily handsome. The offer, along with the appraisal of the young man's facial features, was repeated whenever the teapot became empty. Unfailingly the pot would be refilled, after a click of the camera that had no film inside.

Films were expensive, not to be wasted. The 1949 Civil Engineering class of over 40 strong had no female student. The strength of material class had but one woman, an architecture major. It was not surprising that the comely and artistic young lady would find the course rather mechanical and inartistic, yet troublesomely demanding. A chivalrous classmate, normally a loner and a bit of a "teacher, teacher"—a title Pengxi had coined to be conferred on someone the roommates considered sanctimonious or prudish—volunteered to tutor her. The contents of the tutoring were unknown to any outside observer. But, the tutor's patience and solicitude were plain to the world, at least to those sharing the library with them, and it would make Confucius blush with envy. The tutelage took place on the ground floor of the Low Library. In order to record the event for posterity, Guoda and Pengxi decided to photograph them. To account for the dimness inside, they set the exposure timer to some ten seconds. They slunk to a nearby window, seated the camera on its ledge, focused the noble pedagogic scene, and pressed the button. The timer buzzed, loudly. Too loudly. Guoda turned and ran; Pengxi, grabbing the camera, followed. They stopped behind a tree, panting. Suddenly, Pengxi, still hearing the camera buzzing, pointed it at his roommate and commanded, "Guoda! Don't move!" The precious film could still be salvaged.

Hoping to do a better job at the choir, Guoda enlisted the help of a voice teacher. At the third lesson, the teacher said to him, "My voice is like this." He pointed to the gleaming smooth lacquer on the piano lid, after lilting dulcetly "La—" and his face twitching orgasmic appreciation of his own voice. Then he said, "Your voice is like this," pointing to a spot where the lacquer had peeled with jagged edging. That was Guoda's last voice lesson.

He joined a group to learn ballroom dancing. "Boom—Cha-Cha, Boom—Cha-Cha…" they would intone and practice in the dorm corridor until the supervisor interfered on behalf of those who wanted to sleep.

The supervisor, graduated only a year ago, had to work hard at the role. One Sunday night, after the lights were out, loud talking and guffaws emanated from a room; he knocked on the door and was invited in. He proceeded to lecture the occupants on the rules. They praised his wisdom and leadership. A few minutes later, he was himself lying on an empty bed in the same room, joining in the bull session with Guoda and his roommates.

For all the pranks and shenanigans, that term was for Guoda his best at St. John's. He had a B minus average. To be truthful, however, it was tainted somewhat by an A grade received in dynamics. Professor Mendelker, a short German Jew with a twinkle in his eye, was the instructor. The last class meeting for the course was termed "discussion of grades." The professor would call a student's name, "Wang Xuezhe!"

"Here!"

"I think you've done well in this course. I'll give you a C plus."

"No, Professor Mendelker, I have worked very hard for this course. So hard that I lost sleep and weight."

"All right, a B, or B plus then."

"No, it's got to be an A. I've spent so much time on the course. My mother worried about my health."

"Er…All right, A it is…. Now let me see. Next…Teng Caizi…. I think you've done well…." The whole dialogue would be repeated…. Guoda got his A, the only A he had in engineering at St. John's. He wondered who had more fun, the students or the wily professor from Germany. It was thought then that a civil engineer did not need to be versed in dynamics; statics was necessary and sufficient.

CHAPTER 13

In order to have a chance to graduate with the regular class, Guoda stayed on for summer school. So did his roommates, in their case mainly for social purposes. Together they spent much time with members of the choir, mostly the sopranos and altos. They would go boating in the outlying small towns, bringing food and guitar. Miss Yeats would sometimes be the chaperon and subsidize them with sandwiches and drinks made by a cook and a maid—a brother and sister twosome—that served the unmarried American faculty living on campus.

The group went on a trip to Suzhou. As they came to the foot of the Tian Ping Mountain, a country girl caught their attention. A most beautiful lass with eyes like dew in the morning light was selling eggs hard boiled in tea. The college boys encircled her, asking her about this and about that. "How old are you?" "How come you are so pretty and selling eggs? You should be in the movies." The girl seemed to be used to all that. There was an air about her that kept the young men within bounds of propriety. Yet they wouldn't let her alone. Their female companions tried to get their attention, reminding them it was time to climb the mountain. They, however, either didn't hear or ignored them. Propelled by anger, the girls shot up to the peak like rockets, leaving the boys at the foothill, milling about the maiden like a swarm of worker bees around the queen.

Her name was Ah Xiu (The Graceful). Later they were told by an elderly villager that indeed some movie people from Shanghai had asked her to go to the big city for a tryout, but her parents declined. It was so wise, the college students sagely agreed. They passed the night in the Suzhou home of a schoolmate. Lying in bed, Pengxi kept calling out agonizingly "Ah Xiu! Ah Xiu!..."

Guoda associated her with the second movement of Beethoven's *Pastoral*, that he had heard in Miss Yeats's living room.

In the backyard of Miss Yeats's little house by the chapel, sometimes they would have post-swimming parties. The swimming pool on campus allowed mixed-swimming three days a week—usually before the water in the pool was changed, once a week. It was well water. After being pumped up, it would feel ice-like until it was warmed for a couple of days by the atmosphere. During that time, only males were admitted; for best hygiene, the swimmers were not allowed to wear anything. There would be middle and high school kids around too. Targeting them, some college boys, including Daigu, would tell sexual stories, and when the narrative waxed graphical and heated, one by one the young schoolers would hop into the cold water. Plump-splash! Plump-splash! Legs sticking out of the water like frogs' before the body was immersed.

On some afternoons of summer storms, the roommates would play bridge in the loggia overlooking the inner court inside S.Y. Hall, their summer dormitory, the rain splattering on the balustrades. When hungry, they could just shout their orders downward toward the "small kitchen" on the floor below, and such dishes as pan fried soft noodles with pork chop and onion would be brought up a few minutes later.

After the rain had stopped, at sunset, some of the less choosy young ladies that the roommates had come to know at the swimming pool would appear under the bell tower of S.Y. Hall, calling them to come out. They would hesitate, feeling like maidens in medieval castles. Then when the real maidens held up plates of juicy cubes of cut watermelon, their reluctance melted like ice cream in the sun.

In the flurry of sun and fun, Guoda and Juan would meet also during the week, but generally in group settings. Their regular Saturday night rendezvous became irregular and the relationship seemed to be disengaging. One evening, he was returning to the dorm. Before he turned toward its rear door, he saw dimly past the Gymnasium the backs of a couple strolling near Shu-ren Hall on the High School grounds. The female shape gave rise to his suspicion. He followed them surreptitiously and confirmed that it was Juan. The man was tall, long-legged, and had a graceful way about him, like a well-born, cultured athlete. I can't compete with this guy, he told himself. It bothered him. A couple of days later, he had one of those night rendezvous with Juan. He asked her about the person. She said that he was a senior at St. John's High School, and

"...We are only ordinary friends..." Guoda's relief lasted only a flash as she continued, "just like us...." She smiled; the dimpled, pumpkinseed-shaped face suddenly struck Guoda as so much more attractive now, though a little cold, distant, even cruel.

That was the beginning of the end of his first romance. The reconstruction of past sweet moments, again and again, lost...lost...the doubts, regrets—perhaps I have taken her too much for granted...and the humiliation—beaten by a high schooler! He lost sleep. All and all, the pain felt much worse than the kind his father's bamboo ruler had delivered.

Sometime mid-summer, Fuli was in Shanghai on business, staying in a hotel. He had visited Guoda on campus once before in the spring. That time he had come unannounced, only Daigu was in the room. Guoda was surprised—shocked, actually—when he returned to the room. They had lunch together at a restaurant outside the campus. Guoda waited for the lowering of some boom. None came. Fuli was almost cordial. They went over generalities like how are you doing with your courses. For that term, Guoda could honestly respond with "rather well." He was under the impression that his father was doing even better. He was in a good mood. The only admonition was: "If you have to smoke, pick a good brand, like Lucky Strike, not Chesterfield; it has counterfeits on the market." Guoda mumbled and let it pass. He dared not admit outright that he smoked, let alone asking would there be counterfeits of Lucky Strike too? Later, Daigu told him that his father had looked into his drawer and found a pack of Chesterfield. Actually, unlike his roommates, he did not smoke much. He did it occasionally to be fashionable and sociable.

For this summer visit, Guoda felt more at ease; there was no surprise. In fact, he was glad that his father would want to see him on this day. He arrived at the hotel around six o'clock. Fuli wasn't back yet, and he waited in the lobby. Sometime around seven, he saw Fuli, smartly dressed, walking toward him. He rose from the sofa and said, "You are back. Yaya."

"How long have your been waiting?"

"Not long."

"Fine, fine," Fuli seemed to be a little hesitant, absent-minded. "Sit down," he motioned Guoda to the sofa. "How is school?"

"I am doing all right."

"You think the summer school would enable you to graduate with the regular class?"

"Yes. Yaya, you know practically all my classmates had begun their preparation for engineering before college."

"I know, I know. As long as you can graduate with them, that'll be good enough."

"How are you, Yaya?"

"I am fine. Busy though. A lot of work, very busy."

"How is mother?"

"Your mother is fine. Your brother too," Fuli said and took a look at his watch.

Under the light Guoda noticed Fuli's face look flushed. "You still have business to attend to to-night?"

"I am afraid I do."

Guoda felt that he should leave. "Then I'll go back to school."

"That's fine. You need money?"

"No. I am all right."

Fuli reached in his pocket and gave Guoda three bills anyway, each 50,000 yuan. "Take it."

Guoda took the money (worth about five U.S. dollars) and said goodbye to his father. He had assumed that he would be led to Fuli's room to talk and have dinner together. But he was glad he wasn't called on to defend himself on anything. And glad to leave to find a place to eat, for he was hungry. Alone in a small restaurant, he told the waiter, "I would like to have a bowl of noodle with beef." One always has noodles on one's birthday.

Guoda had a fairly advanced case of varicose veins in his left leg. He would tie a handkerchief around the largest bulge that was just below the knee for support. Miss Yeats had noticed it. One day she said to him that a Dr. Miller at St. Luke's Hospital downtown would see him free of charge. He went and the doctor suggested an incision in the upper thigh.

The relatively minor operation was done in the hospital after the summer term had ended. On the second day in the hospital, his friends had visited him and left before dusk. After night fell, out of the blue appeared a young woman's face by the lamplight, fair with deep-set eyes, big, black and glistening. He had met Lian Chanli but a few times. A freshman, she had come to the choir occasionally. She told him that she lived just next door, on the grounds of St. Luke's Church, where her father was a minister. She came the next evening too. Shortly after he left the hospital, they went to see *Yearling*, starring Gregory Peck, at the Roxy Theater.

Soon the fall term started. One evening he went to the city to visit her. He found her playing the piano in the church, a picture of sanctity. She was luke-warm at first, saying with some irony, "What wind blows you over here?" When he returned to his room that night, his roommates laughed at the lip-stick residues on his face, saying that he should have removed such evidence of "crime." He wasn't sure whether he had left them on semi-intentionally, as a badge of accomplishment or mark of recovery. The pain of the thigh wound was gone, so was that inflicted by that long-legged high school athlete.

He again had a heavy load, including the time-consuming and physically demanding surveying course and the intellectually challenging differential equations course. Two weeks after the previous call, he went downtown to visit Chanli. She was patently cool; the dialog was mostly non sequitur. He couldn't fathom the cause. He didn't call her again. It was a shallow relationship. Easy come, easy go, he told himself. The second time seemed much easier to handle.

He was having difficulties with differential equations. One of the choir altos, Mei Helei, a bespectacled, petite but shapely physics major and a wizard at mathematics, heard about this and offered to help. The tutoring was done at her home, a three story house on the faculty compound. The sessions were serious, initially. After he got on track of the mathematics, they began to have extracurricular breaks. All this took place in the first floor parlor; she had told him that her father—Controller and Vice President of the University—was sick in bed upstairs. Shortly afterwards, he was shocked to learn that her father had died. He did little to comfort her, largely because he didn't know how. He kept telling himself he had no idea that her father was that seriously ill. Never-theless, he felt guilty, suspecting himself of taking advantage of a young woman needing emotional support.

He also struggled with the fieldwork of surveying. Sometimes, he would have a headache after hours in the cold air of late fall. Once, the traverse passed by Miss Yeats's cottage; she invited him to stop by after he was done. He did, and mentioned his headache. She told him to sit down, saying "Poor Guoda…" with her thin-lipped pouting and fussed over him with a hot towel on his forehead, calling the maid to make tea. A veritable in loco mater.

Schoolwork was going fairly smoothly now. He had an additional room-mate. Tall, thin and several years older, Ah Yu impressed his roommates with his easy self-confidence and sophisticated talk, like dancing with the "profes-sionals" at the Paramount Parlor. He led them there one night to its glass floor and taxi dancers.

Guoda didn't enjoy the experience at all. The girls seemed either wooden or insincere or both. And he never did even think of plucking the brassier strap at his partner's back in rhythm with the bass beat, as Ah Yu had coached them to do (for that and his thinness they called him "bra-strap" thereafter).

At Guoda's next meeting with Helei, they were sitting on the steps of the chapel's side door, near which the male servant of the American singles faculty would sit during service and start to pump the organ whenever he heard knocks on its side.

"Haven't seen you all week. Working hard?" Helei asked.

"Most of the time," he said. The trees rustling in the breeze, the air smelled fresh and pure, a lot nicer than the stuffy, smoky, noisy dance hall. "It's so quiet and peaceful here. Have I told you about our new roommate Ah Yu before?"

"Yes. Does he come to the service?"

"Him to church?" Guoda chuckled, and unthinkingly he continued, "You know he led us to quite an expedition the other evening."

"What's that?"

He couldn't go back now. Might as well go straight ahead. He proceeded to tell her of the dance hall escapade, treating it as a joke, since he felt at bottom it was like one.

After he finished, she was silent, looked blandly ahead.

In a moment, she said, "Who do you take me for?"

"What do you mean?" An embarrassment set in.

"Telling me this base behavior in your cigarette polluted breath." Her almond eyes turned bug-eyed.

"You are making too big a deal of this. I didn't do anything base. It was meant to be innocent fun! I told you I didn't enjoy it at all. It was boring, and a waste of time."

"It doesn't sound so innocent to me." She stood up and strode off with her (proportionately) long legs.

What a "teacher, teacher!" Guoda thought. He let her go.

Later on, he knew he had made a mistake, not particularly in having gone to the dance hall—although he had no desire to do it again—but in presuming that his girlfriend would care for him so much that she would tolerate being told such an experience in her face. The next day he called at her house. Her mother answered the door, went in, came out and said her daughter was busy and unavailable. At the following choir practice, Helei held him off with stiff politeness. After it was repeated the next Sunday morning, Guoda was disappointed and gave up. However, healing came fairly soon, as their relationship returned to one of a genial fellowship of the choir that existed before the romantic interlude.

The choir had a male quartet consisted of the three roommates plus a tenor, Yan Shaohuang. Besides at the church, they would also sometimes sing at wedding parties. Yan, suave—particularly for a physics major—had a soft, floating lyric voice. Taciturn but always with a ready smile, he was good looking with well combed long hair, dressed simply but neatly. However, he was somewhat mysterious to the roommates. Although he would be with the choir and the quartet for practically all their activities, yet he managed to keep a certain distance. In fact, none of the roommates had ever been in his room, which was in a different dorm building. They sometimes suspected that he might even think them juvenile. However, they never considered him a "teacher, teacher." There were some whispers that he might be a "leftist," i.e., a Communist sympathizer, even though they knew of no evidence pointing to it. To them his elegant style seemed so at variance with the loud, crude leftists on campus. A point like that did not bother the roommates one way or the other, as they were utterly apolitical—and innocent and naïve.

Then Christmas came. There were candle light service, and caroling well into the night. Miss Yeats got up from her bed and thanked the carolers profusely at the doorstep of her cottage. And there were parties.

When at last the holiday festivities were all over, Guoda read the news that the People's Liberation Army (PLA) had crossed the Yellow River. He wondered what happened to those Nationalist soldiers he had seen at the Bund, who were being sprayed by American sailors with apparently some kind of disinfectant before they embarked on the moored American naval ships, to be transported north to Manchuria to repel the Communists.

CHAPTER 14

Between the rear gate of Jessfield Park and the front one of St. John's was posted a big truck covered with banners and loaded with boxes of towels and bars of soap. Along with a crowd milling about it, a line, in which most appeared to be peasants or laborers, was passing slowly through a station of two tables set up at the tailgate. One by one, each would be handed a towel and a bar of soap after signing their names or, for those who couldn't write, making a cross on a register. Although the Nationalists were not doing that well in the Civil War, they were going ahead to elect a new National Assembly and Legislature. The Assembly convened in April and elected Chiang Kai-shek President of the Republic of China.

Guoda and his roommates did not even consider voting. In fact, they hardly knew anyone who had voted. Their world seemed to lie in a slice of a few miles extending from the bend of the Suzhou Creek at the inner end of the campus to the Bund by the Huangpu River.

Getting used to the engineering courses now, Guoda felt no particular pressure; all he cared for was a passing grade. However, something else concerned him—inflation.

It had been getting worse. From 1945 to 1947, the cost of living rose about 3,000 percent; from 1947 to 1948, 10,000 percent. He would make out a monthly budget and write to his father; by the time he received the remittance, he could hardly live on it for a week; adjustment had to be made in the next remittance, and the discrepancies with that would be worse. Then, quite unexpectedly, Fuli wrote him that henceforth he was to pick up his monthly allowance from his Uncle Qizhi on the basis of a dollar a day—a silver dollar! His financial condition changed from night to day. Thus every four weeks or so, he'd present myself in the big office of the manager of the Min Sheng Company. Qizhi, who had been promoted to that position for some time now, would rise from his seat and take out some 30 silver dollars from a black safe by the wall, make an entry in a notebook and hand the money to his nephew. All this was done in his usual quiet, gentle, and efficient fashion. Out of the office building, Guoda walked with a heavy pocket but a light heart.

The citizens had no confidence in the legal currency. Peasants carried their produce in big baskets to town. They needed the same baskets to carry the bulk of the bundles of paper money from their day's sales to some jewelry shop to buy a bit of gold or silver to protect themselves from inflation, even in a day. "Silver Cows"—hawkers who bought and sold silver dollars—stood on street corners and everywhere, jangling the oversize coins in their hands. Going to a restaurant, Guoda and his friends would order the food and eat first before they went out to exchange their silver dollars for the legal currency to pay the check. Chances were good that the silver dollar would have appreciated during the meal.

The Class of 1949 was to have their surveying camp in the summer of 1948. However, before that, there would be a lengthy break, and Guoda was going to see his family, which had moved from Nanjing to Changsha a year and half ago. Leaving Shanghai aboard a ship, he stood by the railing amidst the rumbling of water boiling against the hull and watched the harbor lights recede. I'd be a senior next year…. And then…He did not pursue the thought. He disembarked at Hankou and took a train heading for Changsha. On it, he ran into Minister Lu Chongkai whom he had met in his Nanjing home two years ago and had called him "Uncle Lu."

The minister was gracious, but a little more reserved than previously. Having arrived at their common destination, he gave a perfunctory invitation to the college student to visit his home in town.

Fuli was now the manager of the branch office of the China Merchants and Steamship Navigation Company in Changsha. The volume of the shipping business here was much smaller than that in Nanjing. During the winter months, the Xiang River, that connects the city to the Yangzi River, was often too shallow for navigation. Fuli was nevertheless happy with the change, returning to his hometown a man of considerable status in the community. Besides, being the boss, instead of assistant boss, had its obvious attractions. (Rende told his brother that the manager of China Merchants in Nanjing had found their father not particularly malleable and recommended his promotion to get him out of the way.)

Rende, while working for the Shanghai Commercial Bank, had guaranteed a friend's loan and entrusted the friend with his personal chop. The man used the chop to procure another loan. When it was not paid on time, Rende was indicted and threatened with a jail sentence. The case was tried and he was cleared as the judge was convinced that he was essentially the victim of a theft. Fuli told him to return to Changsha and made him an employee of China Merchants as Assistant to the Manager. Rende had married there over a year ago. His wife, Zhang Aili, petite, comely and silent, came from a Shanghai business family of long standing. They and their infant son now lived with his parents, although she preferred otherwise.

These days Fuli was generally in a good disposition, content with his lot. His demeanor toward his sons also indicated some recognition of their age and development. In particular, he seemed to accord Guoda a measure of respect, no harsh words, not one, that summer, let alone punishment. Guoda welcomed the change.

When he first returned, he was still bothered by a pounding of the heart caused by a lack of sleep and the "no-doze" pills taken during the days of final examinations. Qisheng set out to collect a dozen eggs, one from each of a dozen families, and cooked them with a turtle. She had him take the concoction. The pounding stopped. He wasn't sure whether it was due to the remedy or just the rest. Qisheng told him that she had learned the prescription from his grandmother, who had gone to live with her second son in Chongqing. Qisheng missed her, and so did Guoda.

One night Guoda and his father were resting behind the house with wisteria on the back wall and bamboo along the other sides of the yard. The atmosphere was relaxed.

"Do you have a girlfriend at school?" Fuli asked.

This presented Guoda a dilemma. Not so much about girlfriend. But because his father had spoken in English. He thought it embarrassing, bad form actually, to converse in English in a totally Chinese surrounding, yet to reply entirely in Chinese might offend his father. So he would begin the first sentence in English and the rest in Chinese. (A practice he had followed later on in life in similar situations.)

"No one special (in English). But I have come to know some women fellow students at the church (in Chinese)," Guoda understated.

"From St. Mary's or McTeiyre Girls' School?"

"Oh yeah, some of them are," Guoda thought his father was well informed.

"Let me tell you. You'd better watch out...." Hearing no response from his son, he continued, "Don't ever get into *a relation* with them. Once a child is involved, you are stuck, for life."

That's what he meant by *relation*, Guoda thought. He kept quiet, feigning an expression of total innocence, incomprehension even.

Fuli continued, "You know, after you graduate, I would like to send you to America for graduate school."

Whoa! Graduate school! In America! I could hardly keep my nose above the water as an undergraduate here in China. He croaked some sound to indicate that he was listening.

"I've heard that a school called Purdue University has a very good engineering college," Fuli added.

"I haven't heard of that school before. Our dean, Dean Lin, had graduated from MIT," Guoda stayed neutral.

"Of course, I have heard of MIT, Cornell, etc. But they say Purdue is just as good, although the others are better known."

All this talk is irrelevant, Guoda thought.

After a pause, Fuli said, "Now you are growing up. Whom would you emulate to be in the future?"

Guoda wasn't prepared for this. Dean Lin? Not really. His uncle Qizhi sprang to mind. However, he remembered Fuli's occasional criticism of his brother-in-law, told to Qisheng, "...That brother of yours is just on the lazy side...." and "...With his talent, he ought to..." and "...He is too soft, wimpy even..." Guoda couldn't help feeling sometimes that his father considered his Uncle Qizhi a competitor. So, he replied, "Yaya, I think you have been doing very well." That was not a lie, although it did not really answer the question either, but it sufficed.

"I must say that I have been rather fortunate," Fuli smiled. "Too bad, I can't show you my new office overlooking the Xiang River. The construction of the new building is soon to start."

"I know. Brother has told me."

"Your brother...He has performed well for the company.... Has he told you about a fracas he got into lately in western Hunan?"

"No."

"Well, I'd sent a supervisor along with your brother to western Hunan to purchase coal for the company. The supervisor reported the incident to me. A hassle developed between them and a local operative near the entrance to a mine. Shortly, a group of miners approached them threateningly from down the path, some with picks in their hands. Old Chen, the supervisor, admitted that he was 'scared to death.' Rende took a shovel that was lying nearby, stepped onto the middle of the road, squared himself to the miners, raised the shovel horizontally in front of him with spread hands and shouted: 'Who wants to come first!' his teeth baring and eyes glinting with ferocity. That gave the miners pause. A third party came up and mediated the exigency; no physical harm ensued for anyone."

"He is fearless and brave."

"He is Hunanese. And you...too much of a Shanghainese." Fuli chuckled.

Guoda didn't particularly appreciate the implication, but mentally he partially agreed with his father.

"You know sometimes, thinking back, I had...in the past perhaps been a little too anxious to cultivate you two brothers."

What is this? Guoda thought. Is he trying to apologize now? He kept quiet.

Fuli took a drink of tea, looked around him, the house, the yard, the bamboo, and said, "All this is very nice.... But I am concerned about the Communists. They are such insidious pests."

The Jing and Lu families then belonged to what might be loosely termed an "upper crust" of the city. They would form a social relationship even without previous ties. Now Mmes. Jing and Lu would meet often at mahjong parties. Once, the Jing brothers were walking home together; as they turned into the lane of their house, they saw two shoeshine boys squatting by the roadside, playing cards. A well dressed, tall and thickset pedestrian, having reached the spot, kicked their boxes, and the kits tumbled on the ground. "You useless little rascals! Gambling in public, eh?" he shouted. The boys picked up the cards and boxes and scuttled away. The man walked on. Rende told his brother, "He is an Assemblyman of the province, used to be a police chief in some city." The Assemblyman was a guest at their house that afternoon, and a participant of a mahjong game.

One afternoon Qisheng was going to visit Mrs. Lu, and asked Guoda to come along. The rickshaws crossed a stretch of a thoroughfare and turned into a maze of narrow side streets with small shops on both sides, clothes hung only a few feet above their heads from the second story of low, dark, gray two-story houses. The rickshaws pulled up at a bookstore. Qisheng led her son through a narrow corridor and exited a back door. Suddenly appeared a wide courtyard, paved in new concrete with shrub edgings. Behind, stood a big modern house with a balcony, bright windows and elegant marble trimmings. It was the 16-room residence that Minister Lu had built so recently that the road to its front door had not yet been paved and thus a side door had to be used.

The minister was not home. In the front hall, Qisheng introduced his son to his "Aunt Lu," who expressed her welcome. Her appearance and mien impressed him, as her husband's had. He thought that she and his mother had met their match in each other in presence and looks. Then a troop entered. Mrs. Lu introduced her children and suggested that they play host to the college student from Shanghai while she visited with his mother.

Guoda found himself in the inner parlor, with six girls (actually four young women and two little girls) and two boys. Miss Lu No. 2 (The eldest daughter was married and living out of town) was about his age. Her next three sisters and their first brother were about a year apart, followed by two much younger sisters and another brother. Misses No. 3 and No. 5 were vivacious and, Miss No. 4 seemed somewhat pensive. He found Miss No. 2 most intriguing. She had short hair, used no make-up, dressed simply in a gray cheongsam, wore canvas shoes, and said very little. She fitted his idea of the charms of a classical Chinese maiden, free of the Western styled affectations that he had observed of some young women in Shanghai. The sisters, led by Misses No. 3 and No. 5 taking advantage of their number, teased Guoda by cajoling him to sing and then mocked him afterwards. He got through the experience without undue damage to the name of "a college student from Shanghai."

That summer he visited the Lus several times, including once joining them to visit Hunan University on the slopes of the scenic Yuelue Mountain across the Xiang River. The young people hiked on the hilly paths. The sisters, excepting Jiafeng, Miss No. 2, had a good laugh when he "happened" to be walking abreast with her, and their brothers sang Wagner's wedding march behind them.

His stay in Changsha was ended by a call to the surveying camp. He returned to Shanghai by rail via Nanchang and Hangzhou. The camp was in the county of Changshu, about 100 miles from Shanghai. It was organized into teams, five students to a team. Each team would survey a stretch of a road in the town's outskirts. The region was noted for its fertile land and natural beauty with green hills, clear streams and ponds rife with caltrops. At breaks, the engineers-to-be would eat the succulent caltrops in the sun.

When not working, the college students would strut around town, flaunting themselves. For one thing, they dressed differently and sloppily. One student had on himself a pair of swimming trunks so short that they were covered by his loose shirt. When some townspeople stared at him, he would say to them, "Look! Look! If you are interested, then look!" as he lifted his shirt.

One rainy day, some of the idled students played bridge inside a pavilion in the town park. The town struck back. Accusing them of gambling in public, the police detained them and confiscated the cards as evidence. A big broadside notice, posted on the wall of the town hall, reported the violation and pronounced that, at such and such a time and date the cards would be burnt in public at the town square to show that law and order prevailed. The news brought Dean Lin pronto from Shanghai. After some negotiations including an explanation of the game of bridge, which the dean himself loved (told his students: "always draw the trumps first"), the detained students were released, and the cards-burning ceremony was cancelled. But the two decks of cards were retained by the local government as a measure of compromise. Other than that imbroglio, the camp operated smoothly.

The national government would have hoped that the economy would operate smoothly. To fight the rampaging inflation, it proclaimed a new money system—the "Gold Yuan." The old money was to be surrendered in exchange for the new money at a ratio of three million old yuan to one new yuan. Gold, silver and foreign currencies were also to be turned over to government banks in exchange for the new money. However, the drastic move did not succeed, and inflation raged unabated under the new system, giving rise to increasing public resentment, and more intense teeth gnashing for those who had surrendered their protection against inflation, such as gold or American dollars, for the new money.

Guoda returned to campus and waited for the fall term to begin. One night, Ting Zhougao, now associate editor of the school weekly, came to the room to see the soccer players and found only Guoda. He sat down anyway and visited over cups of tea and some peanuts. They would agree that the times they were living in were quite unusual and it would be very worthwhile to write about it, and perhaps they could join hands. It was just young people talk, of course.

CHAPTER 15

To maximize his chances to pass all the courses he yet needed to take in order to graduate with the regular class, Guoda moved out of the room he had shared with his old roommates. They understood, and he continued to socialize with them when his studies permitted. He now roomed with two freshmen, Wei and Zeng, from Szechuan province. Initially he assumed a senior's condescending pose. In time it appeared to him that these freshmen in some ways were more sophisticated than he. For one thing, he noticed, on the second floor of Social Hall on campus, that they were better ballroom dancers than he. And another, they were not virgins, at least they had intimated that much.

He would eat with them in the "Big Kitchen," organized by the students. The meals cost much less than those at the privately run "Small Kitchen." But he didn't get the same kind of food either. He could have three bowls of rice in the Big Kitchen and would still be hungry. There was simply not enough fat in the food. His First Aunt, Qizhi's wife, would every so often invite him to have lunch in their apartment, and on his departure, hand him a jar of diced dehydrated soybean cake and pork cooked with much lard. That helped as long as it lasted. Sometimes, feeling filled and yet still hungry, he would simply go to the Small Kitchen and have an order of yellow croaker.

Once, at the Big Kitchen, as his jaws clamped down on a mouthful of rice, he heard a little explosion in his head. A piece of a tooth had been chipped off against a grain of gravel. He stopped going to the Big Kitchen.

Early fall, 1948, the two major cities of Manchuria: Mukden and Changchun, fell to PLA. Growing bolder as the Communists' power became apparent, the "leftist" students provided more substantial information on the state of the war than in the government controlled newspapers. For the first time Guoda read of such names as Lin Biao and Peng Dehuai. The government built up much hope on the engagement looming over the city of Xuzhou where one million men would do battle. The paper predicted a sure victory for the government forces—even though they no longer enjoyed the four to one ratio of man power; the ratio now was more like one to one—because of their advantages in artillery and tanks and absolute dominance in the air. The armies clashed in October. Thousands upon thousands of young lives ended in the field, and the injured moaned and cried out for mother.

Some 700 miles southeast of that battleground, on the campus of St. John's, Guoda lived a relatively charmed life, needing only to manage his studies, reinforced concrete bridges and such. After mid-term, it appeared that he had them under control and had energy to spare.

One weekend, his ex-roommate, Daigu, invited him to accompany him to visit his girlfriend's home. Qian was the eldest daughter of Professor Zhao, Head of the Department of Economics, who was at the time on a fellowship studying in America. A medical student, Qian practically had to study constantly. Daigu would study with her and be in the Zhao house much of the time. Mrs. Zhao, Qian's genial mother, invited Guoda to stay for dinner. Daigu's place at the family's dinner table was taken for granted. (In fact, at times he appeared to be "the man of the house" there.) Guoda stayed for that dinner—a modest one, vegetable and preserved pork, a bit too salty—and a few more at the same table in the following couple of weeks.

Mrs. Zhao had three more daughters and a son. One evening at the dinner conversation, it was revealed that Xun, her second daughter, had found a tutoring job in the city. The mother was concerned about her safety in crossing Jessfield Park in near darkness when returning from the tutoring. A freshman in biology and one of the better sopranos in the choir, Xun was tall and statuesque like her mother, and an excellent swimmer like her sister Qian. Later on, in private Guoda told Daigu that he wouldn't mind escorting his girlfriend's sister through the park. A couple of days later, Daigu told him, "You are on."

Shortly afterwards, in addition to walking across the park, Guoda and Xun were strolling along the banks of the Suzhou Creek and going to movies and eating at small restaurants. Meanwhile, elsewhere in the country, Deng Xiaoping had captured the Nationalist's Commander in Xuzhou, Lin Biao taken Tianjin and Beijing, and Peng Dehuai overrun the western provinces.

Soon the PLA was poised to cross the Yangzi. Shortly Guoda read on the leaflets, which appeared overnight by the doors of the dorm, the charge—"Command To Advance On All Fronts"—given to the PLA by Mao Zedong. Guoda was surprised by its righteous tone. While growing up he had always the impression that the Communists were bandits in matter and in mind. Recently, in matter the Communists were not only substantial but seemingly winning. Now one wondered about the mind part.

The front that had the most attention was the shores of the Yangzi by Nanjing. Within days the river was crossed and the capital taken without a fight. (It was reported that the government garrisons turned their cannons 180 degrees just before the battle was supposed to start.) How true it was: "When an army falls, it's like a collapsing mountain."

"It is getting serious, really serious..." Fuli's letter told his son; the family would have to move soon. It was understood that Guoda would be joining them.

In spite of its almost dire situation, the government decided to go ahead with the National Athletic Meet in Shanghai. Xun, on the Shanghai swimming team, made past several heats but failed to qualify for any of the final rounds in the breaststroke events.

A few days later, she went with Guoda to see *For Whom The Bell Tolls*. When they came out of the Roxy Theater, it was already nightfall and raining. Inside a covered pedicab, after the driver had hooked on the front awning, they were again enveloped in near darkness. The cab started to move. In the warmth of the spring night air, the rain lightly beating on the tarpaulin about them, and her head in the bend of his arm, Xun remarks, "I like the way Ingrid Bergman said, 'I always wondered where the noses would go.'"

"You are an expert now," Guoda moves her closer and kisses her. She responds. Gradually it becomes heated, the tongues working. The rain raps noisily now as the cab struggles against the wind. Guoda withdraws his hand from behind her head and moves toward her front to unbutton her sweater and shirt. A sliver of light flashes past the narrow openings of the awning, showing two halves of her white robust breasts. He changes from caressing to kneading them. Rolls of thunder accompany the rocking of the vehicle. The air is charged. Her hand moves toward his thigh. He reciprocates. They fondle, massage, bite, suckle, squirm and twist—all with controlled movements to avoid the driver's suspicion. The soul-melting moments come. And leave.

Catching her breath, Xun tidies herself and Guoda with the help of her handkerchief.

They had the kind of experience before; only her fear of pregnancy and his of moral responsibilities prevent them from the ultimate. She again nestled her head in the crook of his arm. "Ingrid Bergman is a great actress. So beautiful too," she said.

"Great actress, I agree. Beautiful too. But not as beautiful as you."

"You mocking me?"

"Don't scare me by such talk. How could I dare?"

She chuckled, "Then try to be just a little more credible even in flattery. You have heard that flattery would get you nowhere."

"Flattery? Honest, at least, in physique, you are the better.... You have the best breast I've ever known."

"How many breasts have you known?"

"You are twisting my words. I think yours are even better than Venus's. That doesn't mean I have *known* Venus's breasts."

"So you mean mine are better than those made of plaster."

"You are twisting my words again. I mean yours are soft, stout and warm and of such perfect honey-peach form."

She seemed to be convinced that there was at least some sincerity on his part. "OK. That's enough," she said.

"Sorry if I offended you."

"You did not, but I don't like to be compared with a thing."

"I was just comparing you with Ingrid Bergman and Venus."

After a while, she said, "Flattery has gotten you somewhere. You know that." There was a distinct change in tone from the playfulness that prevailed in the enclosure before. Guoda felt a bit of pressure; it was relieved some as the cab slowed down and stopped at their destination.

In the Small Kitchen they had curry beef noodles. They talked around things, like the noodles and her father's impending return, not important matters on their mind. The mood decline started earlier seemed to continue. The rain had stopped. After they reached her house, she said to him, "Come in. I have something for you." She led him to her room, which she shared with a younger sister, who would graciously stay away when he came. Xun sat down at her desk by the window and motioned him to take the chair beside it. Her eyes looking into his, she said, "You know I've given you everything that a woman can give to a man short of the ultimate."

"Xun, as I told you before, I don't deserve what you've given me," he tried to summon all his concentration. "And I am grateful."

"That's inane talk. It sounded...distant.... Have you decided?"

Of course, she was referring to the question of his leaving Shanghai or not. He had told her that his parents wanted him to leave Shanghai and join them as soon as he graduated. He gave her the impression that he had not made up his mind, although he had not really considered not joining them. On the other hand, he had never enjoyed such ecstasy and female sweetness before, but he was fearful of the direction it was headed, the responsibilities that would go with it and his ability to meet them. In the back of his mind lay his father's admonition of what a *relation* would mean. "Frankly, if it's only me, I'd stay. But under the circumstances I may have to leave."

"I knew that before. You were just trying to spare me from disappointment."

It was obvious that her disappointment had only been delayed. He felt her hurt. Her words were an accusation of an injured. They remained quiet for a moment. She opened her desk drawer, took out a small box and handed it to him, saying, "A present for you."

A little surprised, he gave its blue velvet top a look, and rolled it up. A gold ring. He felt a current of emotion. It ran in a sea of realities. "I don't deserve this," he said, tears coming to his eyes. "You are such a good, decent person. You know that I am only a mediocre senior, struggling to graduate. To tell you the truth, I worry about meeting your father next week when he comes back from America. He'd find out soon enough how poor a student I am."

"You have told me all that before. But grades are not the only thing. You told me you had not been properly prepared for engineering. Have skipped many grades and all that."

"Thanks for trying to save face for me. But about yourself. You are talented, good-looking, and a good student. I am positive...that you'll meet someone more deserving than I."

"What are you trying to say?"

"It's not that I don't want the ring. As I said, I don't deserve it. Honestly, I think it's better for you to keep it. The circumstances are too fluid for either of us to be tied down right now."

"I know you don't want to be tied down."

"Not so much that. *You* shouldn't be, Xun, honestly. I speak from my heart. Right now, I don't know where I'd be a month from now or what I can make of myself in this world."

She kept silent, looking out the window at the boat lights moving along the dark Suzhou Creek. Tears dripped down her face.

"Do you want me to call on you again?" he asked. No answer. "You don't want me to call on you again?" No answer.

The boat lights glided past, slowly, getting dimmer.

The school authorities gave notice that in view of the special circumstances, graduation would be moved ahead of the scheduled time and there would be no ceremony, and that those students who had fulfilled the requirements should present themselves at the registrar's office to receive their diplomas. The instructors posted their grades. Having passed all his courses that term, Guoda went to the registrar's office to check his status. He was told that while he had completed all the required courses, he was short, by two credits, of the total number of credits required for graduation, because of the number of D's he had gotten. A D-grade earned only two thirds of the full credit for a course. He had figured previously that he should have barely enough. He carefully compared the registrar's record with his own and discovered that his work on a debate course and a chemistry laboratory course, one credit each, had not been entered.

In only the nighttime natural luminosity—the PLA was said to be near; no artificial lighting was allowed at night—he rode in a pedicab first to Dean Lin's house. The dean certified his successful completion of the one credit debate course. He timidly asked him to write for him a "To Whom It May Concern" letter of recommendation. The obliging dean, typed out the letter himself under a shaded lamp. What could one say to recommend this mediocre student? Beside some boilerplate lines, he wrote: "...Mr. Jing is a young man who knows himself...." Guoda had no time then to wonder what it meant.

With some difficulty he located the home of the chemistry laboratory instructor. She similarly issued a note certifying his work of one credit. The next day, at the registrar's office he got his diploma, stating "...Bachelor of Science in Civil Engineering...to enjoy all the rights, privileges, dignities and honors..."

A couple of days later, he stood with the choir—sans Yan Shaohuang, the suave tenor, who had simply disappeared for some weeks now—holding hands in a circle on the lawn in front of the chapel, and sang *Auld Lang Syne*. Later, passing the stone memorial arch of S.Y. Hall, with a lingering look at the chapel, past Social Hall, and a final glance at the big camphor tree, with his trunk at his feet and a couple of bags beside him in the pedicab, Guoda left the front gate of St. John's University, a fledgling leaving its old nest.

CHAPTER 16

❀

He left his trunk in his Uncle Qizhi's apartment and went to stay at his friend Ni Zhiyu's home. At night, rumblings of cannons could be heard.

Surprisingly it wasn't difficult at all to get an airline ticket to Guangzhou. He said goodbye to the Ni family. Zhiyu's parents told him be sure to return if the airport ceased operation.

A warm day in late May, the city seemed uncharacteristically quiet and subdued. On the plane there were only a handful of passengers, all young men like himself. Nearly all those who wanted to and could leave had already gone. After one stop at the port of Shantou, where he had gotten off the plane to vomit because of airsickness, he arrived in Guangzhou.

Rende met him at the airport and told him that their father was waiting to have his money transferred to Hong Kong before taking the family there. Owing to housing shortage, the family rented a rundown place, which used to be a small temple. In the "sitting room," elevated like a stage, Guoda was reunited with the rest of the family.

The next morning he went out with his brother to buy powdered milk for his nephew. Guangzhou seemed a boomtown. The restaurants were full, the shops busy. They were accosted on the street by hawkers and solicitors and shown pornographic pictures, which Guoda had never seen before. He was curious but not curious enough to buy. Instead, at a bookstore, he bought a copy of Rousseau's *Confessions* and Dickens's *Bleak House*.

In the afternoon, Fuli said to Guoda, "I haven't seen your diploma yet." He showed it to him. Fuli took it in his hands, examined it a while and obviously pleased, commented, "At least you have brought this home." Guoda was relieved. Then, Fuli said, "I saw in your photo album several pictures of a young woman."

"Yes?" Guoda thought, you have been searching my bags?

"She looks attractive, very good figure. Who is she? A taxi dancer?"

Silently outraged, Guoda thought, my girlfriends are proper, unlike yours. "No, she is a student," he answered. "A first class swimmer, represented Shanghai in the recent National Athletic Meet," he could not help adding.

Later, his parents went out to visit some friends. At night, while washing himself in a wooden tub in a stall by the kitchen, he crooned for amusement: *Like a golden dream in my heart ever smiling, like a vision fair*—With the washcloth dripping under his chin, he caught sight of a rat big as a squirrel slinking in its prickly fur in the dim light. The vision stopped him cold. He watched it crawl into a sewer hole, its fat hairless tail slowly retreating. Vanished with it was his mood for amusement.

The parents returned later. The family chatted for a time and everyone but Guoda went behind the "stage," where crude partitions made for sleeping quarters. He remained, reading *Confessions* under a light bulb dangling from a rafter. In a while, Fuli returned, cast his eyes about for a couple of seconds, turned off the light and went back in. Holding the open book in the dark, Guoda resented the rudeness. He had noticed a change in the air about his father from that of a relative mellowness in Nanjing and Changsha to a sourness, reminiscent of the time in Shanghai during WWII.

In ten days, the Jing family arrived in Hong Kong. They rented a new apartment on Lion Rock Road in Kowloon City. (It was almost like buying; after one paid the "key money," one needed to pay only a nominal rent. Besides, the key money could be recouped from the next renter if one chose to relinquish the tenancy.) The apartment, on the second floor, had two bedrooms and a living room with a porch overlooking the street. The parents would use one bedroom; Rende, Aili and their toddler son have the other. Guoda would sleep in the sitting room, on the floor.

He read *Bleak House*. Afterwards, imitating the early fog scene, he wrote about falling leaves (like the ubiquitous London fog) on the campus of St. John's and along the banks of the Suzhou Creek. Fuli read the scribble he had left in a drawer and admonished him: "I tell you. Literature is a luxury you can hardly afford. It's enervating, particularly in these times. Most people are lucky to be alive. Let alone the hokey stuff you got here, if you could improve it one hundred fold, you couldn't make a living on it."

"I was just amusing myself with it," Guoda defended himself weakly.

"You ought to try to spend your time on the kind of work you've been trained for."

The next day, Guoda placed an advertisement in the *South China Daily News* in the "employment wanted" section: "1949 graduate in Civil Engineering, St. John's University, Shanghai,..." Ten days passed, not a single response. How can I make a living in this world? I am supposed to make a living now. Am I not?

Help came from a friend of Fuli. Tao Bailing, a well-known jockey on the island, had become even more famous by his recent winning of the grand lottery. Not surprisingly, he knew a number of patrons of horse racing who were also established businessmen in the colony, including one Mr. Huang, owner of a construction company and a stable, among other things. On an afternoon, neatly groomed and diploma in hand, Guoda went with Mr. Tao for his first job interview.

Mr. Huang, a short, stout man with salt-and-pepper hair on his large head, and a cigar between his fingers motioned them to their seats. He proceeded to talk with Tao about horses and racing with increasing animation. Following only in part the conversation in Cantonese, Guoda waited demurely, clasping his diploma rolled into a long cylinder and neatly tied with a gold colored ribbon. After a week, it seemed, with a tip of his head in Guoda's direction, Tao said to Huang, "As I told you previously, Mr. Jing here has recently graduated from St. John's University in Shanghai...." Guoda sprang up, approached his potential boss and was about to unfurl his magnificent diploma.

Huang waved him away, saying, "You report to the field engineer tomorrow morning at seven at our Happy Valley Racecourse work site."

Tao led him out. He felt humbled, not only for himself, but for his alma mater also. After all, he could have been a straight A student and would still be similarly treated. Besides, he didn't know anything about the work tomorrow—what kind? Responsibilities? Pay? But, still he was glad, for the first time in his young life, he had a job in the real world—a world in which he felt like a stranger, unsure, uncomfortable and vulnerable.

The next morning he presented himself at the Happy Valley site. The project was to widen the racecourse there. A good part of the work had to do with construction of retaining walls, which required a lot of concrete. The field project engineer told him that he was going to be a construction inspector, to work from 7 a.m. to 5 p.m., six days a week, at HK$60 (about US$10) a month, and the company would provide him with lodging and boarding in a dorm.

The pay sounded nugatory, and learning that in the dorm he would be living with the laborers, he forwent that part of the benefit. It made no difference to either the project engineer or Mr. Huang. He found out that his job consisted of walking about to oversee rows of black-clothed middle-aged women laborers wearing conical hats, who, sitting on the ground, hit brick size boulders with hammers to break them into aggregates for the concrete mix.

Before he left the apartment early in the morning, his mother would give him a few Hong Kong dollars for the day's expenses, mainly for lunch. (Between his father and himself, neither would bring up the matter of money.) When he arrived at the construction site, the pinkish radiance on the horizon would be intensifying with the rising temperature and humidity. His back felt pricks of heat and his heart heavy, thinking that it was only the bare beginning of the day. Too soon the sunbeams would begin to sting; he'd open his tung-oil-treated paper umbrella for shade.

Around half past eight, a black limousine would cruise down the road. He'd descry a former classmate, Li Baoya, in the car with his father rolling toward downtown. Hong Kong was Baoya's hometown. His father, manager of a local bank, had helped his son to get a job as a designer in an engineering consulting firm, a position worthy of and appropriate for a college graduate engineer with a diploma stating "…to enjoy all rights, privileges and honors…." The former classmates would wave at each other.

The Lis lived on Repulse Bay, a high-class area. On Sundays, Guoda would visit them at their fine home and spend a good part of the day under the sun on the white sandy beach a short walk down from their front gate. In midweek, patches of skin would peel off the back scorched by the sun earlier. Guoda thought that very few people who lounged around Repulse Bay on Sundays would spend their time at work the way he did. The hours were long, boring, zero intellectual content, nothing to do really. They don't need me; the job is created for the celebrity jockey. Besides, on his feet all the time, the fullness of his varicose veins bothered him. He'd rather sit down beside the women workers and bang the boulders himself.

When the showers came, usually in the afternoon, he would pick his way up to the sidewalk, cross the street and trot to a row of houses a little ways down, where, away from the mud, gravel piles, and the din of steel hammers on stones, he would find partial shelter under some eave, and himself seemingly back to civilization. Indeed, there would be live piano and singing. Quickly he made out that a singing lesson was in session. It brought memories of his college days—which seemed a lifetime ago—of pure and tender voices and the soft purling of the organ. He would think of his girlfriends on campus. He'd feel pangs of conscience of probably having hurt the feelings of Helei and, particularly Xun, probably having taken advantage of their innocence. But, powerless and wretched, what could I have done—"a clay Buddha crossing a river," hardly able to save myself.

All that physical and mental discomfort for HK$60 a month? Besides, he would now feel sheepish at getting his daily allowance even from his mother, although the manner in which she handed him the money was no different from when she had handed him coins to buy tangerines after school, when he was in his first grade. He needed help.

Guang Pengxi too had come to Hong Kong, living with an older sister of his. A professional piano teacher on the island, she had helped him to earn an income as a violin teacher. But it was hardly enough for a living. On the day he was returning to Shanghai to take an engineering job that a relative had arranged for him, he told Guoda that the father of one of his former violin pupils was looking for someone to translate business letters in Chinese into English. Guoda wrote a letter of application, addressed to a Mr. Kang, the proprietor of a trading company. After he mailed the letter, he suddenly recalled that he had signed off with "Respectively yours," instead of "Respectfully yours." He was utterly dejected; not only his chance for the job vanished, but also it would reflect badly on St. John's.

He got the job anyway, at $180 a month. The possibilities of independence perked me up. However, he continued to live with his parents, sleeping on a straw mat unfurled over newspapers laid out every night on the hardwood floor of the sitting room. Sometimes, though tired and anxious to get enough sleep for the morrow, he had to wait for the room to be vacated, as in the night when his Aunt Qijin, a happy-go-lucky lady, demonstrated with her jolly husband, his Uncle Dazhan, their newly learned ballroom dance steps.

Work now started at 8 a.m., instead of 7—an improvement. In a sheltered office, instead of the open construction field—another improvement. Sitting at a desk, rather than standing on foot with blood-distended veins—still another improvement. All these in addition to a threefold jump in pay. He would translate those business letters that the boss had drafted in Chinese into English when such was needed. That did not take much time. Mostly, he would do such odd jobs as adding up figures in ledgers, quantities and values on lists of commodities, lengths of gabardine, or weights of dehydrated sea cucumbers or hog bristles, and the like, all using an abacus.

Occasionally he was sent to deliver letters, like an office boy. A little demeaning, he thought, but nobody has to know about it. Besides, what is the alternative? One time, a letter was supposed to be hand carried to some place up the hill in Hong Kong. In the heat and humidity, already sweating much in the sun, he showed the address to a passer-by and asked for directions. The man said, "Up there," pointing towards the peak that appeared to be touching the clouds. Guoda wiped his brows and sighed.

Mr. Kang's employees were required to work not only from Monday to Saturday, but also half a day on Sunday. Pengxi had told him that his pupil's mother, Mrs. Kang, was a Christian. Guoda approached her husband one day and asked for permission to go to church rather than coming to the office on Sundays. The boss glowered, looked away for a moment, and with a couple of short nods and grunts, returned to the papers on his desk. Guoda took it to mean yes. He stopped coming to work on Sundays and joined the choir of the Christ Church in Kowloon Tong, one of the finer residential areas in Hong Kong. None of his fellow employees, all older than he, dared to demand equal treatment. They probably had families to support, he conjectured.

The time had come that the boss's only son was leaving for the United States to go to school there. Guoda was asked to write his address in America on some boxes, and also to be just another hand around to help the family see the son off aboard the liner *General Gordon*. Mrs. Kang, noticing the lettering of one who had had a college course on mechanical drawing commented, "You ought to go to America too." The compliment—Guoda thought it was—gave his mind a little twitch.

Mr. Kang would normally come in the office around nine in the morning, read the mail, and make his business moves by telephone, telegrams or correspondence, and see to it that his five employees were kept busy. Then he would leave for lunch, usually at home.

For Guoda's lunch, generally he would call aloud from the window to a coffee stall, a couple of stories below, in his best Cantonese: "Yat Bei Ka Fe, Nien Guo Sai Bien Lo!" (A cup of coffee, two pieces of cake and Lo!—for gusto.)

The boss would return around 2:30 or three, his big belly bulging and moon face flushed, after a nap. Sometimes late in the afternoon, Guoda would be tired and hungry. One such afternoon, the spicy ginger peels that he used to chew to keep drowsiness away did not do the job, and the boss, fresh and alert, sitting there in his catbird seat, caught him yawning. Mr. Kang remarked, "Nowadays, young men are not what young men used to be—no energy." The young employee would like to respond with, "His mother's! You had a two-hour nap!" But of course he kept his nose to the grindstone, and thought that Kang's attitude was the stuff that sows revolution.

CHAPTER 17

Guoda no longer took money from his mother, and he was in straitened circumstances. In fact, earlier with the allowance she gave him, he had better, more substantial, lunch. Besides, his needs were a little greater now, at least greater in transportation expenses. He had heard from his mother that his Aunt Lu had also come to Hong Kong with her older daughters and the two sons; the other children were back in Changsha under the care of a relative. The news that she and the minister were divorced surprised him. Divorce was rare to begin with, and the two, each having apparent impressive merits individually, seemed such an ideal couple. Now the minister had gone to America, leaving his former wife to care for the children.

Guoda went to visit them in an upscale multi-story apartment building, ostensibly to pay respects to the mother as an elder family friend. He also saw her older daughters too. After a couple of such visits, there appeared a recognition among the Lu family that the visitor's main purpose was to see the No.2 daughter, Jiafeng. However, he was not sure of her mother's attitude toward him. She'd be cordial sometimes, but as often he felt a definite coolness. He did not get much encouragement from Jiafeng either; neither discouragement enough to stop him, however. Her siblings were generally neutral. It was a time of uncertainties—in everything, country, family, and even the self. All said, he would usually be allowed to have a time alone with Jiafeng, but so far, those moments were passed in a generally superficial fashion.

One evening, while he was visiting, a Mrs. Liang came to see Mrs. Lu. It sounded they were going to discuss some business matters. Jiafeng said to him, "Would you like to go to the rooftop?" He was of course glad to, particularly nobody else seemed eager to join them. The roof was only weakly illuminated by the scattering of city lights. Standing by the parapet, they listened to the tune of *More* wafting up from a dance hall at a lower floor.

When he heard her humming with the music, he asked her to sing. To his surprise, she didn't outright decline, saying, "I would if I knew the words."

"Well, then sing a song that you know the words," he suggested.

She did a rendition of *How Could I Not Think Of Him* in a light bamboo-flute like voice. He praised her singing and poise. She went on to tell how in her high school, not only did she sing, but she acted also in plays. He talked about his fiddle playing. And then she told more about herself—how she was brought up in Changsha mainly by her grandmother, as her parents often lived in a different city, even out of the country, as her father's work required, taking only some of their children with them. The friendship implied by such conversation pleased Guoda, until she said, "I wonder whether Aunt Liang had left."

He took the hint. By an instinct, as it were, he felt his pocket and discovered that he had no change left and didn't have his wallet with him either. How am I going to buy the ferry and bus tickets to go home? A sweat broke out on his back. I'll just have to brazen it out, he told himself. "I should go home now," he said to her. "Er...But I am embarrassed that I have been so careless.... I forgot to carry my wallet with me and have no change left...."

It took her a couple of seconds to see his dilemma and need. "Oh, really. Let me see." She felt around in a pocket in her skirt, brought out a square of paper, unfolded it—a HK$10 bill—and handed it to him. "You can use this."

"I'll pay you back next time." He took the money, glad that the redness of his face wouldn't be seen in the dim lighting. On his way home, he castigated himself for having spoiled the pleasant evening by his own negligence, ending in a near disaster, just when it seemed that he was making progress.

That weekend he went to repay the money, he was psychologically prepared to face slight, had she told her mother about the loan. Apparently she had not. After opening the door, her mother greeted him cordially. Inside he found Jiafeng and her two sisters (No. 3 and No. 5) all dressed up. (She wore leather shoes now.) They were going to a matinee tea dance as guests of the Liang family, who lived in an apartment two stories below them. He had once met the Liang brothers, sons of Mrs. Liang to whom he had been introduced the other night. The brothers were about his age. The older one seemed a little awkward, but his brother was something else, dark eyebrows and dark eyes, a dimpled chin, and tall, taller than him anyway, athletic—a tennis player, he was told. The college student conducted himself with an air of ease and confidence that he found rather disgusting. He handed the envelope with the money to Jiafeng without being noticed by others. She took it with like circumspection. That was the only comfort he could find that afternoon. He left the jolly group as graciously as he could. At the door Mrs. Lu bid him goodbye with a sadistic smile, as a demonstration of jitterbug to the tune of *Buttons and Bows* was heard from inside.

Obviously, he needed to improve his financial state. A chance appeared when Fuli told him that an acquaintance of his might help him to apply for a job at a British firm. This acquaintance, a Captain Chen—the diminutive gray-headed man indeed had once been a sea captain—was the Chinese Manager of the Lion and Globe Steel Company, a subsidiary of a major steel manufacturer in Sheffield, England. Its Hong Kong office was looking for a replacement for the Chinese assistant to the English manager. An interview with the latter was arranged and Guoda got the job. Afterwards, he observed that Captain Chen's title with the company was very much an overstatement. In fact, the "Chinese Manager" would be paid only with a commission for any business he brought in. That was all. He had nothing to do with the managing of the company—he didn't even have a desk in the office.

The job was an improvement all right. Regular office hours, 8-5, with an hour lunch break. The pay was HK$240 a month, with an official title of "Representative." The young man, who was leaving the company and Hong Kong to return to the Mainland—a move opposite to that which many young people had made at the time—worked with Guoda for two weeks. Their talk at lunch would go beyond office work. The man seemed as sincere in his sense of patriotism as in his responsibleness in helping the firm to train a replacement. The duties paralleled that of Guoda's previous employment: translation and clerking. The first part was mainly oral, between those customers who needed it and the manager. The clerking part involved more.

Guoda needed to learn the fundamentals of bookkeeping and also typing. He bought a book on the former. For the latter, in front of a stationery store window, which displayed a typewriter and a diagram of its operation, he memorized which finger covered which keys, and went on from there. Shortly he settled into the job. There were three others in the office: Mr. Victor Ferrero, the fortyish English manager, Mr. Yao Ning, another Chinese staff member, and an office boy. For the company's products, normally a *consumer* would buy from a *retailer*, which would buy from a *trading company*, which, in turn, would place its orders with the Lion and Globe Company for the products to be shipped from the mill in Sheffield. The Hong Kong office, small as it was, did business directly with all three classes of customers, with quotations decreasing from consumers, retailers to trading companies, in compliance with the commerce system. Mr. Yao, a Hong Kong native in his late twenties, had been with the office for a few years, dealt with the execution phase of sales to consumers, mainly in seeing the goods prepared and delivered, which required the hiring of labor.

Early October the front page of *The Xing Dao Daily News* showed a large picture of Mao Zedong, standing on Tiananmen, proclaiming the founding of the People's Republic of China. Qisheng, looking at it for a moment, said, "Strange! In the past, he looked like a bandit. Now he seems to have the aura of an emperor!" Another illustration of the old saying, "He that succeeds is king; fails, bandit."

That day, Guoda went to visit Wei and Zeng, his Sichuan roommates in his last year at St. John's, who had also come to Hong Kong. They had rented a room on the mezzanine floor of a lumber mill in Kowloon City. The mill was only a few steps away from the bus terminal close to Kai Tak Airport. He had to shout over the mill cacophony for directions to their room. Crossing a floor of saw dust, and making a turn over the steps up a narrow concrete stairway, he found it—a hole-in-the-wall. A bunk bed against the back wall took up much of its space. Sitting on the lower berth, Zeng was writing, using the windowsill as a desktop. Wei was strumming a guitar, *You Are my Sunshine*, on the upper berth. The music had to compete with the downstairs whining of the saws tearing into timber stocks and the rumbles of double-decker buses. Guoda sat on the floor, his back leaning against the doorjamb, one leg in the corridor, which was open but for a parapet on the other side, overlooking a courtyard. Zeng said he was still looking for a job, but just now he was composing a rebuttal to Mao's proclamation. Wei had started to work as a probationary teller in a bank. Likewise Guoda updated them about his circumstances.

However he would like to, he couldn't make himself go to visit the Lu family in the week following the loan episode and the jitterbug demonstration. He couldn't do it the next week, and it became a state that he needed to break out of. Instead, for social activities, he went with Wei and Zeng, who had made friends with an eclectic group of young people including several second or third rate movie actors and actresses. Doris, one of the latter, had given Wei and Zeng and Guoda too—and possibly every halfway decent young man she met—a picture of herself dressed in a dirndl, taken, she said, in her senior year in a (Catholic) high school. In it she looked innocent, almost sacrosanct. She was on the thin side with a somewhat bony face, but not bad looking.

One night, it had been raining intermittently. In the swimming pool of the North Point Amusement Park, there were only a few visitors left beside Wei, Zeng and their friends. The raindrops came down almost warm; the water was warm. Guoda and Doris happened to be standing together in a shallow part of the pool under a loud speaker piping *I Saw The Harbor Light*. Suddenly he felt his lower part being touched over the swimming trunk. Instinctively he bent to evade. His hand was taken under water and moved quickly under her swimming suit. She had a sort of Mona Lisa expression on her. His heart fluttered—with more curiosity than desire. Nevertheless, sensing nothing good would come out of this, he withdrew his hand from a soft mat, saying, "This wouldn't do," in an ostentatiously brotherly way, allowing the whole thing to be interpreted as a joke or prank. Yet he didn't move his person away, thinking it'd be too insulting to her. To his relief, she lowered her head and swam away.

He didn't mention the episode to Wei or Zeng. But it didn't surprise him later to hear them once refer to her as a "supreme treasure," the hand that "eats" (or beats) all other hands in the game of *small pai-jiu*.

For some time now, he had asserted his right to come and go by only telling the family where he was going and when he expected to be back. That rainy night he returned later than usual—than what he had told his parents earlier. Shortly, as he was making his bed on the living room floor, he overheard his father commenting rather loudly to his mother in their room, "I feel we are operating a hotel."

CHAPTER 18

❀

A few days later, when Guoda returned from work, everyone was home except his brother, who was attending an automotive engineering class at a community college. His Aunt Qijing was visiting; all were in the living room. Fuli was finically arranging the newspapers and magazines on the coffee table. He nodded unsmilingly to acknowledge Guoda's greeting. As Guoda was making small talk with the ladies, he went into the kitchen, brought out the broom and began to sweep the floor. Qisheng said, "There is no need to do that. Ah Mei had done it this morning." Ah Mei was the maid, who was out on some errand. Qisheng and Aili knew that whenever Fuli felt that he was not the center of attention at home, he was apt to do something like that—making people nervous.

"That's all right. I'll just get rid of some scraps," he said. A rattler was lying on the floor. It belonged to Xiao Pang, his diapered toddler grandson, who was repeatedly running away from Qisheng and then diving back into her lap. Both Guoda and his sister-in-law offered to take over the broom but Fuli insisted, "It's all right. I'll do it." There was some tension in the air in spite of Xiao Pang's playfulness.

Shortly Fuli sat down in a chair, looked around a bit and clapped his hands at the little kid, "Come, come to your Dia-dia (Grandfather)." A finger in his mouth, the toddler looked at him. Qisheng nudged him to go on. Fuli picked him up and started to toss him from his lap. As the kid dropped down, he opened his mouth and smiled. The next toss, he laughed. The laughter got louder as the toss went higher. Then he screamed. And he spat. The spittle landed on his grandfather's face. Fuli stopped, his face sunk and flushed, and he slapped the kid's face. The little boy was stunned voiceless for a moment and then began to bawl. The women: the mother, the grandmother, and the visiting grandaunt were shocked and immobilized.

Guoda found himself in an existential moment; he said to Fuli, "Xiao Pang is just a baby. He didn't know what he was doing." Fuli turned and stared at Guoda icily and said nothing. The grandaunt took over the crying boy and retreated with the other women to his mother's bedroom. The atmosphere in the living room was leaden. Fuli went inside his room. Guoda was on his feet but didn't know where to go or what to do as though he was stranded on a single-palm islet. Momentarily he heard Fuli declaiming, like he was on a stage, "If you think your feathers are all grown, then why don't you just fly, fly away…" Guoda hurriedly picked up his belongings and left the apartment with two bags.

He went to the hole-in-the-wall. Wei and Zeng welcomed him. At night he lay on the corridor and gazed at the stars beyond the eave. Hollowness, fear. A current began to run inside him. I'll be free. I am free! You can't be free without being independent. Exultation alternated with apprehension. After a time, tired, he fell asleep, oblivious to the roaring airplanes and growling buses. In the morning, after a couple of sneezes, he was ready to begin a new day, a new life.

A few days later, Zeng left to return to Sichuan, resigned to the fact that he couldn't find a job in Hong Kong. Guoda took over the lower berth. The hard part of his new life was at the beginning of a new day—to jockey with the lumber workers for position to wash in the courtyard and to get inside the tiny lavatory with a squat toilet and be done with it in about 30 seconds. If longer, there would be a rapid banging on the door that could louse up a good part of the morning for him.

Nevertheless, he enjoyed his new life immensely. After work he took on reading, mostly novels. Tears streamed down his face as he experienced those segments in Ba Jin's trilogy: *Family, Spring,* and *Fall,* that portrayed "social feudalism," and oppressions in the old style Chinese families. He had no thought of going back to the Lion Rock Road apartment.

But he yearned to go back to that big apartment building in Hong Kong to visit the Lu family. The longer he waited, the less courage he had. Then one Sunday morning in the Christ Church of Kowloon Tong, there they were—the Lu sisters—like a godsend. A new neighbor and friend of theirs had taken them there. Their mother had acquired an apartment in Kowloon City, a few blocks from his hole-in-the-wall, miles of land and a harbor of water away from the Liang brothers. Jiafeng and her sisters seemed friendly enough. He resumed visiting the family and was received with the same fluctuations in hospitality, as if there had been no hiatus.

One day, Rende called him in the office saying that their mother wanted to see him. The family had moved to Lichee Point on Victoria Island. He couldn't refuse to go. The dwellings, on a slope a few hundred yards from the beach, seemed haphazardly put up. The houses themselves were of nameless construction and seedy. The tenants were mostly lower middle class tradesmen. However, some new residents were or had been people of status, including a three star army general and his family—refugees from the Mainland. The Jings considered themselves belonging to that group.

The apartment had no foyer. When he walked in, Fuli was practicing calligraphy in the living room. Guoda said, "Yaya, how are you?"

Fuli turned around, looking slightly startled. "Very well…very well," he nodded quickly with a mechanical smile that he often accorded his first time business contacts, hesitated for an instant and returned to his ink and paper. Guoda went on to greet Qisheng and the rest of the family.

At supper, Qisheng, Rende and Aili kept the atmosphere reasonably agreeable. Afterwards, Fuli went into his room, Aili proceeded to tidy the kitchen, and Rende to bathe Xiao Pang.

"Your brother said that you have been staying with a bunch of laborers in an overcrowded dorm," Qisheng said to Guoda.

"Not really. Actually I shared a room with a former schoolmate. True, it was small. But not that bad."

"Are you all right?"

"I am just fine." He didn't want her to know that actually he felt great for his freedom.

"Is it safe there?"

"No problem." That was not totally true either. One night he was awakened by a loud cry and then heard a rush of running steps on the corridor. His roommate told him that he had been awakened by some sound and noted that someone was trying to fish his pants—hung on an end brace of the bunker bed—with a pole from outside the window. He jerked the pole back toward the window and it gave rise to the cry and the rapid splatter of flight.

"You have to take care of yourself…. Every morning and night I pray for our family to Heaven—Goddess of Mercy, or Jesus, it doesn't matter, all the same. Cha-cha, listen!…" She looked around for an instant, "About that day your yaya spanked Xiao Pang—"

"Yes?"

"You shouldn't overly blame him." She continued, "That afternoon he had just returned from an interview for a job with a foreign trading company. He didn't get it."

Guoda would visit them every two weeks or so. The following summer, Fuli and Rende started a small business of renting out rowboats at the Lichee Point Beach. The father supplied the capital and the son the labor. In their cramped apartment, Fuli still had a desk for his exclusive use, such as to practice his calligraphy. On it was a picture taken of him standing barefoot on the beach with his trousers rolled. It carried his own inscription: "Yesteryear a manager; today a boatman." Guoda thought that he was still a manager (albeit of a much smaller operation), but Rende was the boatman.

One evening Guoda came visiting. Rende hadn't returned home yet, and it was already quite dark. Guoda went to the beach to look for him. His face smarting from blowing sand, he couldn't see five feet in front of him. Suddenly out of the darkness appeared a giant form. Rende emerged, blackened by sunburn, carrying a boat on his bare back. He said that some customers would just leave the boat anywhere they chose to end their pleasure rowing, and he would have to walk all over to retrieve the boats by the end of the day, like a shepherd caring for his flock.

The business ended after only a few months; the parents were leaving for Taiwan. Guoda went to see them off. On the ship, Qisheng found a moment alone with him. "Now you really have to take care of yourself," she said.

He couldn't help smiling. "Look here, Mama. I had been living away from the family essentially since I began college. I am still in one piece."

"That was different. Your Uncle Qizhi was in Shanghai. He could take care of anything. Now, Rende and Aili are expecting to join us before long; you'd be truly all by yourself."

"Don't worry. It is you and Yaya who have to look after yourselves."

She didn't respond to that but took out from her purse a small velvet packet and unfolding it, showed him an emerald ring. Having quickly re-wrapped it, she handed it to Guoda and said, "Put it in your pocket securely. I don't have much to give you. Keep this safe. I hope it would help to tide you over should the need arise." Guoda was moved. So, she is going with her jobless husband to an island, vulnerable to military conflict—should Mainland choose to attack—and still she is giving me her priced possession. Chances are she would need it more than I, as I still have my youth. But he kept the ring, because he knew that was the way she wanted it.

Shortly afterwards, Rende, Aili and their young son left for Taiwan also, as soon as their entry permits came. Subsequently Guoda heard from them that Fuli had rejoined the China Merchants Steamship and Navigation Company. With all the refugees concentrated on the island, resources were strained and living conditions could not be compared with those earlier on the Mainland. Nevertheless, Rende, and later Aili, had also found employment—with the Taiwan Provincial Highway Bureau—earning enough to make a sparing living for their family of three, which now for the first time had their own, though small, apartment.

CHAPTER 19

In Hong Kong, Guoda needed to be frugal too. Yet on an impulse he had bought a watch for HK$120, low for a Movado, but of questionable authenticity. Miscalculating the following payday by a day, he discovered that when one is out of money, he is like a fish out of water. With his roommate spending the night elsewhere, he passed it alone with an empty stomach, the gnawing made worse by the scent of fried fish the mill workers were having and jabbering loudly about downstairs. The next noon, still no paycheck. He took money out of the office petty cash to buy lunch. The money was put back by the end of the day. The penalty came to be no more than a singe of conscience, and a vow never to repeat. He needed more income.

He found himself moonlighting in tutoring English. One pupil was a high school senior, and another a businessman; both were family acquaintances. While the former couldn't wait for the lesson to end, the latter wouldn't let it end on time. Once, while practicing conversation, the businessman was dragging on. The tutor asked, still in the tone of a continuing lesson, "What time is it?" The man looked at his watch and said, "It ees...ten minutes...past line O'clauck." "Don't you think we should stop now and continue next time?" To the surprise of the eager student, the lesson concluded thus. The pay pretty much lifted the threat of running short, but still he led a largely hand-to-mouth life.

Mr. Ferrero the boss was going to England on home leave for six months. Sheffield had earlier sent another Englishman, Richard Birdwhistle, to the Hong Kong office. A graduate from some trade school in London, Birdwhistle was in the beginning courteous and friendly to everyone. But the membership of the colonizing race gradually worked on him, as it had on many Englishmen past the Suez Canal. Although he remained proper, even polite, to Guoda, he became less patient and acted haughtily with Yao and the office boy when there were problems in communication. Nevertheless, just being English did not suffice, he was deemed not experienced enough to run the office, a Mr. Arthur Black was sent from Sheffield to relieve Ferrero.

Black was an "old China hand," having worked in the company's Shanghai office for some years before WWII. For a smooth transition, he had arrived in Hong Kong a month before Ferrero's departure. One mid-morning, both Yao Ning and the office boy were out; Black, noting that he had run out of tea, said to Guoda who was sitting at a desk facing him, "Jing, would you get me some tea?" He spoke in an even tone—most natural, like to a waiter in a restaurant—and returned to reading a document with his forehead in a palm and a frown from concentration.

Guoda was dumbfounded and then felt hot all over. "I don't make tea here," he tried to keep his voice from shaking. Ferrero's desk was close by; he stepped over and mumbled something to Black. They walked out of the office to the lobby outside. After they returned, all acted as though the request or order for tea had never been issued.

To Guoda, "Jing" rather than "Mr. Jing," was already a slight. He was uncomfortable with that when Ferrero called him Jing in the beginning, although the boss would conscientiously refer him as Mr. Jing when speaking to Yao or the office boy or any customer. Ferrero called the young Englishman Birdwhistle by his first name, Richard, the first day they met. The address matter could be swallowed, Guoda thought, but making or pouring tea? Ferrero is never like that. In fact, Guoda considered this Englishman rather enlightened—in some respects, more than himself.

In the retail part of the company business, labor was usually needed to cut the tool steel bars to the lengths the customer asked for and then deliver it. It was Yao's job to hire such a worker. Once in talking about the delivery of a fairly large order, Yao gave the impression that he was going to ask the one laborer that he had regularly used to do it all. Guoda didn't think it a problem. Ferrero objected, saying it would be too much for that one person. (The chap did appear in the office once, a rather emaciated looking soul.) Guoda was embarrassed, ashamed, that a foreigner was able to see too heavy a burden being placed on a poor, disadvantaged Chinese and interdicted, and yet better off Chinese, like himself and Yao, were so insensitive about a luckless countryman of their own that they either couldn't see the situation or wouldn't act on it.

Nevertheless, the colonial environment seemed to degrade all. One rainy afternoon, Guoda had accompanied Mr. Ferrero, a graduate of metallurgy from the University of Sheffield, to a toy factory to heat treat some dies made from a Lion and Globe tool steel. On their return, they stopped by the post office. Ferrero walked in, pigeon toed and cock-like, the elevated balding head pitching to and fro in synchronization with the steps and the beat of the ferrule of his umbrella on the floor. As they reached a window, a Chinese clerk, his head down, was fumbling with some papers. The Englishman thrust his chest, raised his umbrella and banged on the ledge, "Wake up! Wake Up!" he commanded. The clerk raised his head, jumped up and piled a ton of smile on his face, "Yes, sir…" The scene saddened Guoda. He had considerable respect for Ferrero—for his business and technical competence, commonsense and common decency. It was the system.

In time Mr. Black's temporary assignment of seven months was over. Missing his family in Sheffield badly, he was anxious to go home. Ferrero's return was for some reason delayed. Black left anyhow, thanking Guoda and giving him a modest raise, but handed the power of attorney to Birdwhistle. Guoda felt that any Englishman, irrespective of his character and ability, when landed in Hong Kong would be his superior, even after his hair had turned gray like Captain Chen.

Yet it would be Guoda who would go over the accounts, draft the quotations, write the checks and such, and ask Birdwhistle to sign. He'd ask Guoda, "Is it all right?" in his cockney accent. "Of course." While signing, he'd say, "I hope I am not signing my life away."

Ferrero returned about a month later and soon discovered that since Black's departure, Guoda had virtually run the office. The returned boss seemed vexed with everyone in the office. It bothered Guoda. However, after a couple of weeks, almost abruptly, Ferrero's displeasure toward him changed to something almost like respect. It puzzled Guoda. He conjectured that the boss might have been initially troubled by the greenness of Birdwhistle as well as a suspicion that the young Chinese clerk might have taken inappropriate advantage of the situation, but in time he was convinced that the firm's business had gone on properly before his return.

At the time the more China shut herself off from the world, the more Hong Kong gained in importance, and the business of the Lion and Globe Company grew with it. So did Guoda's experience and contacts in the steel business on the island. And the trend was growing.

He would be invited by customers, or potential ones, for lunch. He was aware of the likelihood that his host was only trying to pick his brains, or worse, offering temptations to reveal company proprietary information. Those he would of course shun, but not legitimate opportunities. At a luncheon, a customer told him that he would like to procure good quantities of high speed steel and stainless steel. Guoda said why not just place an order with Lion and Globe; he did not mentioned there were other manufacturers of tool steel too. The man said that the delivery time was too long; he wanted the material in short order and asked whether Guoda could help, promising a commission. Afterwards, Guoda hustled to contact several dealers whom he knew probably had the kinds of steel in stock. The man got his goods, and Guoda his commission. A whopping sum—for him—more than two years of his wages.

That evening after he picked up the check, sitting by the railing on the upper deck of a Star Ferry boat, he felt like in a dream until a sea breeze woke him. His mind glimmered like the lights on the waters. He sensed possibilities but they were vague at the time.

His effectiveness and reliability led to more similar opportunities for brokerage. As he had accumulated enough to be reasonably called capital, he proceeded to set up a company of his own. For that, in Hong Kong at the time all one needed was to choose a name, have a company chop made, and open a bank account. He bought some commodities himself and waited for the prices to go up. Almost invariably they would. His financial state improved rapidly, almost a quantum leap.

In his social life, courting Jiafeng had turned out to be a lot more difficult than his previous experiences. That, along with her limpid eyes, caltrop-shaped mouth and her strong character, kept his interest in a continuous heightened state. Recently, it appeared that he had made some good progress, aided by his improved income that enabled him to take her to movies and dinners. However, Liang Feisi, Mrs. Liang's younger son, remained a challenge, particularly now she had enrolled in the same college as he had been going to.

In the meantime, her mother, together with some friends, had been organizing a clothing company with investments, in addition to their own, from others including Feisi's mother. Mrs. Liang had told her that she could double the investment after she talked it over with her husband. Mr. Liang, an executive of China Petroleum Corporation, was visiting in the Middle East.

This day the phone rang, Mrs. Lu answered. "Oh…Feisi…How are you?…Good…. Your mother?…Good…. Your father?…Still there…Good…. She is home. Wait just a moment." She called Jiafeng from her room. After the daughter had completed the phone conversation, "What does he want?" Mrs. Lu asked, although she had a good idea about it as she'd overheard her daughter.

"He is inviting me to a party."

"Are you going?"

"I don't know yet. But he'll call back."

"You and your sisters said you all enjoyed that party with the brothers."

"We did."

"Then what's the problem?"

"There is no *problem*." Jiafeng said. She was thinking about how would Guoda react to this. She had been going out with him on a fairly regular basis now. Her mother's attitude toward him seemed to have actually improved some lately. Perhaps such recent gestures on his part as to have invited the Lu family to a dinner had helped. Yet one day Mrs. Lu asked Jiafeng,

"Does he still live in that lumber mill he told us before?"

"Yes."

"You've been there?"

"The mill?"

"His room."

"No."

"Don't go if he asks you."

Jiafeng was annoyed. She probably would have gone if invited, she would trust him that much. Yet she could empathize with her mother. Just divorced, responsibilities with the children. She agreed with her mother when she told her daughters: "…for a woman marriage is the most important thing in life. It's essential that 'Men Dang Hu Dui' (The gate and the door—statuses of the families—ought to match)…" The situation now was that she and he both came from respectable families; however, one lived in a nice apartment and the other in a niche in a lumber mill.

That evening Guoda came calling. When alone, Jiafeng told him about Liang Feisi's invitation.

"Are you going?" he was glad she told him about this but nettled at himself for asking the question.

"I told him I'll think about it."

Now he was more nettled that she'd so plainly told him that she might choose to go.

She did go to that party and enjoyed it. She enjoyed jitterbugging with Liang Feisi, so sure with his lead. Charming smile, white teeth, he was carefree, easygoing—a style Guoda at times seemed to desire for himself yet it did not appear to be his real nature. Just a bit uptight at times, serious, she thought. If I am looking for a dancing partner, Feisi would be more fun. Well, he hasn't even finished college. Guoda is a minor clerk, but he talks as if he wanted to aim higher. He does seem to be doing better now than that time he borrowed ferry fare from me. Wonder what Mother would react if she knew that then.

The following Saturday, after a movie, she was surprised that Guoda took her to the famed Three-Six-Nine Restaurant. Over her objection he ordered lobster just for her—because he was allergic to shellfish—shark's fin soup and a couple other dishes plus wine.

"Are these overly extravagant?" she was concerned about the cost.

"It's OK. I don't do this everyday," he smiled.

"What's the occasion?" she asked.

"Do you need to ask? You are the occasion. Anytime you are with me. It's an occasion," he grinned at her.

"You think you are cute, eh?" she smiled.

"Don't worry. I got a pretty good commission yesterday."

He had mentioned to her about his broker activities before; it gave her the impression that they only augmented his wage at Lion and Globe (in the Lion and Globe books, the Chinese employees' pay went under a 'wage account' and the British a 'salary account'), certainly not to the extent that his new activities almost made that wage unimportant.

She waited him to ask. He didn't.

"I went to that party," finally she said.

"Oh," he affected nonchalance.

"But don't worry." She was in high spirit, lifted in part by the wine.

"Who is worrying?" He softened the challenge with an exaggerated smile. "Enjoyed the dancing?"

"Yes. It was fun. But don't worry."

"Here you go again," he said, allowing that needling and teasing were all fairly typical female tactics, and he wasn't entirely without tactics himself. "You know, when I first saw you back in Hunan, I'd never have thought you'd enjoy ballroom dancing so much." He left off fashionable dresses and make-ups.

"I know. How would a country girl—in drab clothing and canvas shoes as you said before—like ballroom dancing." She never forgot people's remarks about her, even in jest.

"I don't mean it that way. I mean in relation to temperament."

"You could read my temperament then?"

"I tried."

"What is it?"

"I thought you'd like quietude, serenity…"

"Simple like a country girl. Is that what you mean?"

"No. Not necessarily. Whatever, canvas shoes or high heels, quiet serenity or lively fun. It does not matter. I think you do have a good heart."

Off the double-decked bus, they strolled around Kowloon Tong for a while and sat on the knoll by the Christ Church. Under the stars they kissed for the first time, for the second time, then the third…. Both were intoxicated, she by her first intimate contact with a male, and he by the slightly fragrant and musky scent from her mouth.

Since nearing the end of the Civil War, people had been swarming into Hong Kong; its population swelled dramatically. To exert some control, the government decided to issue identity cards to its residents. An Office of Registration of Persons was set up. Jiafeng took an examination, passed, quit school and became an employee of the Hong Kong Government to work in that Office.

Guoda had long been looking for a better place to live even though he had had the small room all to himself for several months now since Wei had moved out to stay with his girlfriend's family. He asked Jaifeng's opinion on some possibilities; she would actually go with him to look at them. The places for singles would seem not good enough as long as he was going to make a change. The nicer units would appear to be too large for a single person. The thought occurred to him that he could get married and settle down. He proposed to her. She hesitated at first. But the idea that it would lighten her mother's burden and make it unnecessary for her to defend herself before her mother, every time she went out with him, appealed to her. She accepted, saying her salary could be added to his income for their livelihood.

The parents had some reservations but not enough to object. The lovers were married in the Christ Church. The reception was held in the Peninsula Hotel, after which, the newlyweds rode to the Clear Water Hotel in Clear Water Bay in Baoya's father's black Lincoln Continental, the one Guoda saw in the mornings when he used to pace among the conically-hatted, hammer-wielding women on the Happy Valley racecourse. Returning from a week's honeymoon, he sold most of the commodities he held and bought American dollars and gold bars with the proceeds. When he first entered into business of his own, he was relatively bold, thinking that if he were to lose every dollar, it wouldn't matter because he'd started with nothing. Now a married man, he needed to play a little safer.

CHAPTER 20

❀

The newly weds had a flat formerly occupied by the family of the high school student whom Guoda had tutored before. They had moved to Australia. It was a modern apartment on Prince Edward Road. A maid, a refugee from the Mainland, took care of them.

On weekends, there would be parties—mahjong in the afternoon and dancing at night. They danced on the polished parquet floor of the parlor to the *Emperor Waltz*, the *Gold and Silver Waltz* and the like. Wine and spirits on the sideboard. Their guests would include Baoya and Amanda, a St. John's alumna, whom Baoya had married shortly after he had been the best man at Guoda's wedding, other old schoolmates like, Ting Zhaogao, now a reporter for the *Hong Kong Standard*, and new friends in the Christ Church choir. Some nights, in evening gown and tuxedo, they'd visit nightclubs, such as the Lido on Repulse Bay.

After weeks of such days and nights of wine and roses, an uneasiness began to grow in Guoda. He enjoyed the merriment—but only to a degree. After a time it turned vapid. He didn't like the life of a broker, the labored sincerity, the forced bonhomie, and an acute feeling, warranted or not, that he was not really a productive member of society.

He tried to cultivate himself and hired a teacher of Chinese classics to give him lessons, and correct his essays. At 21, what was his long-range goal? He had fancied going back to the Mainland, like his predecessor in Lion and Globe, or Pengxi, to work in engineering to serve his countrymen. But the idea evaporated as he acknowledged the near irreversibility of that kind of a decision, and more importantly, the realities of the differences between the social justice the Communists preached versus their undemocratic and harsh actions. He didn't want to go to Taiwan; the Nationalists hardly inspired him.

He had so far kept such thoughts about making major changes to himself. He presumed that Jiafeng was quite happy with their lives, and with good reasons too. Besides, what specific plans could he propose? One evening after returning home from a farewell dinner for a church friend—who had graduated from Hong Kong University and was going to England to do advanced work—Guoda said to his wife, "I have been thinking."

"Yes?"

"I have been thinking whether we should continue to live in Hong Kong."

"What's up? Is anything wrong?"

"No. Nothing is *wrong*. I've just been wondering about this way of life."

"Not good enough?"

"Not that. No. It's actually very nice—a small party every three days and a big one every ten. However, I thought: Will it last? Should our lives be on a more solid foundation? I don't really enjoy this broker's life. The work of a middle man is totally dependent on others' initiative."

"What are you going to do about it?"

"Of course, I may be fantasizing, totally unrealistic. I thought perhaps I could go abroad to get additional education and a fresh start academically."

She was silent for a moment and said, "You did not surprise me. I have sensed that you have been restless. Have private lessons with your tutor and have those philosophical talks and compose essays about purposes of life and such. I suspect you want more. Now more studies. On what?"

"Civil engineering, of course, what else could it be?"

"You already have a degree in that. You said it doesn't mean much here."

"That's because it was not a British one. I was thinking if I consider going to England to study, then why not America?"

"Hum…. America…. It sounds good. You may want to mull it over some more, though."

"To me the big question is how. But do you really agree it's a good idea?"

"Why should you think I might not agree?" she said.

He took the question to be a positive enough answer. "You have surprised me again."

"I know, I know. A country girl in Hunan who had become a most vain city woman in Hong Kong, high heels, Max Factor products, jitterbug…" she smiled.

"Don't forget the willfulness."

"Yes, I am willful too."

"If you are not willful, we would have that flat I preferred on Argyle Street with a view of the hills," he said.

"Do you agree now that this is better, more convenient, practical?" she challenged him.

"Hum...I suppose" he smiled.

"Well then..."

"I presumed that you are happy with our present way of life. You have your promotion, a chance for a government housing. Now to give that up for an uncertain prospect—"

"Yes, I am quite content with my job. When you mentioned the possibilities of leaving Hong Kong, the first thing that came to my mind was losing the chance of a flat with a view of the sea. I was in my supervisor's flat the other day. The seascape was simply splendid....But what you are talking about is entirely a different matter.... I could see the point of it. We could give it a try. Nothing needs to change now. We'll cross the bridge when we come to it."

Guoda wrote to several universities in the United States, stating he was willing to do remedial work if admitted. None gave him any encouragement. He was frustrated. She suggested he write to her father in America. He hesitated.

It was late 1951, St. John's University in Shanghai finally closed operation. On her way back to the United States, Miss Helen Yeats stopped by Hong Kong. Guoda took her up to the Victoria Peak and had tea at Dairy Farm. She said she was happy to see him apparently doing well. However, Guoda revealed to her that actually he didn't find his work that stimulating and he was trying to resume his studies, hopefully in America. She said to him, "Guoda, there is a will, there is a way."

After she returned to America, he wrote to her for help, laying everything open, his aspirations as well as his poor grades. She wrote back, saying that Mr. Miller might be able to lend him a hand. A professor of mathematics at St. John's, and brother of Dr. Miller who had treated his varicose veins, Mr. Miller was a long-time close friend of Miss Yeats. Subsequently, Guoda received another letter from her, saying that Mr. Miller had contacted a Professor Heinze at the University of Virginia about his case, and told him to write to the professor himself and to note Mr. Miller's suggestive role. She added that the professor was a fraternity brother of Mr. Miller, and no less than the Dean of Engineering at the university.

Guoda followed up. One late afternoon when he and Jiafeng returned from work, the maid handed her a letter. Having a look at the envelope, she gave it to Guoda, saying, "It's from the University of Virginia." He took it and went over to the dinner table to sit down, opened and read it. Jiafeng watched him. She had never seen his expression so serious before. It was apparently a short letter; his hands and eyes seemed hardly to have moved; he must have been rereading it.

"What did it say?" she asked.

"They've accepted me as a special undergraduate student."

Jiafeng thought that he should be jumping with joy. But she had come to know him to be not the demonstrative type. Noticing the flush on his face, she said, "We have come to that bridge. Haven't we?"

He advised Mr. Ferrero of his intention to leave Lion and Globe. The boss made an effort to keep him, saying he understood his perception of his limited future in Hong Kong, but suggested that he could be transferred to Japan, or possibly to Sheffield. That sounded a bit far-fetched to him. When Ferrero realized that he was very much in earnest, he alerted Guoda that "the school might be one for Negroes."

Jiafeng also resigned from her job with the Hong Kong government. To cut down expenses, they moved out of the Prince Edward Road apartment and rented a cheaper one at Temple Street in Hong Kong. The neighborhood of small shops was noisy, yet if the windows were closed, heat rashes would erupt on the back overnight.

Getting a visa to the United States was no simple matter in ordinary times. The Korean War made it a lot more difficult for any applicant who had come from the Mainland. The reason was vigilance against Communism. It would be easier in Taiwan, a bastion of anti-Communism. But it was almost equally difficult to get an entry permit to Taiwan for the same reason.

Quite excited about the prospect of his son's going to America, Fuli worked hard for the young couple's permits, which required two guarantors to vouch for their political cleanness. As the fear of Communism ran wide and deep in Taiwan, a guarantor's commitment was no ordinary favor; it offered one's total fortune as hostage to someone else's political leaning, which could be quite volatile then. (In America, it was the McCarthy era, even Miss Yeats, an Irish American from San Diego, California, mused over her possible liabilities, because she had voluntarily stayed on in Shanghai for two years under Communist rule.) However, a person's common decency, such as not to hurt one's benefactor, is a safer bet. Anyhow, Fuli convinced two of his friends, who were probably even closer ones of Jiafeng's father, to be the couple's guarantors.

Guoda and Jiafeng arrived in Taiwan and stayed with his parents. The plan was that Guoda would go first, and Jiafeng to follow after he had found a footing. Fuli seemed to have done away with his past domineering attitude toward Guoda. He and Qisheng were appreciative that Guoda had regularly sent from Hong Kong merchandises that were costly or hard to get in Taiwan. They were also amiable to the ex-minister's daughter, now their new daughter-in-law.

Guoda received his visa after a wait of two months. With a US$450 one-way ticket, he landed in America first at the airport in Seattle, Washington. It looked so clean, the lights so warm, and the air so fresh, carrying the haunting song of *You Belong to Me* (a rendition by Jo Stafford, he found out later).

In New York, his father-in-law met him at the airport. Lu Chongkai was working on a doctoral degree at Columbia University. He showed his son-in-law the skyscrapers of the world's most famous city. However, Guoda couldn't muster much interest for he was dizzy out of motion sickness. The next day, Guoda boarded a train at the Grand Central Station, as people pricked up their ears to the radio broadcast of a baseball game—they called it the World Series—between two teams, named the New York Yankees and the Brooklyn Dodgers. He arrived in Charlottesville, Virginia, two weeks after the fall term had already begun.

CHAPTER 21

In Dean Heinze's office, Guoda thanked him for his help and promised his own best efforts. The laconic administrator seemed unimpressed and curtly referred him to the Chairman of Civil Engineering Department. Guoda appreciated the chairman's solicitude in asking him about his physical condition and mental comfort level after such a long journey.

He had no strong preference at the time for any particular area in civil engineering. The chairman told him, as an advanced undergraduate student, to take Soil Mechanics, Dynamics and three other courses. "Let's see how you handle these."

Guoda went out and bought the textbooks for the courses, school supplies and several apples—the largest, and shiniest kind he had ever seen. In his dorm single room, he scanned the books while he ate the fruit in lieu of cafeteria food because of residual motion sickness. None of the passages in the Soil Mechanics book looked familiar to him. In the dynamics book a symbol that resembled the treble clef puzzled him for an instant, then he recalled that it was the integral sign. "What am I doing here?" Suddenly he was afraid. He wasn't sure that he could manage. His head spun. Scenes of the easy times in Hong Kong flashed—waltzing on the parquet floor, body surfing at Repulse Bay. He went to the window, pulled down the shade and knelt and prayed. The agitation subsided, and he started to work.

By Thanksgiving Eve he had caught up. He began to have some social life. On weekends, when the university cafeteria was closed, he would walk with Hu Zhaoxu, a graduate student in chemical engineering from the National Taiwan University—frail-looking, thin-lipped, the Chinese stereotype of a "pale faced scholar"—to some local cafeteria for meals. Sometimes they'd play a few games of ping-pong in the dorm basement before Guoda wanted to return to his studies. Around midnight some Saturdays, Roger Deng, an ethnic Chinese from South Africa and undergraduate in political science, whose Cantonese was even inferior to his, would knock on the door. He would just be returning from some party. They would chat for a while. Big-eyed and soft-spoken, Roger had asked Guoda "How can you keep at this without having some fun?" pointing to the work on the desk. "I had my share of college fun," Guoda replied.

There were no more than half a dozen ethnic Chinese students in the whole university, two of them were female, an undergraduate and a doctoral candidate in education. Hu had related to Guoda that once he had gone to see Dean Heinze on behalf of a classmate in Taiwan for possible admission, and the dean replied, "We don't particularly want that many Chinese students in the college." Guoda thought that although Ferrero's conjecture on the racial makeup of the university was wrong, the idea behind it wasn't totally off.

One morning he was brushing his teeth in front of the washroom mirror that ran the length of the wall; a big burly, red-headed student, naked but with a towel around his loin, was shaving beside him. Tarzan turned around and glowered at him, saying, "You know we could be shooting at each other."

Startled, Guoda said, "What? Why?"

"In Korea."

"Oh, oh,…but I am from Formosa." For geopolitical reasons, the United States administration preferred Formosa to Taiwan. There was no pride in his replying so, but one needed to be practical. He had heard that some windows in Chinatown were smashed.

Came Christmas break. He thanked his father-in-law for inviting him to New York, but decided to stay in the dorm to study for the coming final examinations. After the term ended, he was admitted to the master's degree program on the strength of his straight A's.

The school report had been sent to his "home address" in Taiwan. Fuli wrote to him: "…Your grades indeed surprised me. I am very glad…." Guoda was pleased to read this. "…I hope that you'll continue your efforts to maintain such excellent performance…." The exhortation didn't surprise Guoda either. "…As for myself, my environment at work has not been that ideal. Before long, I suppose, with your graduate degree you can find a good job there. I hope that you can get one with the United Nations. In that case, I can also come to America…." Guoda wasn't sure why the U.N. would hire a civil engineer. He went to the registrar and changed his home address to his at the university.

Jiafeng came down from New York. She had arrived there with the help of her father. Staying in the Jefferson Hotel of Charlottesville, she and Guoda had their second honeymoon—made sweeter by the long separation and big change in surroundings.

"The place is small, like a matchbox," Guoda warned his wife before moving into a university housing unit for married students on Copeley Hill. It wasn't quite a hill, but there was a definite slope to it. They had one of the stationary trailers, left over materiel from WWII, arrayed on the incline. Though small—approximately 20 ft. by 15 ft.—each trailer had all the essential conveniences including a lavatory (with a shower) and a kitchen that resembled one in a commercial airplane. After looking around a bit, Jiafeng said, "This isn't so bad. I had wondered what would it be like when you said matchbox."

There were bus services to the university and downtown. Heating came from a potbelly oil stove close to the front door. Residents fetched their oil from a community center "up the hill" where people also did their laundry using washing machines with hand operated wringers. Walking up the slope with an empty can and down with it filled was easy. However, Guoda dreaded getting past one trailer that kept a barking, leash-stretching boxer. The owner would sometimes come out, "Brutus, come on. What's the matter with you. Just one of your neighbors," and turning to the scared passer-by, "He is completely harmless! You can pe-E-t him. He won't bi-II-te." How sweet! Guoda thought, you won't be the one to get the Pasteur needle in the belly if the brute broke my skin.

In the spring, he bought a used Desoto for 500 dollars. A neighbor, Melvin, took time from his graduate studies in physics to teach him to drive. After he had his license, he taught Jiafeng, and she got hers. Friends told him that to have successfully taught one's wife to drive was a major accomplishment in life. He agreed.

Summer time, he put a coat of silver paint on the black tar roof to provide "air conditioning." It was a pleasant environment. Melvin and his wife, both Jewish and from New York, lived up-slope next to them. Diagonally down-slope behind them were a graduate student in jurisprudence and his Eurasian wife, both from Iran and supporters of Mussadegh. The three families, sometimes also joined by another Jewish couple a few units away, would get together every now and then. More often, it was only the wives that would congregate under a big magnolia tree in the middle court bounded by the trailers, while their husbands studied inside. Planning to resume her college education, Jiafeng worked on her English, which improved rapidly, thanks to her close contacts with the neighbors.

The university was almost lily white. Guoda had met only one African American student, who usually ate alone in the cafeteria. Guoda joined him a couple of times but did not get to know much about the reticent person other than that he was in Law School.

There were two ethnic Chinese faculty members at the university. A middle-aged professor in the Medical School, who also worked as a pathologist at the University Hospital, liked to tell grisly tales in his practice—"a little change in my interpretation of the slide would mean a lot as to how much the surgeon would cut." He would tighten his lips, chop down with his open hand, and conclude with a sadistic grin. Other than that he was an affable person.

The Chinese students enjoyed their gatherings more at the home of a younger assistant professor in the Woodrow Wilson School of International Law and his wife. He, who had grown up in Chengdo, Szechuan—a place with a rich and expressive dialect—was witty and broadly informed. Some Saturdays, chatting late into the night, the cluster of compatriots would let their hair down and regale themselves with reminiscences of the old country, in particular, the different kinds of foods and delicacies that they missed. The guests would guffaw wildly at the hosts' performance of pas de deux as they expounded on the differences between classical Chinese dancing and the ballet.

By coincidence, Miss Helen Yeats was teaching at a village school only 20 miles or so from Charlottesville. The Jings drove out to visit her through the winding roads in the foothills of the Blue Ridge Mountains. They had lunch with the school assembly. As the principal, a middle-aged woman in an ankle-length plain black dress, introduced them, the girls and boys first looked on them with curiosity. Afterwards, they applauded heartily; it touched the visitors. Since their arrival in America, there had been no major surprise until now regarding her general image they had in China. Indeed, it was an orderly and prosperous society, and above all, of high standards of living. However, this school appeared to be an exception. It seemed seedy; the students, all Caucasian, were shabbily dressed; some didn't even have shoes on.

The Jings were invited to the principal's home. Wearing a tight smile and with large bulging eyes behind her thick glass and her mouth working a little, the principal sat stiffly in a chair and watched a somewhat nervous Miss Yeats—who seemed to be out of her element—tell them about the students and the curriculums. Before she finished, the principal jumped up with a coarse yell, "Damn!" and stomped toward the kitchen. Guoda did also smell something like food burning. He felt sorry for his erstwhile choir conductor, a lady of gentle dignity.

Mr. Miller, accompanied by Miss Yeats, came to visit the Jings at Copeley Hill. While Jiafeng was preparing as good a dinner as she could manage in the tiny kitchen of the trailer, Miss Yeats waited on her long-time friend hand and foot. He lounged on the lawn chair with his long legs crossed at the ankles and extended far into the dandelions. With one eye closed, he expounded to Guoda the definition of "just right." In the old South, a white man gave a cigar to his African American servant. A couple days later, he asked the servant, "Have you smoked the cigar?" "Yes, sir." "How did you like it?" "It was just right, sir!" "What do you mean by 'just right'?" "Well, sir, if it was bad, I would not have smoked it; if it was any good, you wouldn't have given it to me."

Guoda realized that he had been given a second chance at formal education, if not at life. He was not going to let it pass. As it had happened to other souls, before and since, he had now developed a liking to studies after he had graduated from college. Sitting at his desk by the tiny propped-up window in the trailer, he enjoyed the hours of mental exercises—with the books, notes, paper, and slide rule—in the quiet of the morning, or in the lamplight while it was dark outside, sometimes accompanied by the gentle tapping of rain on the tarred roof and the wooden steps of the trailer. Some nights he'd put on a record, such as Pachelbel's *Canon* for Jiafeng as she went to bed. He worked late and rose early. During one intense stretch, the sensation of heart throbbing returned. He quit smoking. It didn't help. He went to the university clinic. An elderly doctor queried him about his life style and told him afterwards, "You are not living right. Don't work so hard, relax and go back to your smoking." He slowed down some and the throbbing sensation gradually went away. Came summer—his varicose veins acted up in the humid and hot weather. Having the leg propped up by a pillow in bed helped some at night, but such relief was not available in daytime. Finally, the university hospital provided the needed service—segments of the abnormal veins were stripped. He was told to wear an elastic stocking for support for the rest of his life.

Miss Yeats had told him that an American student, an acquaintance of hers, when asked about Guoda at the university, had replied, "He was just like anybody else in the school." Guoda was pleased at hearing this. Yet he knew it was not totally the case. For example, when he used his abacus during an examination (which needed the summing up of short columns of numbers). It elicited some ribbing from his classmates. He considered it to be all in the spirit of collegiate fun—thinking of his own St. John's experience—and took it as a good sport. But he stopped bringing the tool to class afterwards.

Another time, near midnight, somebody knocked on the trailer door. He opened it. A well-dressed young man said, "I am sorry to disturb you at this hour. But you may be able to give me some help. I am a Law School student. I heard that you had used some ointment during examinations, which apparently worked well for you. I wonder I could get a little of that. I am willing to pay for it." Guoda recalled that when taking a test, he had sometimes rubbed "Tiger Balm," basically a menthol-type ointment, onto his forehead. He let the night caller have a tiny can of it for goodwill along with a word of caution not to overly depend on it. When he related the story years later, some friend said in jest, "The night caller might have been Bobby Kennedy."

But it was Joe McCarthy time. Guoda listened to some of the hearings on the radio—the Senator's mesmerizing low-pitched voice, "Mr. Chairman...Mr. Chairman..." He also heard Counselor Welch's cry, "...You have done enough. Have you no sense of decency, Sir, at long last?..." That expression—and its reception by the American general public—drew Guoda closer to America as a people, as a nation. The word *decency* moved him, exerted on him a quantum pull toward his host country.

He was hired as a research assistant in the Virginia Council of Highway Investigation and Research, an organization housed in the university but financed and administered by the Virginia Department of Highways. After some initiating assignments in the Soils and Concrete laboratories, his main assignment for the Council was an investigation of "Laterally Loaded Pile Foundations," which would also be his thesis.

In the spring of 1954, the department chairman suggested that he continue his studies at some other university, since the University of Virginia then did not have a doctoral program in civil engineering. When he first came to America, the thought of a doctoral degree would be mocking to him. He would be satisfied with a master's degree and then some appropriate professional employment. But now he was encouraged by the professor's suggestion, and also by his father-in-law's example, who had recently obtained his doctorate at Columbia University.

He wrote to his parents about the possibility of his going on for a doctorate, thinking he'd surely garner some praise, in particular, from Fuli, for he knew his mother would defer such matter to her husband. However, he was surprised that Fuli was rather lukewarm in his support—"...a doctorate degree could narrow your future to an academic career...but you are in the best position to judge...."

Guoda proceeded to contact several top engineering schools. He received admissions from all, but only Johns Hopkins University and the University of Illinois offered financial support. He chose the latter.

By August, he had received the master's degree, and with Jiafeng, hosted a dinner party—borrowing the young Chinese-American professor's house—to thank his teachers. The Jings packed their belongings in the Desoto and said good-bye to Jefferson's university and Charlottesville.

CHAPTER 22

Guoda and Jiafeng drove up to New York City. Her father had remarried. His new wife, who used to be on his staff, received the young couple hospitably. After a couple of days, they headed west.

When they got on the Pennsylvania Turnpike, it was almost twilight. Ahead, the clouds glowed fiery on the horizon. The car window down, Guoda took a deep breath in the buzzing air stream. It felt cool and bracing. It was all freedom, exultation, and anticipation! Open road and little traffic. He accelerated and pointed at the speedometer to Jiafeng, "Look, 70 miles an hour!" No sooner had he said it than he heard a big pop. The car ran with rapid jerks and swerved into the other lane. There was no other car near. He slowed the vehicle down back to the shoulder, stopped, walked back a way to retrieve the hubcap. With the car jacked up, noting that there was still enough daylight, he asked her to get out the camera and take a picture of him working at the tire changing, which she did.

When they approached Pittsburgh, it was nightfall already and raining hard. The road was hilly and visibility limited. They arrived in the city and settled in a motel. As he was going to sleep, it suddenly occurred to him what their lives would be like had there been a car in the other lane when the tire blew. Next morning, they decided to take it easy and not use the turnpikes.

Having arrived in Champaign-Urbana, they moved in a university apartment in Stadium Terrace. Like the trailer in Charlottesville, the unit was also of wartime temporary construction, but much bigger than the trailer. It had a living room and two good-sized bedrooms; one would be used as a study. All at $45 a month, including utilities. With little or no insulation, it would get hot in late summer afternoons. They bought a big fan from Sears Roebuck that blew out from a living room window to cool the rooms at night, one at a time, by closing all the other windows except one in the room being processed.

The Department of Civil Engineering here was a much larger operation than that in Charlottesville. Guoda reported to Dr. Nathan Fineman, Research Professor of Civil Engineering, who was in overall charge of research in structural engineering, the largest such program in the country, possibly the world. The structural research annex at the corner of Green Street and Prospect Street, housing a good number of the structural research personnel, was like a little United Nations. While he used to have only three or four classmates in a graduate course in Charlottesville, now there would be twenty or even thirty, from all over the world.

Jiafeng resumed her studies, enrolling in the Business College of the university. The number of Chinese students in Charlottesville was single digit; in Urbana it was triple. It was observed, with some slight exaggeration, that during such holidays as Christmas, when native students went home and the restaurants were closed, the streets in Urbana were teeming with Chinese students walking around with no place to go. Similarly, the number of ethnic Chinese faculty and staff was also much larger than in Virginia, running into the dozens.

As a research assistant, Guoda was assigned to the Bridge Dynamics project. It was under the direction of Simon Segal, a full professor. Its execution was the responsibility of Xiao Tiebao, an assistant professor. Xiao, a Qing-hua Scholar (winner of a Boxer Rebellion Indemnity Scholarship), seemed to be a modern version of a Chinese "wild scholar" of old—brilliant, proud, almost arrogant, upright and scornful of worldly successes and those who openly seek them. He reminded Guoda of the prized gold fish at his grandmother's house in Changsha—the "Heaven-facing Dragon" kind—although proportionally his skyward eyes were not nearly as big.

In addition to his studies and research, Guoda also prepared, with the support of Dr. Fineman, a paper based on his master's thesis. It was presented at the Annual Meeting of the Highway Research Board in Washington D.C. and subsequently published.

He assisted Xiao in a study of "impact factors" for bridges under vehicle loads. The sponsors of the research met annually to review its progress. Since Xiao was unenthusiastic to make a presentation before the committee, the job fell on Guoda. He did the best he could, talking about Lagrange equations and such—all mathematics, no bridge or truck. At the coffee break after the presentation, a silver-haired representative from the Bureau of Public Roads called him to the side and told him that his report was "clear as mud" to him, and the man wasn't smiling. Guoda felt hurt.

Something else was hurting him also. It was his abdomen. He underwent a successful appendectomy. In the two weeks connected with the episode—observation, operation and recuperation—he studied French. The following winter, he signed up for the examination on translation of technical French to English for doctoral students. Luck had it that on the sheet in French there was a figure with all the mathematical notations of a deformed beam. He knew the contents before reading the text; he passed.

He reckoned that he couldn't count on having the same kind of luck with a similar exam for German. He prepared for it methodically. He would assign himself to memorize a few new words for each daily chore, such as three or four words while taking a shower. He passed it the next fall.

Basically a mechanist and applied mathematician, Xiao considered the applied nature of the project not challenging enough intellectually. Once Guoda found him reading the score of a Beethoven symphony on his desk. Another time, Xiao told Guoda that he had already done the project work for the next year but would only release the results piecemeal. That was shortly before he resigned to return to China. In the research annex, there was a consensus that he should have been promoted a long time ago. In fact, full professors from other schools had traveled to Urbana to seek the technical advice from this assistant professor. Dr. Fineman went to his home to ask him to change his mind and offered him a promotion to associate professor. It came too late.

Xiao and his family soon left the United States for China through the intermediary of the Indian diplomatic service, since there were no diplomatic relations between the two countries. Assistant Professor Theodore Agnew became the supervisor of the project. A graduate of Robert College in Turkey and former student of Fineman, he was bright, focused and hardworking—a rising young star of the faculty. Guoda had taken two courses from him. He also became Guoda's academic adviser after Fineman succeeded to the department headship. (For "defensive purposes," the renowned researcher told Guoda some years later—presumably against the possibility of an under-appreciative new department head.)

It was time for Guoda to take his preliminary examination for the doctorate, to be administered by his guidance committee, which consisted of Professors Fineman, Segal, Agnew from the Civil Engineering Department, and two professors from the Department of Theoretical and Applied Mechanics, his minor field. The examination would be in two parts. First the candidate would be examined individually by each committee member. The second part would be an oral examination given jointly by the committee. Word had it that the preliminary examination was the main hurdle for the degree. Horror stories abounded. Candidates sometimes froze, unable to speak. A couple of years ago, one had to be carried out of the conference room.

Guoda passed the individual tests in mechanics without unusual strain. Segal's test was to discuss certain sub-sections in the newly released Design Code of American Concrete Institute. After reading his report, Segal told him that the work was publishable. Agnew's test took him a couple of days. There was only Fineman left. Guoda felt pretty good about the progress, as, according to the grapevine, the busy researcher-administrator was usually less demanding than most. Unexpectedly on the morning of his appointment, Dr. Fineman's secretary called that her boss wanted him to report to Professor Fields first. Now the candidate's optimism was dampened. Fields wasn't even on his doctoral committee. Instead, he was the Chairman of the Committee on Licensing of Structural Engineers for the State of Illinois. Anyway, Guoda had no choice.

Professor Fields drew on the blackboard a frame supporting a crane and asked, "Mr. Jing, could you tell me how would you size the girder?"

"I need first to find out what are the internal forces in the member."

"Good. Tell me what are they?"

"I have to analyze."

"What are they?"

"I need to calculate, writing the equations of equilibrium and compatibility of deformations…"

"Can you give me an estimation *without* writing equations?"

Guoda detected a note of disdain in the term of "writing equations," but couldn't come up with an answer to the challenge. In silence, he stood there, feeling hot. After a pause, the professor said, "All right, you go ahead and *write your equations and do your calculations.*" And he left the room. In humiliation and apprehension, Guoda plodded through the calculations and went to see the professor. He examined the results, nodded, and said, "All right, I'll see you tomorrow, same time."

The next day, the questions were along a similar practical vein. After a couple of hours, the same parting words from the examiner, "I'll see you tomorrow." The next day, the same. Guoda realized that his weakness was exposed in full—a deficiency in practical experience. He returned to the apartment, exhausted, and told Jiafeng, "It seems that I can't make it here. Let's go to Milwaukee or Chicago to find a job."

"What happened? Did the old man flunk you?" she asked.

"No. Not yet…. But he wants me there again tomorrow."

"Well then, don't worry. We'll cross that bridge if we come to it," she said.

It was snowing when he left the apartment to see Fields for the fourth time. At the end of it, the professor with his bow tie, gray hair and draping eyebrow, extended his hand and said, "Mr. Jing, I'll let Dr. Fineman know that you have done well."

Back inside his Desoto, Guoda felt like a prisoner declared innocent and released. Snow was falling heavily, and seeing no cars near, he let out a big yell: "O—Kay!" Then he collected himself. Don't make too much of this, there is still a way to go.

He told Jiafeng simply that he had passed Fields's gauntlet. She seemed benumbed for a few seconds. "Uh…. That's good. So I need not to think about moving to Milwaukee or Chicago," she said quietly.

He sensed that like himself she probably didn't want to let the extent of her gladness show either. "At least, not now," he responded. He suggested they go out for supper. She said she already had it prepared; besides, there was so much snow outside. She made an additional dish—slices of Virginia ham with pepper and onion. They finished eating. He just couldn't stay still. Had to get out. The snow had piled up so much that there was no bus. They trudged to downtown and saw *Josephine*, starring Marlon Brando and Jean Simmons.

The examination with Fineman himself was the easiest, done in about half an hour. The grapevine was formally true. At the oral examination before the entire committee, the members began by reviewing the candidate's record. Segal commented, "All A's but one, eh? I wonder who was the son of a gun who gave you the only B." He was being ironic. He had given Guoda that B. It was for the last course Guoda needed to take to complete the course work part of the degree program. The grade for the course depended entirely on a take-home final examination. He had felt that if ever there was one course that he was sure of an A, it would be this one, because he had two weeks to write the examination. So he did the best job he could. He even submitted the paper with much fanciful trimming with table of contents, indexed separators, etc. It might have backfired. The doctorate preliminary examination had come after that course. He felt that had the order of the two examinations with Segal been reversed, he might have gotten an A for that course too. That part of the doctoral preliminary exam was indeed later on included in a paper with Segal and himself as co-authors. Although the constitution of the experience was minor, it confirmed for him that never count one's chickens before they are hatched, no matter how good the eggs look.

The oral examination by the committee as a whole was almost perfunctory, done in about an hour. Now he had only a thesis to do. He was promoted to Research Associate and placed on full time. His project work would also be his thesis. While congratulating him, a friend of his, an assistant professor in mechanical engineering, said to him, "The period in which one works on his doctoral thesis is the easiest time of his life." The friend might have exaggerated it a bit, but that observation wasn't too far off for Guoda, in comparison with what had gone on before and what was to come.

CHAPTER 23

❀

Guoda and Jiafeng would now join their neighbors to have a beer or two on some weekends. One such night, the hour was getting late, the party waning. The conversation came to jobs and opportunities after school. Perhaps too much alcohol, their downstairs neighbor Todd Timmerman lamented the rapidly vanishing opportunities for shouldering the white man's burden. "Now in our prime," he said, "we send out dozens of resume, hoping only to get a job in America. Even outside the country, we'd be working for some goddamned cooperation as some goddamned employee.... It used to be that you can sail to some place in South America, Asia or Africa and set up a business, an empire, like Rhodes, or at least, a plantation, train some goddamned natives as employees to run the goddamned thing. But now all those banana republics in Central and South America, and little god-forsaken land-locked states in Africa all have their own leaders, all dictator bastards...." He bobbed his head and burped.

"You have had too many, Todd," his wife said.

"No. I'll have another one. Maybe a little later," he burped again.

"Todd, you major in business. Right?" Guoda said. "Speaking of training natives, I think there ought to be an optimal level of education, technical or otherwise, that the developed countries should let the underdeveloped ones have. Too little, you are not making good use of the vast available resources, here we are talking about the human kind, not oil or minerals, and lose out in competing against other developed countries. Too much, those people in Africa, Asia or South America may take such ideas as freedom, democracy, even honor and dignity too seriously that they would want to be competitors rather than employees…. You could get a paper out of such a study, if not a research grant."

Todd's wife cast Guoda a judge's eye and said, "Are you serious?"

"Not totally," Guoda smiled and retreated.

"I think Guoda is drunk," Jiafeng told her, "He can hardly take any alcohol."

Guoda also took part in some social activities within the university, like playing the fiddle accompaniment for a Chinese woman student singing the Beijing opera aria, *The Inebriated Royal Concubine*, on the "International Night" program.

The university had a winning varsity basketball team that year. They enjoyed watching the team on TV, even when the game was played on home court, since going to the field house would be too costly in money and time. Not owning a TV set themselves, they would go to the home of Professor B. T. Qian to view the game.

The professor and Mrs. Qian were a generous couple. An apocryphal story about the professor went like this. When he started his academic career at the university as a research assistant, he already had his doctorate in mechanical engineering from Edinburgh University in Scotland. Before long he was promoted to research associate. He stayed at that position for years. Traditional Chinese culture would restrain a scholar even to appear to care, let alone ask, for recognition. Qian never complained until the day when one of his former students, who had graduated and stayed on the faculty, was promoted to associate professor.

He went to the head of the department and said, "I quit."

Surprised, the head asked, "Why?"

"Look here. I have been at the instructor rank too long. And now even my student has been promoted to two ranks above me."

"Oh, so you are not happy?"

"You bet!"

"Why haven't you said so before?…Don't quit. We'll fix it."

After that, he was promoted each year. At the third year, he was a full professor. The experience probably initiated him to university politics; later on he became the head of the department.

Guoda and Jiafeng had thought of getting a television themselves but wavered, concerned that it would be too distracting. Finally they relented and bought one. Each noon he'd pick her up at the Library and they would rush home to watch the soap opera *As The World Turns* (wondering whether Penny would find out her friend Ellen's father's lover was her own Aunt Edith), as they ate leftover rice warmed in boiled Campbell chicken noodle soup.

Now Guoda being a full time employee of the university and thus no longer qualified for married student housing, they rented a small one bedroom house on Busey Street in Urbana. They had stopped birth control after his preliminary examination. Jiafeng became pregnant. It would interrupt her college education and gave added impetus to Guoda's work.

It was bitter cold the day he took Jiafeng and Michael home from the hospital. The water pipes froze. Diapers couldn't be rinsed in the toilet bowl until a plumber was called to rectify the situation. The baby fussed all night. The parents took turns to comfort him. Guoda held him and paced in the living room while watching the pale dawn emerge. Jiafeng took over. Instead of going to bed, he went to school and took the final examination of the Tensor Analysis course that he had been auditing.

Life was frantic—cooking, washing, feeding, burping, changing and rinsing diapers, washing bottles and making and sterilizing formula. Then the baby had a cold; they called the doctor, got the Neo-Synephrine to help drain the baby's nose so that he could sleep and they could too. One night when he was a couple weeks old, waiting for the arrival of Jiafeng's father and sister Jiayin, they were awakened by the visitors. They had come in the house—with Guoda's keys in the door—while the new parents had fallen asleep from sheer exhaustion.

In a few weeks, things began to settle down. Only then, one night, lying in bed, Guoda suddenly thought, "My goodness, there is another person in the room, and I am his father." When the baby was one month old, they took him out for a drive. Coming out of the apartment, Guoda was holding him. It was icy; he slipped. While falling, he made sure that his body was between the ground and the baby. Fortunately, his own clothing, including a thick cashmere overcoat that he had made in Hong Kong, was between his body and the frozen ground. No one was hurt.

Overall his thesis work progressed well, though not without the usual ups and downs of research. In a year, seeing light at the end of the tunnel, he started to send out letters of job applications to industries and universities and received a few promising responses. One morning, the department office called: Dr. Fineman would like to see him. The upshot was that he was offered a job at the university as assistant professor—contingent upon his completing the degree program. He gathered from the conversation that Dr. Fineman had received inquiries about him in relation to the letters he had sent out. He accepted the offer so that he could concentrate on the thesis without the distractions of job hunting.

He did his research largely independently. Every two weeks, he would submit a brief report to Ted Agnew, who was usually supportive. However, nearing the end of the work, disagreements between them surfaced. None had to do with theory or analysis. They concerned the practical side of the work. Technically their differences were not major—generally matters of form rather than substance. Nevertheless, each thought he should have the "final say." The student considered that the work was his thesis, and the supervisor regarded it his project. Before their discussions reached an impasse, Guoda would capitulate. He thought he would suffer the "injustice." He wrote in a large size the Chinese character: *Ren* (To bear or be patient) on a sheet of paper and kept it in his drawer. He also remembered the saying that "The head of the character *Ren* is a sword." (Indeed, the upper half of the character *Ren* is itself a character meaning sword, with the lower half meaning mind or heart.)

He received his doctorate. Now an assistant professor, he got an appointment to see the department head.

"Dr. Fineman," Guoda began, "I knew you are busy—"

"Guoda, I am not that busy to hear what you have to say," Fineman smiled and leaned back in his executive chair.

"Thank you…. I am a little embarrassed to bring this up with you—"

"It's O.K. Speak your mind."

"Yes. Ted had been my thesis supervisor, and project supervisor, which he still is…. I respect him. I've learned much from him, particularly about technical writing. I am indebted to him and have told him so. But I have always felt somewhat uncomfortable working with him. Somehow our personalities don't seem to jibe…. You have promoted me to my present position in the department. I am grateful. I value the opportunity and wish to do my best work for the department…. But I honestly felt I could do a better job if I didn't work directly under Ted, and—"

"Say no more. I understand what you are telling me," Fineman said. "I know and appreciate your attitude toward work. We certainly want you happy at your work, not just for you, but for all of us. As you grow, the department grow with you," he unfolded a smile and paused, and folding back the smile, "About your request...I suppose we can do something about it. Let me talk with Simon Segal first. Either he or I will get back with you."

"Thank you. Perhaps I should have waited—"

"Guoda, you need not feel embarrassed. You are not the first one to have difficulties with Ted. He can be...too intense at times."

"It is not that. But—" Guoda stopped, seeing Fineman's secretary standing at the door, trying to get the boss's attention.

"I'll be with you in a minute," Fineman said to her, and returning to Guoda, "You need not explain further. We'll get back with you on this."

"Thank you." Guoda was now on his feet.

"By the way, Ted has always spoken highly of you," Fineman remarked casually, as Guoda started to turn.

Guoda muttered a thank-you one more time and left quickly. The last obiter dictum felt like a blow to the stomach. He began to think that Fineman, overseeing more than a hundred faculty members, besides being still professionally active, probably did not have sufficient firsthand knowledge of his progress. Agnew, although only an assistant professor himself, but as his supervisor, might have a lot more to do with the job offered to him than he had realized before. Have I been unfair? Small minded? It troubled him.

Shortly he was transferred to a new project as its supervisor. He and Agnew co-authored a paper based on his thesis, which was also issued as a project report. They remained on friendly terms, even after both eventually left Illinois.

He was Agnew's first doctoral student. A couple years later, one midnight, he received a phone call from another doctoral student, asking for advice as to how to deal with his adviser, Professor Agnew. Still a couple years later, while walking on a concourse in Chicago O'Hare Airport, he heard rapid footfalls behind and then somebody calling his name. It was yet another thesis student of Agnew, seeking similar kind of advice. In both cases, Guoda told the troubled graduate students that Agnew was a decent and honorable person whom they should not fear, and to be patient and to look at the big picture. He learned later that both had obtained their degrees without undue delay, as he had.

Guoda's specialty, structural dynamics, a relatively new field in structural engineering, covers such sub-fields as bridge vibrations and earthquake resistant design. Agnew, who taught a basic graduate course on the subject, was going to MIT on a sabbatical leave. Guoda had hopes that during that period he might teach the course. It surprised him to learn that the course would not be offered in Agnew's absence. Thus, he wondered whether the University of Illinois was the optimal place for his professional development.

It was a propitious time for new doctorates in engineering. The Soviet Sputnik was recently sent up there orbiting the globe. It was perceived as an indication of a threat to American security. The Soviet breakthrough was also thought to be due to their emphasis on theory in their sciences and technology in contrast to the American preoccupation with practicalness, an attitude that could be an impedance in modern high technology. To meet the Soviet challenge, the case was successfully made for *basic research and graduate studies* for engineers and scientists. The former was defined as research that would create new knowledge for its own sake, not necessarily for any immediate practical application. To both quality and quantity ends, a host of federal government programs were initiated to support colleges and universities to take part in the effort. Grants were made available to cover faculty salaries and other associated costs of research including university overhead. *Basic* emerged as the new paradigm in engineering research. Often higher mathematics and physics were put forth as a manifestation of that character. Equations would be worked out in scalar form and then recast in tensor form to impress reviewers. A doctoral degree became a prerequisite for new engineering faculty. Money and prestige joined hands to influence academic planning and policies. Guoda entered that market.

Virginia Polytechnic Institute offered him a promotion in rank that he didn't take because he thought he didn't particularly need a promotion, and the town of Blacksburg was too small; the nearest hospital was in Roanoke, some 20 miles away. He wrote to Wisconsin Technical University after learning that it was looking for new faculty in engineering. He had a brief meeting with Chester Gordon, Chairman of its Civil Engineering Department, at a conference of the American Concrete Institute in Chicago. It was followed by a formal interview in Orchid City, and later by an offer, which amounted to a level transfer between the institutions. He accepted it as an opportunity for a faster professional development. Fineman made no attempt to keep him, at which he felt a brief disappointment. As Guoda thanked him for the growth he had attained at Illinois, Fineman said, "I appreciate your contribution here too. We are all even. I am sure you'll do well in Orchid City." What a gracious administrator, Guoda thought.

Priscilla Jing was born before they left Urbana. The infant had colic; every night each parent would take two-hour shifts to comfort her. On a late afternoon in early February, they left Urbana, dog-tired from packing and cleaning the little house. At night they checked in a motel near Kankakee, Illinois. The next morning, Guoda woke up to an unusual quiet, only low sounds of breathing. He felt relaxed and refreshed—a rare state for him in recent months. The baby had slept through the night. The colic had passed! Over ice covered roads they arrived in Orchid City, Wisconsin, in a winter storm, but safe and sound.

CHAPTER 24

❀

The Jings had a two-bedroom brick apartment in the university Oak Lane housing complex. It was a homogeneous community in which all fathers were busy, mothers were young, and children beautiful but required lots of unglamorous work. Jiafeng quickly made friends with the wives of a couple of assistant professors as well as of an assistant basketball coach and a librarian. A full-time mom now, Jiafeng, with one eye on Priscilla in the portable car-crib, would lead Michael and his little friends in the living room to waddle, clap and sing, "Little white duck, swimming in the water, little white duck, swimming in the water…"

For the Spring term, Guoda proposed a new graduate course in structural dynamics, like the one that he had hoped to teach at Illinois. When the proposal was presented at the department meeting, Allen Graham, the most senior member, on the faculty over 30 years, asked gravely, "Who approved this?"

"I did." Gordon, the department chairman, responded with an equally stern countenance.

"When we use our resources, we ought to bear in mind what our kids would be doing after they get out of here. They'd be designing and building water treatment plants, laying out drainage systems for subdivisions, etc.," Graham said.

The implication seemed to be that the proposed course on dynamics was too specialized. Guoda thought of the reason he got his only A at St. John's—statics is necessary and sufficient for civil engineers, i.e., dynamics is not really necessary. Nobody gainsaid the senior professor's statement, neither the proposed course. No debate. No vote. Thus the faculty was duly informed and consulted on the new course. The meeting went on to the next item on the agenda.

The brief skirmish was not unexpected from what Guoda had gathered on his earlier job interview. The university started as a land grant college. After WWII ended, enrollments swelled with veterans entering under the GI Bill. The college grew and succeeded in substituting "University" for "College" in its name, aided at the time materially by the success of its football team. A name did not a university make. Traditionally, the engineering college at WTU emphasized practice; its production of graduate degrees and research was not comparable to the engineering colleges at most other major universities. To justify the name of a university and to join others to meet the Sputnik challenge, the administration set out to upgrade its engineering college to be more active in graduate studies and research.

James Carr, Chairman of Electrical Engineering Department at the University of Michigan was hired as Dean of Engineering to do the job. Young for his position, and energetic, he in turn proceeded to assemble young and energetic new leaders for the various departments. Gordon had been recruited from the National Science Foundation, an organization with obvious affinities to the new goals. Before long some older faculty would regard the new leaders and their newly hired colleagues as interlopers. Power struggles ensued. Carr, physically a big man, would also enjoy good administrative battles, which the older faculty were to find out to be usually one-sided. For example, when one senior professor refused to vacate his old office to move to a smaller one, the dean simply had the lock changed.

Battles were fought on all fronts: the department, college, university, alumni, board of trustees, and public. The president of the university, more importantly, the times, were on the dean's side. The old timers lost practically every round. When Guoda came to the school, the strife was nearing its end. The old guards had either left, retired or given up, though occasionally they would exercise their academic freedom to grumble a bit but discreetly avoid real unpleasantness. Thus they were left alone to do their teaching and lead peaceful lives—as long as they didn't challenge the administration.

Such was not the case for the new faculty. The real authority of the new administrators did not come from their titles, but from the expectation that they would deliver the goods—in the form of research (measured in publications and grant dollars) and the number of graduate degrees awarded. The production of such goods fell mainly on the new faculty.

The whole engineering college here was somewhat smaller than the Department of Civil Engineering at Illinois. The pace was slower and less intense. At night or weekends the Engineering Building seemed deserted, while at Illinois there would still be lights on in the Structural Research Annex and Talbot Laboratory and people digging. Almost every workday Chairman Gordon would come to get Guoda to have lunch together. At Illinois he had dined with Fineman but once, in his home, as one of the three newly hired assistant professors in structures that year. Sometimes, it would be Dean Carr himself leading a lunch group from the Engineering Building, past the North Lawn and its flower beds, toward the Union cafeteria. In summer, the atmosphere was even more relaxed. The older faculty, almost all teachers of undergraduate courses, would be out of the campus, some enjoying their lakeside cottages. In his first summer term, Guoda taught a "Special Topics" course on structural dynamics, emphasizing recent developments, an emphasis to foster the instructor's research potential as much as, if not more than, the students' education.

One day on the way to the Union for lunch, the dean asked Guoda, "How are you doing?"

"Pretty good, I think. I have six in the class, two from outside the department actually. All seem quite enthused, and I am asking them to—"

"I am talking about your research," the dean was curt and unsmiling. As he raised his right shoulder and heaved his chest with a tic of his jaw, which he was wont to do, the six feet and some boss looked to the new hire seven feet eight.

Guoda quickly sobered up. "Oh, I am preparing a proposal for the National Science Foundation." That seemed to stop the dean's tic. He went on to ask Guoda amiably whether he had yet come across a good Chinese restaurant in town. Guoda was tempted to say "Not only that but also a good enough Chinese laundry." But he told himself not to be so darn sensitive.

The proposal—on the subject of safety of bridges—was submitted at the end of the summer. A response from the Foundation came back three months later with a query from one reviewer. After it was rebutted, the grant came through early winter. It covered half time salaries for him, as the principal investigator, and two graduate assistants for a period of three years, expenses for experiments and travel, plus an overhead of some 40 percent. He knew that he had gotten on the right track.

He was now more or less considered in the college as a "research man." The dean seemed to think that a transformation of the college to one with steady-state ongoing—vis-à-vis fitful—research activities couldn't be accomplished just by having progressive department chairpersons. He looked to the younger, newer ones for more agency to his mission. To this, he needed to be discreet. The university was administered along lines of command. Sometimes, when he wished to see certain things done in a department, he'd go to a faculty member—to whom it was not clear whether or not the dean had first talked to the chairman. Some unwary faculty, feeling so honored by the dean's visit would over-interpret or misinterpret the situation or even take it as an opportunity to challenge, full of passionate intensity, his chairman. If and when a confrontation ensued, more often than not, the faculty would discover that the dean had left him holding the bag. In a few instances, the disillusioned one even found it best to pack his bags. Thus goes the saying, "The company of the sovereign is like that of a tiger."

The dean had come to Guoda's office once to tell him, "Haven't you noticed that one of the most desirable large rooms assigned to your department is being used just to store surveying equipment?" Guoda hummed a vague response but wouldn't follow up. It is really none of my business, he thought. It was almost public knowledge that the dean would like to see surveying dropped from the curriculum.

The dean had also said in Guoda's office, "We need to realize that for the education of a modern engineer, a bachelor's degree is only the first step." Guoda thought for institutions like Cal Tech or MIT, it may be, but not for a state university. But he did not speak his mind. Another time, the college was to interview someone for a full professorship. The dean asked Guoda to talk to the man and write a report to him. Throwing his chest, Guoda thought, "Gee! An assistant professor interviewing a potential full professor!" He did what he was asked, handed his brief report to the dean's secretary and stayed away.

For the first time, the Jings bought a house (on mortgage of course), a bi-level on a slope, with the living area on the upper floor. One side of the basement was level with the ground and walled in with glass panels giving out to a small garden. The whole downstairs was semi-finished with a study and a large recreation room. The original owner had added another sizable, nameless room at the ground level. Not quite finished either, it had a fireplace foundation and a couple of marble slabs left over it, with which Guoda went on to build an indoor flowerbed over the foundation. It was completed on the day that he, Michael, and Priscilla welcomed home from the hospital Jiafeng and the newest member of the family, Paul.

Behind the carport, a middling silver maple served as the centerpiece of the small garden, which was a few stone steps higher than the driveway and featured a bed of snapdragons and marigolds at its front. At the back, a hedgerow separated the garden from a gently rising sodded backyard, on which Guoda put up a swing set for the children. They enjoyed the unusual topography of the house and the grounds as well as the tomatoes and raspberries the previous owner had planted in the backyard. There Jiafeng would have the wash hung on clotheslines, and everybody liked the smell of the sun on their clean clothes.

The university had one of the most beautiful campuses in the country. Some weekend afternoons, Guoda would take the family and wander through the arboretum behind the Library to the banks of the Blue Orchid River. Jiafeng would hand pieces of stale bread to the children, who would tear them and throw the crumbs to the ducks, gathering under the redbuds' pink clouds. With such outings, he would find some relief from a guilt for not having spent enough time with the family, a feeling almost unknown in his father's generation. Nevertheless, the feeling was real, as the changes of environment and culture were.

In 1962, he was to go to Lisbon, Portugal, to present a paper at a conference. He planned to take the opportunity to visit Paris and London. Still holding a Chinese passport issued in Taiwan, he met with much red tape in getting the visas for France and England. For a short visit to these countries, the holder of an American passport would not even need a visa. That year he was promoted to associate professor. The dean's letter stated, "…As Associate Professor, you will have tenure when you become a citizen of the United States…."

Jiafeng purchased a set of sofa for the living room and asked him to repaint the room. He enlisted the help of Yan Qiunan, a biologist friend. On a Saturday afternoon with sunlight streaming from the picture window, they chatted relaxedly while working with the brushes. Casually, Guoda remarked, "I wonder if this is all there is to life."

"What do you mean?" Yan asked.

"You know. Working hard, getting promotion…" At once he regretted the slip of the tongue and quickly added, "Do you think what I just said sounded like 'De Yi Lao Sao' (a smug complaint)?"

"I am afraid I do," his friend was unforgiving.

Guoda was embarrassed, but he felt misunderstood. Yes, he wished for something more, yet he hadn't given it enough thought to properly express what it was.

Before he left Virginia, he had applied for permanent resident status in the United States. After moving to Illinois, he had an interview in Chicago with an officer of the Immigration and Naturalization Service (INS). At its end, the officer told him that he was going to recommend approval of the application. Then he added solemnly, "You know, this country is mainly for Europeans." Guoda wasn't sure where the gratuitous remark came from. He was tempted to reply with, "Oh, I see. That's why Chief Illini danced with such joy because he had been admitted to this land." (At football games of the University of Illinois, a Chief Illini mascot would perform a spirited dance with the band.) Of course, he didn't say that. Giving the officer a polite nod, he stole away. Shortly he received his green card. Subsequently, Jiafeng obtained hers too.

Some years hence, he had received reminders from INS that he was eligible to apply for American citizenship. He had put this on the back burner. After all, giving up one's nationality of birth is not something one could do without serious thought. And he was busy, occupied with his work at hand. However, that experience with the French and British visas and the tenure issue pushed the citizenship question to the fore.

After summer school that year, the family rented a cottage by Lake Geneva, to swim, fish and generally relax. One night, after everyone else had gone to bed, he stayed up by the reddening potbelly stove (in Wisconsin some September nights needed that). I can't renounce the fact that I am Chinese. Giving up the citizenship of one's birth country is almost like renouncing one's parents. Or is it? Where is your country? China. On the Mainland? Taiwan, or Formosa? (The latter, a name of Portuguese origin for the island, would dilute the Chinese claim that the island was part of China.) How much loyalty do you feel toward the government in either place? If not that much, what is it you are loyal to? A Chinese heritage? What does it mean? Does becoming an American citizen violate that heritage? Would staying in a country and yet not merging with its people and culture cause one psychological discomfort? Would it also be unethical? It might be all right for a short stay. For a prolonged period, let alone an indefinite one, would it be unfair to the host country as well as to the person himself?

I would probably have little problem. I know who I am. I'll contribute my share to the society from which I derive my sustenance. I know my roots; they are in China. But I have also been growing new ones here. The soil has been most congenial. It has given me no cause to complain. Any discomfort I have occasionally felt originates from my emotional grounding of the past; that is not an unusual state of mind for an immigrant, any immigrant. This land is full of immigrants. Besides, up to now a third of my past, two thirds of my adult past, has been already in America.

He gazed at the door behind which his children were asleep. How about them? They know little of China, never having been there. They know America. Is it fair to have them carrying the burden of living in a place and not being full members of its society? Of feeling guests in the land of their birth? He recalled one evening he was playing the Chinese fiddle for amusement in his study, and Priscilla stepped in. She watched for a moment, and then pointed at him with her forefinger, "You, Chinese!"

After the vacation, Guoda and Jiafeng sent in their applications for citizenship. On the day of swearing in at the court, the presiding judge remarked to the new citizens that new immigrants from different cultures to the nation were like alloy to steel—just a little could do much to strengthen and toughen it. A "steel man" of sorts himself in his Hong Kong days, he appreciated the welcoming remark, and it helped to thin the shadow cast by the parting comment of that Chicago INS officer. He took the oath of allegiance to the United States of America, like the signing of a contract, thus ending his refugee status. It struck him how fortunate he and his family were, now a finite fraction, though small, of this great new country.

In the fall that year, he was in San Francisco for a meeting. Sitting by the window on the second floor of a restaurant in Chinatown and hearing brassy marching music, he looked out down on the street, a troop of Chinese American boy scouts was marching behind an American flag. The scene blurred as his eyes filled.

On that trip he also visited the University of California at Berkeley. He had previously felt that American college students were a rather docile lot, vis-à-vis their counterparts in China, who often spearheaded social/political movements. (Not the group he had belonged to, though.) That time at Berkeley, the feeling changed. He saw students talking excitedly and milling about stalls and tables with plaques, signs and handbills that advocated their causes, mainly for civil rights and against the Vietnam War.

Although he was immersed in his work, back to Orchid City, he was motivated enough to spend one Saturday afternoon canvassing his neighborhood to distribute decals of a "clasp of a black hand with a white hand" and ask people to place them on their picture windows or doors. At the college he volunteered to be a tutor of minority students. He had an African American sophomore from Chicago as his protégé. The young man seemed bright enough but he surprised Guoda when he informed him that his social life always came first. Guoda tutored him algebra with spotty results. The young man eventually left the university. Afterwards, Guoda gave up volunteering—in the meantime suspecting himself of tokenism. He poured practically all his energy into his own technical career.

CHAPTER 25

The new emphases on basics provided for Guoda challenges as well as opportunities for career advancement. For structural engineering theory, his general field, the fundamentals lie in mechanics and mathematics. The field had been advancing rapidly. Again he felt that he was behind and needed to catch up. He enrolled as a graduate student in Physics Department and took for credit courses in mechanics and in advanced mathematics. Just to keep up, to understand what the other person was talking about, to debunk, to guard against bluffing. Or to bluff, when needed?

He studied, on his own, such new subjects as matrix theory of structural analysis, plastic structural analysis, and random vibration. Shortly, he taught these subjects as "Special Topics" to graduate students and felt guilty because he did not yet have full command of the material himself. He would partially justified the initiatives by the thought that it was better than teaching the students material that was obsolete or soon would be.

All too often, going home late afternoon after he had taught classes, attended committee meetings, counseled undergraduate and graduate students, yet he would think: "I haven't done a thing today." "Thing" meant research and/or new knowledge. As a rule, he would pack books and notes in his brief case for the night's work, and on Saturdays, Sundays, he would be working in the office. He knew he couldn't survive by teaching alone. He had to manage to write papers, get them published; write proposals, get them funded; and attract graduate students, get them supported and graduated (sometimes help them find jobs).

He developed stomach problems: cramps, diarrhea, weight loss. He went through a battery of tests. Upper GI, lower GI, allergy, amebic dysentery, parasites, diabetics. The family doctor couldn't find anything organically wrong with him. Then he went to the University of Wisconsin Hospital. Some of the tests he had before were repeated. The principal physician, after reviewing the results and some questioning, asked further, "What is your field?"

"Civil engineering."

"And rank?"

"Associate Professor."

"You involved in research?"

"Yes."

"I am not surprised," the physician turned around to the gaggle of young interns behind him. "Pressure from work could do that to some people."

He was told that before by his family doctor. But he was still concerned about the possibility of organic causes. "What is the probability that I have cancer?" He had felt bulges in his abdomen at night.

"The same that I have—about one in 200,000."

That gave him much relief. The doctor then told him, "I know it's difficult for you at this stage of your life and career. But take my advice. Try not to work too hard. Find more time to relax; get your mind off work."

He discovered that he could get his mind off work by watching baseball games on television. On Saturday afternoons he'd sit with Michael and be glued to the TV set. It did get his mind off work—during the game. But afterwards, a sense of regret and guilt would take over, even if his team won—for having lost valuable time on something not really that worthy. Yet as the next working week wore on, he'd be looking forward to the Saturday game on TV.

As a baseball fan then, he was perhaps not that different from many of his colleagues or millions of conscientious American workers who would find in spectator sports diversion and relief from pressure at work. A colleague's wife once complained to him about her husband. "He watches all kinds of sports on TV—football, baseball, basketball. You name it. Now the habit has so degenerated that he'd watch golf, and even bowling!"

After that consultation at the University of Wisconsin Hospital, his stomach trouble eased. However, it would flare up every so often, usually in correlation with pressure of work.

He would avoid greasy or spicy foods, and alcoholic drinks. Once after a conference in France, he was in a roadside café in Paris, having pastry and milk for his afternoon snack. Another customer, a young man, who had watched his earlier awkward exchanges with the server, sneakingly moved his chair and himself toward Guoda, a little at a time. When he was close enough, he leaned over and said to Guoda, "Zee meelk ees...very good...for the ba-BEE!"

In the evening, he joined a bus tour of the city. Near the end, the sightseers were led into a bar. While everyone else was ordering alcoholic drinks, he ordered milk. An elderly man came over, took off his hat and bowed deeply to the abstinent young man. Guoda sportily returned the reverence, smiling a little like a saint, accepting the approbation of a forced virtue.

Back in Orchid City, he kept grinding away at his work.

In his sixth year at WTU, he planned for a sabbatical leave and to take his family to Taiwan to visit his parents and let his children meet their grandparents for the first time. After corresponding with several schools, he chose to go to Stanford University. Jiafeng like the choice too, since her mother was then living with her sister Jiaxuan's family in Belmont, California, twenty minutes away from Palo Alto.

After the Board of Trustees approved his sabbatical, along with his promotion to full professor, he anxiously awaited the trip with the family to California. It was one of those golden falls in lower Wisconsin. They would drive their new Pontiac station wagon to see the glorious multicolored leaves, exploring the charming secluded lakes around the border of Waukesha and Walworth counties. Leaves fell on sunlit water—gold upon gold. In quietude, the reflections of the dark trees, the blue sky and the white clouds were more beautiful than oil paintings. Why would anyone want to go some place else?

They did—Chicago, St. Louis, Springfield, Missouri, Oklahoma, Route 66 to Amarillo, Albuquerque and beyond. Early in the morning they would load their baggage on top of the car rack and cover it with a tarpaulin, and hit the road, the shadow of the car leading the way. They'd stop for breakfast. For the rest of the day they would go with the flow. Paul, two years old, sat in a car-seat between his parents in the front; his siblings, Michael, nine, and Priscilla, seven, in the back, telling jokes, singing such songs as *Winchester Cathedral* and *San Jose*, or competing to be the first to correctly call out whether or not the oncoming car was a station wagon. Entering Arizona, they tarried a while at the Petrified Forest National Park. At the Grand Canyon, the family waited in darkness for the sunrise. As the horizon began to glow, Guoda heard the drum and the first bars of *Thus Spake Zarathustra*. Crossing the deserts of Arizona and California, passing the greenery of San Joaquin valley, they arrived in Palo Alto.

They rented a little stucco house on Cornell Street near the campus, and Michael and Priscilla could walk to the Escondido School. Guoda sampled a number of courses and settled on one in Operations Research and another in Computer Science.

In April, at a conference in Seattle, the head of Department of Structural Engineering at Purdue University approached him to ask whether he would be interested in joining them. It plucked a heart string. He thought of that summer night almost 20 years ago when his father mentioned that he might send him to the same university. How different were the circumstances. He gave the possibility some thought, and said thanks but no thanks, an answer he had given in the past few years to several other schools, none more noted than Purdue, though. He felt quite comfortable at WTU. Changing schools, chances are that one would have to prove oneself all over again.

Socially the Jings visited most often with Jiafeng's mother and her sister Jiaxuan's family, the Hos. However, on Memorial Day weekend, he drove the family to San Diego to see Miss Helen Yeats, who had retired to her hometown for some time now, and to visit that city's famous zoo.

She lived in a small apartment attached to the back of her sister's house above a ravine. Flowering plants climbed up the patio posts, and potted ones bloomed on the porch. The air was fresh and cool. Her aging gray eyes sparkled as she saw her young choir member matured, and bringing his family to pay their respects. She fussed over the kids as she did over their father, like the time when he had a headache from surveying in a cold afternoon on St. John's campus. She had two meals with the Jing family. Before parting, she and Guoda had a hearty embrace.

"Daddy, I have never seen you hug anybody so close before," Michael said to him in the car; Priscilla giggled; their mother snickered, and Paul too joined in the fun.

After the school year ended at Stanford, the family headed for the Far East. First they stopped in Tokyo as guests of Guoda's friend, Professor Yamamoto of Tokyo University, and his family. In the lobby of the Hilton Hotel, they ran into Dr. and Mrs. Fineman. Guoda and Jiafeng invited them to a dinner, which cost him the whole stipend from a seminar that he had given there earlier. All had a delightful time besides some short shoptalk between the men. Fineman was expansive, commenting broadly on his own faculty. X hadn't published anything in two years and still considered himself a researcher; Y nibbled at the same thing for years on piddling support from a stagnant industry. But he also lauded others—doing pioneering work in probabilistic methods and computer utilization.

After a short stopover at the University of Kyoto, the Jings flew to Hong Kong, where Li Baoya and Amanda met them at the airport. As they rode in a taxi on the busy Nathan Road, two-year old Paul marveled at the throngs, "Wow! Big Chinatown!" Guoda went to the Lion and Globe Steel Company, and had lunch with his old sidekick Yu, who told him that Mr. Ferrero had retired to England. Guoda had corresponded with the latter a few times in his graduate student years. Ferrero's letters, written in his exquisite penmanship, were friendly and unaffected, the last one advising Guoda "not to lose his British accent" (which he never thought he had one). Guoda's last letter to him had addressed him as "Victor" and it was not answered. Guoda suspected that perhaps even for this rather enlightened Englishman, the erstwhile young Chinese employee might have crossed some kind of a line.

When Dr. J. K. Chung, Professor of Mechanical Engineering at the National Taiwan University, was in Orchid City several years ago as a visiting professor, the Jings had invited him to their home a couple of times for dinner. Before Guoda left Stanford, he had written to him about his coming trip to Taiwan, hoping that the professor would arrange for him some professional contacts in Taiwan. Dr. Chung replied to offer more. As the new Minister of Education, he proposed that Guoda come as one of the lecturers at the Summer Science Seminars that were under the joint auspices of the National Taiwan University, Qing Hua University and the Academia Sinica. The remuneration terms were quite generous, including housing and a salary. Guoda followed up and soon accepted an appointment as a visiting scholar and lecturer.

CHAPTER 26

❀

Guoda, Jiafeng and the children were welcomed at the Taipei airport by his parents, Rende's family, Aunt Qijing and Uncle Dazhan. Truly an occasion of great joy. The new arrivals checked in President Hotel, since their housing at the National Taiwan University wouldn't be ready until a few days later. His parents, Guoda's liaison for housing matters, had been advised also that their son's family would have one of the houses built for foreign visiting scholars in a compound close to the campus.

In the absence of Fuli, Qisheng said to Guoda and Jiafeng, "I went to see it myself. It was the largest one in the compound, very impressive, the Chinese palace style, large rooms, high ceiling. They were being repainted."

"Royal treatment, eh?" Jiafeng said to Guoda.

"And Rende had already hired a maid for you." After a pause, Qisheng said, "I was thinking...since we have lived so far apart, on this occasion having you two and the children all together, perhaps, your yaya and I can come and stay with you all for the summer."

Guoda liked the idea on first hearing. On second thought, he said, "That would be very good, but wouldn't it be inconvenient for Yaya?"

"I know what you mean," Qisheng said. "I've also thought about that too. He has mellowed. In any case, this is such a rare opportunity."

Guoda had to agree with the last point.

"I think it would be nice for the children too to spend more time with their grandparents," Jiafeng said.

Guoda appreciated her attitude. Turning to his mother, he said, "Have you talked with Yaya about this?"

"Yes. He said it'd be very nice."

"Everyone is for it; I am too," Guoda said.

They all moved in. There were window air-conditioners but none worked. The daily temperature and humidity hovered around 90-90. However, the tall ceiling and large windows did help to make the house reasonably comfortable. In front of the walled-in grounds was an experimental rice field. Some evenings, after a hefty shower, Guoda thought he could hear the young rice stalks grow in the warm, humid island air.

Fuli and Qisheng had one bedroom; Guoda and Jiafeng another, and the children shared the largest. Every workday morning, Guoda taught a two-hour class at the university, Fuli went to his office at China Merchants downtown, and the two older children walked to a nearby house to have an hour and half Chinese lesson taught by a tutor as arranged by their mother.

The general atmosphere in the house was similar to that when Guoda and Jiafeng were staying with his parents, when years ago he was waiting for his visa to America. There were some significant differences, however. Jiafeng would now be the mistress of the house, giving instructions to the maid, etc. Qisheng was happy with her role an honored guest. Guoda's heart warmed to note his mother wearing much of the time a smile that showed her neat teeth.

Fuli seemed a little unsure as to how to conduct himself with his grandchildren from America. Nevertheless, he was delighted with them. They did not know enough Chinese to carry on a conversation in the language. Now it was a fitting time for Fuli to speak in English, which he always enjoyed. But the experience wasn't as satisfying for him as expected, because often he couldn't understand them. Then he would turn to their parents, "What did he (or she) say?" And he was the more annoyed because he felt he couldn't very well question the authenticity of the children's language, however not quite textbook-proper it might be. He would not hesitate to challenge the English of any other whose native tongue was not that, in the same vein as he would sometimes comment on a Beijing opera singer whose rendition he did not like—"A mouthful of shit!"

Once over dinner, he proclaimed, "If only I had a million dollars!" (he meant American dollars, as a lot of people in Taiwan, and the world, were wont to reference money), and with a wide upward sweep of the hand, like a field commander issuing an order, "All these kids will stay right here!" Guoda let his father's flight of presumptuousness pass, conserving his own energy.

Later Fuli decided to take on some new responsibilities—to the grandchildren. Every other day or so, he would teach them some basics of Chinese culture, starting with *Zhong Xiao Ren Yi,* (Loyalty to country, Fealty to parents, Benevolence and Righteousness), with particular emphasis on the second. He also tried to get them to recite a simple Tang quatrain by rote.

The children had had some Chinese lessons in Orchid City with a class organized by the local Chinese community. Their interest faded after a couple months. Guoda, wishy-washy on such matters, wouldn't want to force anything on the children unless he was sure of its necessity. He wouldn't even arrange to have them baptized, as some of his church friends had suggested. He thought they could make up their own mind about religion later.

Now with the new demands being put on them by their grandfather, the children began to grumble. "It was not fair. We already had Chinese lessons in the morning in Teacher Lai's house." And "Grandpa wanted me to make ink. It's so *boring.*" And "I had already turned the TV so low I could hardly hear it. He still said it was too loud." One time his grandfather told Paul to pick up the plum stone he had spitted out. The boy started to cry because he had never been confronted with such a stern face before.

Fuli suggested that Guoda pay respects to some of his friends, and he would accompany him. Guoda remembered his experience last time when he was in Taiwan before he left for America—Fuli took him around the city to visit his friends. For some whom Guoda knew fairly well he didn't mind. But he thought it made no sense to visit Fuli's new friends whom he had never met before. Rende had told him, "He just want to show you off." This time Guoda simply declined.

In the third week, Qisheng asked Jiafeng, "Is it all right that Yaya have several friends of his come here for dinner this Saturday night?"

"Saturday? Aren't we supposed to go to Aunt Qijing's place?"

"Oh, yes. I was going to tell you. They have agreed to change the date for that."

"In that case, of course, we can have Yaya's friends here."

When she later told Guoda about it, he complained to his mother, "I'd rather spend time with Aunt Qijing and Uncle Dazhan. Why can't Yaya invite his friends to a restaurant?"

"I suppose they like to see the house?" Qisheng said.

The guests arrived. In the parlor, Fuli motioned them to sit down, told Qisheng to have the maid serve tea, and introduced them to Guoda and Jiafeng as Uncle X, Uncle Y and Aunt Z. They exchanged pleasantries; the guests praised the architecture of the house. "We rarely see such high ceiling and spaciousness for residential buildings."

Jiafeng told them dinner would be ready soon. She had most of the dishes delivered earlier from a restaurant.

"It'd be nothing elaborate. Just some homely food!" Fuli made the usual hostly remark.

The dishes were on the table. Before Fuli could do it, Guoda stood at the head of the table, spreading his arms in a hospitable gesture, said, "Please take whichever seat that's convenient," ignoring Qisheng's anxious look and Fuli's glare.

The dinner passed, during which Fuli said very little.

That night, Jiafeng told her husband, "Yaya didn't seem too happy during the dinner."

"I know. I wasn't too happy before it…. Perhaps I over-reacted." He had a singe of conscience.

The next morning, Qisheng told Jiafeng after both of their husbands had left for work, "I think we better move back to our apartment. Your father couldn't sleep too well with the frogs behind croaking all night, and that dog of the German professor's family started to balk even before daybreak."

His parents moved back. Guoda regretted that his lack of forbearance and generosity of spirit had unfairly curtailed at least the togetherness of Qisheng and the children. Afterwards he found Fuli somewhat cool, distant and overly polite, whenever they met, mostly at dinners invited by relatives. That didn't surprise him. Two weeks later, at a dinner that Rende and Aili hosted, Guoda was glad to notice that his father's coolness seemed to have gone. His Uncle Dazhan started,

"How did the President look?"

"Frankly, he looked kind of feeble to me," Guoda said. "Nothing like the erect commander-in-chief I used to see him in the pictures. I think he had rouge on his face and I smelled whisky. But his eyes still have that penetrating light."

"Did Minister Chung take all the scholars there?"

"No, we had our separate invitations," Guoda said. "It was kind of funny. I was lecturing. Suddenly a smartly dressed, young, strapping officer strode into the classroom. I stopped talking. The officer nodded and asked, 'Professor Jing?' I said 'Yes.' He stepped onto the dais and laid his attaché case on the table, opened it and took out a big envelope and handed it to me. It had my name and Jiafeng's on it. On its left side were printed, in large size, Chiang Chung-cheng (Chiang Kai-shek's other name) and Song Meiling. I took out the contents—an invitation. Out of a habit grown in America that I would check with Jiafeng for any social engagement involving us both, I was thinking whether Jiafeng would be free for this one. The officer hardly gave me any time to think. He pointed at our names on a registrar and ordered, sonorously like a drill sergeant, 'Sign here!' I meekly followed the instruction. The officer straightened himself, nodded, turned around and semi-goose-stepped out."

"Don't blame the American custom of checking with the wife. Admit you are hen-pecked," Rende said. That drew a wave of laughter.

"When have I offended you, Brother?" Jiafeng protested.

"How did the interview go?" Dazhan asked.

"I nearly blew it at the very beginning. Our group was headed by a Professor Zhu from MIT. We sat on a long sofa, facing the President in a chair with a uniformed aide standing behind. Professor Zhu had forewarned me that I needed to be prepared for some substantive questions from the President.

When it came to my turn, the President read from a notebook in his hand and muttered slowly, 'Jing Guoda...Hunan, Changsha...' Lifting his head, he said, 'Professor Jing?' 'Yes, President Chiang.' 'Changsha, a fine place...a fine place,' he hummed. I nodded a little, smiled a little and tried to look respectful. Then I heard, "Gui ken do sou?" From the tone I knew it was a question, but I did not understand it. The embarrassment only seemed to have lasted too long. I felt pokes at my ribs. Professor Zhu was hitting them with his elbow and said under his breath hurriedly, "How old are you? How old are you?" Then I caught the literary phrase the President used in his heavy Zhejiang provincial accent. 'I am 37, President Chiang.' The crisis passed. He wanted to hear my suggestions for Taiwan regarding the education and training of structural engineers. I was prepared for that...."

Through all the narration Guoda noticed that his father, with a smile on his face, was listening with obvious pleasure. His eyes would circle around the table as if to make sure that everyone was paying attention to his son, whose name was on every newspaper on the island as one of the visiting scholars from America, for whom the President and Madame Chiang had hosted a party.

"A close call," Guoda's Uncle Han, the former minister to France, said.

"You almost bring shame to the Jing name," Fuli said, but his tone of voice and facial expression appeared to mean the opposite. Then turning to Jiafeng, he asked, "Did you speak with Madame Chiang?"

"Just briefly. She did almost all the talking, saying that she'd have us all back for good once the Mainland Communist bandits are defeated by our counter-offensive."

For the rest of his stay in Taiwan, twice a week, after class, Guoda would go to his parents' apartment. Qisheng still complained about poor health. Dreadfully afraid of draft, when she went to restaurants or visit relatives, the first thing she would do was to look for a spot to seat herself where the air was still. The windows of her room were usually closed. It was one of the few instances that Guoda would feel sorry for his father. When he came home for lunch and a midday rest period, she would allow the front door to be open to let some breeze in. Most of the time, before he returned, she would chat with Guoda about relatives while she sat in her bed. She would bring up things of the past, such as Fuli's philandering, saying that she still had to watch him.

Soon the summer session was over. Too soon for Guoda, those rare days with his parents, brother and other relatives would become just memories.

CHAPTER 27

The Wisconsin Jings stopped at Hawaii. Resting on the beach, watching the kids having fun with their mother, Guoda mused over the Taiwan experience. It would be nearly perfect if he hadn't reacted so wilfully when Fuli had his guests in the house. Overall the family reunion was made all the more gratifying by the visiting scholar appointment—in particular, the publicity of which seemed to have brought so much pleasure to his parents. He wondered about the role of chance in life—the shear luck that he had come to know Dr. Chung, which had brought about the appointment.

A year after returning from the trip, they had a new home built on a wooded lot. All bedrooms were upstairs. In his study downstairs, Guoda could gaze out the window and see the white trilliums and pink cranesbills, fireflies swimming in blue lagoon, yellow elms and scarlet maples, and squirrels hopping holes in snow. The children called the backyard the "jungle," as the wooded grounds behind the house were left wild. Flocks of pheasants would in the morning traipse across it to the fields to feed, and in the evening return to the stands of tall trees to roost. He worked steadily in the study with a tranquil mind. The tranquility in the backyard lasted, but not in the mind for long.

In the late 1960s, an environmental consciousness—raised by such works as Rachel Carson's *Silent Spring*—and the Anti-War campaign coalesced into a general humanistic movement surging across the country. It blamed the "industrial-military complex" and technology in general as major causes of modern society's problems. Engineering was of course identified with technology. Furthermore, engineering works and thus demand for engineers were tied to the business cycle, which was then in a downturn. Engineering enrollments dropped.

To counter the decline, admission standards were lowered, and spokesmen were sent to high schools to persuade potential college students that technology was the tool needed to solve society's problems. Nevertheless, a sluggish economy tightened budgets. The government squeezed the university; it squeezed its colleges; they the departments, and down the line. Administrators in the engineering college had reasons to be nervous. While economical conditions seemed to be restraining or even contracting almost all technical fields, they did not slow the advance of electronic computers.

It was not surprising that the dean would want to establish a new Department of Computer Science. The bright future of computers was for all open eyes to see. The problem was money. Tight budget would mandate a reallocation of resources within the college. Existing departments found themselves vulnerable. Civil engineering in particular, as the oldest and perhaps least sexy among the major engineering disciplines, felt the threat.

In early spring, 1969, the gentlemanly Chester Gordon announced his intention to resign from the chairmanship after his current term, which was to end in June. The dean directed the department to elect a three-member Search Committee for a new chairman. Guoda became one of the three. The committee met and agreed on a choice.

James Mitchell, a professor in Mechanics and Materials Department, was one of the most respected faculty members in the college, having a reputation of excellence in teaching, scholarship, good sense and personal integrity. He and Guoda had joined efforts and set up a graduate program in structural mechanics that would enable students to work in traditional civil as well as other fields of engineering such as aerospace and automotive.

However, to the Search Committee's inquiry regarding his availability, Mitchell reacted negatively, citing health reasons. As the last days of Gordon's term drew near, the dean asked the department faculty to elect an acting chairman, and Guoda was chosen. The dean told him that his new position made him a likely candidate for the regular job, and if he liked that, he should resign from the Search Committee. He did.

As acting chairman, one of the earliest decisions he had to make concerned the reappointment of a young assistant professor in his own field. For the past two years, he and Larry Hanson often had lunch together, alone or joined by others, and he had come to know the young man professionally rather well—a competent and conscientious teacher, but not particularly interested nor productive in research. He was aware of that before, but now it became his responsibility to act. He talked to people in and outside the department, put it aside and came back to it. Before he made the decision, he went to see the dean, wanting assurance that the position would stay in the department if the young man was let go. He got that and went ahead to recommend no reappointment. He was keenly aware that Hanson, who had a wife and a young child, now had to find a job in an uncertain economy. The young man left without coming to see him. Guoda regretted that and the missing of a chance to explain his reason—that the department needed research to compete and survive. On the other hand, he was relieved that he didn't have to face what could be an unpleasant experience.

Closely following that case was a request for an extension of a sabbatical leave in Europe from a colleague who had a joint appointment with the Department of Mechanical Engineering. Its chairman had already given his approval. Guoda read the papers and thought that the man had been essentially having a vacation sabbatical. He disagreed.

The man returned from Europe. In a chair across Guoda's desk, he said, "Jack had okayed the extension. Why did you block it?" (Jack was the other chairman.)

"Look. It was nothing personal. It's my job to optimize the use of department resources."

"So a couple of lousy months don't meet your criteria of optimization. Don't give him that optimization crap that you picked up at Stanford. OK? You told us yourself all about those Chinatown dim sum and trips with children to the San Diego Zoo on your sabbatical."

Things are getting out of hand, Guoda thought. "At least, I have offered a new course on Operations Research Methods," he said, hating that he was defending *his* sabbatical.

"How do you know that my extension wouldn't be worthy?"

"I don't think 'travel and consulting' is a good enough reason in our current tight budget situation."

"I tell you why you torpedoed my plans. You wanted to show everybody, the dean, in particular, how tough you could be!" He stood up, eyes glaring, nose flaring, like the Hulk.

Guoda was concerned that the person, probably twice his weight, might be losing his marbles. Guoda's chest simmered, belly tightened. "Well, if you think that my action was inappropriate, you can always go to the dean, or the Grievance Committee."

"Grievance Committee! Give me a break!" He stomped out.

Guoda was relieved. I don't want this damn job, he said to himself.

The job also required him to make out contingency budgets—three percent and six percent reductions—and to write the annual department report showing "progress," in a time of retrenching. The couple of baptismal months as an administrator taxed his capabilities. It wore him mentally and physically. His stomach problems, which had been more or less under control recently, flared up again. A strict diet didn't help. One night he woke up, feeling nauseated with the stomach cramping. He went downstairs to the kitchen to warm up some milk. Suddenly the discomfort and the nausea intensified and he went to the sink and retched. The pain reached a crescendo. He saw a white light and slumped. He heard Jiafeng's cry, a thin voice, as if from faraway, "Michael, come quickly," and then it was all peace and quiet. No pain, no nausea.

Examination in the hospital showed that he had stomach ulcer and had lost much blood through internal bleeding. He felt fine after a couple of days. Friends and colleagues came to visit, and he talked with them animatedly like a well man. During a visit by Mitchell, conversation turned to department affairs. He advised Guoda to put his own health above the administrative job. Guoda replied, "That's a foregone conclusion," implying that he wouldn't take the regular chairman job. He was released from the hospital a couple of days after the bleeding had stopped.

At a following check up, he asked his family doctor's opinion about the possible chairman job. "Let me put it this way," the doctor counseled, "You don't need it." Guoda mulled over the remark but did not withdraw his name from the list of candidates.

The chairmanship was offered to him. He was apprehensive—of his health, his temperament, i.e., his fitness for the job. But an eagerness for a new kind of experience and a healthy (or unhealthy) dose of "honor and glory," or just plain vanity, prevailed—they had all along. He accepted the offer.

The budgets of the university, the college and the department remained tight. Every Friday morning, the College Administrative Committee—consisting of the dean, his main aides including the Director of the Division of Engineering Research, and the chairs of the departments—met to discuss the operations within the college. The meeting was dubbed the "Friday morning tea-party."

The sobriquet might be fitting for good-times. In tough ones, the meetings often became contentious and tense on interpretation of statistics, responsibilities, etc, in particular, when considered in relation to resource allocations. Clarence Munro, Chair of the Department of Mechanics and Materials, a Scottish-American physicist and a frequent correspondent to the city newspaper's opinion page, once made the suggestion that Civil Engineering Department be transferred to the newly established College of Urban Affairs in the university. His logic was that such usual civil engineering concerns as traffic, housing, roads, and water supply had much to do with the urban environment. Guoda was miffed less at the narrow view of the profession than at the transparent local economic-political motivation. The move would result in a transfer of the cost of Civil Engineering Department to the College of Urban Affairs, which, in the current political climate, would have little problem in absorbing it. In the meantime, the move would free a lot of money for the College of Engineering. Besides, he felt that whatever politics there was in the College of Engineering, it probably would be child's play as compared to that in the College of Urban Affairs.

"I don't worry about the affairs of departments other than my own. Doesn't your department have problems that deserve your thought?" Guoda attempted a retort. Indeed, Munro's department had the most serious low enrollment problem in the college, and it was also deficient in external research support.

"We are a democracy here. I can do whatever I damn please," Munro asserted gruffly. Guoda had no short answer to that, and a long one would be distracting. He took it, unwilling to contend with Munro unnecessarily.

At the time, Guoda was also Chairman of the College Committee on Admission of Foreign Students. It had gone against admissions submitted by Munro, who in some cases, had acted as though applicants from countries in Africa were African-Americans. Guoda understood the sentiments, but as a policy, he thought it ought to come from a higher level than the college, or even than the university itself. But he understood privately that Munro was just trying to do his job as the chairman of a department facing problems of survival. In spite of their differences of opinion in matters of college business, outside the conference room, they were civil, even friendly, to each other. In fact, Munro, a tennis buff, regularly put in Guoda's mailbox sports page clippings, plus his own complimentary remarks, on Guoda's older son Michael's successes on high school tennis courts. But the boy's father continued to have a tough time in the dean's conference room.

CHAPTER 28

A year earlier, a professor in the water supply area left the university to join another, and the position was lost to Civil Engineering Department. It was presumed that the resource had gone to the new Computer Science Department. Now at a "Friday morning tea-party," routine business items, such as a date for the next college open house, were over. The next item was "research in environmental qualities." The dean opened the discussion, "We all know that the economy has been sluggish. The war in Vietnam has been drawing much resources. Support for aerospace research has peaked since after the moon landing. The issue that has the public's attention nowadays seems to be environmental quality. How are we, as a college, responding?"

"Yes," said the Chair of Chemical Engineering. "The squeaking wheel gets the grease. So, the caterwauls of the likes of Carson and Commons have finally gotten to the politicians...."

"Are you being ironic here about Carson's book?" Guoda said.

"I know the title of her book. The attention-getting effect is the same, greater perhaps," the chemical engineering chair said. "To get back to the subject, Brian, one of our younger guys, has been interested in air pollution and is making contacts with Wisconsin Power. He is also planning an air pollution seminar for next term, hoping to develop it into an advanced undergraduate-graduate level course."

"I understand Brian has been talking with Dick Peterson in our department about that. Dick has contacts with the agricultural industries, dairy, hogs, poultry. Besides the power industry, they have shown interest in supporting work on air qualities too," The Chair of Mechanical Engineering remarked.

"Bob Snell in our department is looking into noise control," Munro said.

"That's interesting," the dean commented. "He seems to be the only one so far in the bunch of aerospace specialists we had hired in recent years who's willing to look beyond their own field. Now the support of that is weakening…. We may have to keep them for the next 15 or 20 years." Nobody followed up on the point. The dean continued, "But noise control? How big a problem is that?"

"I don't know. I suppose in big cities, factories, the noise level would have a significant effect on health," Munro said.

"In fraternity parties too," jested the Assistant Dean of Undergraduate Studies.

At this junction, the Director of Research, giving his upper body a sideways tilt, straightened himself in the chair and said, "I am not saying that you guys are barking up the wrong tree. The areas, just brought up, particularly air pollution, may well give us much support. But right now the big money is in water pollution…."

"That's true." "No question about it."…The chairs agreed. "Early this week," the director continued, "Carl Grappe of the Department of Biology came to my office. He is privy to the fact that the new National Water Quality Council would need to lay out ten million before the end of the fiscal year—"

"Otherwise they'd lose it," some one interjected.

"And get less for the next year," another added.

"So far," the director resumed, "There are only a few proposals pending, generally each in a few hundred grand range. Grappe said that any reasonably decent proposal sent in before the end of the next month would be sure-fire."

Eyes popped.

"Water quality. That's really an area in civil engineering. Isn't it?" the Chair of Electrical Engineering asked.

"So, what has our Civil Engineering Department done about it?" the dean turned to the spokesman for the department.

Guoda had been thinking about water quality too, particularly the man in water supply who had left. Guoda felt he was being embarrassed. "You may recall Ben Walters who had left us last year. When he told us the offer by Iowa Tech, we didn't make an effort to keep him. He was our only water quality man. And our department lost that position too…. I don't know how to put it. I think the situation is somewhat like…first you castrate a man, and then dangle two fat breasts in front of him and mock him for not being able to perform." The crudeness was deliberate, aimed to shock.

A couple of weeks later, the dean told Guoda that Civil Engineering Department would have two new positions. They were filled fairly expeditiously, not as expected in the prevailing culture of the engineering academe—to jump on the current gravy train of environmental quality research—but to firm up some much neglected but essential fields in the department's purview. In his new job, Guoda had became more aware of—nearly alarmed by—the inadequacy of the teaching resource in the department. For example, there was no specialist in the fundamental area of hydraulics.

Both teaching and research resources reside mainly in the faculty body. To promote research, the dean had set up the Division of Engineering Research in the college. The director, who happened to be a most amiable person, but (rather surprisingly) no engineer nor researcher, and (unsurprisingly) a confidant of the dean, understandably had a job to do. For a given amount of resource, or faculty, more research meant less teaching and vice versa. When research monies were brought in by faculty from outside, there would be an issue as to how would they, the overhead part in particular, be distributed among the units in the university. The dichotomy in the management of the faculty into teaching and research gave rise to a tension between the departments and the division.

Before taking on the administrative job, Guoda was essentially neutral on those issues. He sensed that the disadvantage of having two bosses to report to was balanced by the advantage of having possibly two sources of support. They might compete for his efforts, if not loyalty, even though he realized that, regardless, it was his actual production that counted; shallow politics were illusory, at least at the faculty level.

After he took on administrative responsibilities, he felt that the Division of Engineering Research was in some ways a check on the work of the department, and the dual loyalty of some faculty members an impedance. He began to speak for the principle that research, as teaching, ought to be the departments' responsibility. The principle was for focus and efficiency, and it was the practice at most major universities. Nothing novel about it. But, at WTU, it would increase the power of the department chairs and lessen that of the Director of Research. While the dean had essentially a supervisory role over the departments, which were the basic administrative units of the university, he had a more direct control over the Division of Research. It provided him with greater flexibility to allocate college resources and perform his mission—to build a name for the college in graduate studies and research.

On the matter of faculty responsibilities, Guoda went a step further. As many did, he believed that doing research also makes a better teacher. Every faculty member ought to do research, he advocated, because that was what characterizes a university faculty. The dean did not disagree with that. The disagreement revealed itself in the definition of research. According to the dean, implicitly, it was externally supported, or at least as a prelude to that. Guoda took the classical definition that research, as curriculum, should be defined by the faculty as long as it was recognized by his colleagues as scholarly work. On this issue, the dean was on the side of the real world; perhaps over 90% of engineering colleges in the country operated on that basis. But Guoda thought he had the idealistic, academic high ground within the ivy-covered walls. He grasped that vine and contended with the dean and the Director of Research. He knew that he could survive as long as he had himself an external grant in force. He also knew that he was fighting a battle he couldn't win. He fought, nevertheless. The strength of his conviction came from his observation that much of the research energy seemed to be expended on factitious claims, not so much motivated by scholarship as by money. It wouldn't be so bad if the ineffective use of resources affected only research, but it affected teaching by taking resources away from it.

Many a night, or in the wee hours of morning, he'd sit at the kitchen table, sipping warm milk to nurse his aching stomach, and wonder what was he doing to his life. Was he burnt-out? All this to make a living?

He turned more philosophical, and started some reading outside his technical field. The horizon painted by Toffler's *Future Shock*—the threat of obsolescence—frightened him. The energy and time spent on administration would certainly be a waste so far as guarding against professional obsolescence was concerned. Then books such as *The Greening of America* by Reich seemed to offer an alluring, even elegant, way out. He felt an urging to back away from the worldly strife, to look in a non-technological, humanistic dimension, to seek something more spiritual. In that frame of mind, he writes:

A Caveman

A golden bird sings on a bough.
Atop the cedar muses an owl,
 watching the sparrows chirp and hop,
 pecking a grain or two, blink and stare.

Suddenly the crows rive the air;
flap and caw, "Go! Go! Go!"
Into the woods withdraws the golden bird;
the silent owl departs without a word.

I must go to the shop now
to make efficient tools
to push the boulders up and down
the dusty mountain route.

It wouldn't be too long; I'll return
to the golden bird to hear it sing
songs of meadows, forests and blessing.
I'll seek again the owl
and look into its cool eyes.
Do I see a sparrow pecking, a crow hustling,
Or, a caveman fumbling, by a primordial fire,
his little stick upon the wall?

However, he cautioned himself not to stray away from the realities of the world. He thought about his job: at bottom the raison d'etre of a college of engineering was to produce engineers, who serve society by doing engineering, like building skyscrapers and constructing highways, and not to train applied mechanists or mathematicians. Gradually he appeared to metamorphose into a spokesman for the old guard of yore, like Professor Graham, who had retired. While the dean would not fault him on that per se, the corollary that moneyed research was not mandatory was not operable for him, nor for his boss, the provost, and so on, up the ladder. Guoda had felt for sometime that he wasn't doing his job as expected of him. When the dean said to him at a Friday morning tea party, "I trust you read the papers every morning and are reasonably informed of what's going on in the world," he knew it was time to leave administration. He tendered his resignation as chairman, two years ahead of a five year term. The dean graciously returned it the first time, in the manner of a polite audience's applause inviting a return bow by the mediocre performer, but accepted it the second time. The Peter Principle netted another example.

The responsibilities of chairmanship led Guoda to a broader view of the department, his relation to it, and his own place in society. He had been a "researcher." But his research interest was based mainly on what he thought could attract external financial support, not on what the profession needed most. He did not know what the profession needed most, because he had never been a professional engineer. Is it preposterous for someone who has never really been a practitioner of a profession to head a professional department? Most of his colleagues were "registered professional engineers" with a record of substantial engineering practice. He came to feel that even to be a bona fide member of a civil engineering faculty, let alone its leader, one should be a professional engineer. A full professor and ex-department chairman, how could he begin to be a real professional engineer? Once again he felt he was behind.

CHAPTER 29

Guoda had wondered what the practice of his profession was really like. Before he left the University of Illinois, he was once told by a senior colleague that when the department was considering offering him the assistant professorship, the venerable Professor Fields had suggested that the candidate be allowed to leave the campus and get some industrial experience first. Dr. Fineman replied that "Then he might not choose to return," and made the offer to him anyway. Guoda knew that it was not that rare in other professional fields, such as the legal and medical, for one to mature and prosper almost entirely situated on an academic base. In engineering, for example, Fineman, essentially a research man, had never left the University of Illinois since he was a graduate student, yet no one would question his eminence in his profession.

But Guoda also knew that he was no Fineman. He contacted some local engineering/construction companies and was told politely that he was simply overqualified—"We seldom have the kind of work that needs your expertise." Expertise? Indeed, he had been hired as consultant or expert witness regarding matters on which he would give his opinion based on book knowledge. Although nobody, not even the lawyer on the other side, ever challenged him on his lack of practical experience and a professional license, now he meant to rectify those shortcomings for his own satisfaction and confidence.

It was the golden age of the American nuclear power industry. He talked with the representatives from Continental Power Corporation, who were on campus to recruit new engineers. At a subsequent visit to the company's Madison office, he received an offer as a full-time Consultant in the Civil/Structural Division. He took the job after getting a leave from the university with the support of the new department chair, a bright and coolly efficient professor of transportation hired from Northwestern University.

At Continental Power in Madison, Guoda worked in the Office of the Chief Engineer, who appreciated his purposes and gave him a variety of assignments, ranging from ordinary designs, to unusual ones, such as the design and construction of the inner steel shell of a nuclear reactor containment building, to highly theoretical ones, such as the probability consideration of an errant broken turbine blade hitting the reactor. Before long—it took much less time than Guoda had anticipated—he felt like a real engineer.

The following May, he took two weeks off to prepare for the professional license examinations. In July, he became a bona fide professional engineer.

In Madison he stayed with the Yans three nights a week, returning to Orchid City on Wednesday and Friday after work. Yan Qiunan, his biologist friend, had joined the faculty at the University of Wisconsin several years ago, and Mingfen, his wife, a literature major turned chemist, was a researcher at its Medical School. That year Guoda lived like a regular office worker—vis-à-vis an engineering research professor—of 40 hours a week on the job and not bringing work out of the office. At the Yans's house, he was allowed to help out with the cooking and washing the dinner dishes, which made him feel at home. They enjoyed the evening sessions of conversations. He had not felt more relaxed for a long time. He dabbled a bit more in poetry. One afternoon after work, he writes:

A Pebble

The sun thinning on the parking lot,
like a call from a friend long lost,
a pebble gleams on the ground.
I work my legs and kick it about,
and watch it bounce and skip
like a kid romping on a playground.

Early one morning, he writes:

A Stormy Night

The curtain lights up and is gone.
The heaven cracks open and growls.
I wrap the blanket tight around.
The rain begins to hit the roof,
like hordes of little horses on fast hoofs;
drips drum the gutter; gush splashes on the ground.
I bend my knees and wriggle my toe;
waves of night wind come and go.

Late fall, he composes:

A Song of Autumn

I

To the sunset recedes a vee of geese.
Fallen leaves, freed from shriveled stubble,
tumble and skid in chilling breeze.
Dazed bees stumble in the yellow mums.
Laughing children run together,
homeward, toward supper and dear mother.

II

When will the curtain fall?
shrouding the actor in long disguise.
Has the mask the masker possessed?
A small peddler, crippled by anxieties,
chained by vanities, walks a tightrope,
hanging between the seen and the unseen,
and clings to a thread of the soul.
Loose skin sags over tight joints;
pale truth stretches the bowls taut;

he travels and smiles
at arrogance of power powerless to defy,
rudeness of youth sans youth his own to bear,
neither a name to forestall the slight,
nor talent to match the pride.

III

Halt! Turn and behold!
Oh! the colors! Gloria of the woods!
Upon the river bend and up the hill!
The splendor, the grandeur!
What rhythm! What dignity!
A full blast of a magnificent symphony!

IV

Through tender budding in the chill,
gusty storms, blazing heat and summer hail,
greedy caterpillars, sloppy fowls and pests,
the leaves, in dried sinews, blotches and festers,
have survived and provided
for aging roots, arching branches, and sweet fruits.
Even the lowly brambles by the road
are exalted in bright red and gold!

V

The colors soon will fade, and woods grow
dreary with indifferent snow.
Don't let the thought trouble you.
Think of the verdant years,
soft words stroking your ears,
spoken in the morning mist of spring
in the rose-scent of a summer night.
Think of the tribulations in the ancient land,
of the journeys and transplants,
and of the blood, red and black,

in building a nest
in the erstwhile foreign forest.

VI

Therefore, hold your cup, not full, but fully earned.
Hold it by the crackling wood slowly burned—
a sip for the bitter, a drink for the sweet.
Rest, you will rest this autumn eve.
Mind not the wind ravages the leaves.
Come spring, it'll bring the resurrection.

At the end of his consultantship, Continental Power indicated an interest in having him on a regular basis. He equivocated, saying that contractually he had to return to the university for at least a year.

That summer he returned to the university with full pay but no specific assignment except to do scholarly work. Instead of writing research proposals, he wrote class notes and designed and built experimental set-ups for teaching, such as that to relate the mathematics of the buckling of columns to the physical phenomenon. It was an easy summer. He had more time with the family. Regularly they would have cookouts at the backyard patio. Jiafeng would have the meat already marinated, when he got home to start the fire. Michael, Pricilla, and Paul, now 17, 15 and 10, all helped out. They had even gone once to see the Chicago White Sox.

He was trying to define a new life, for him, of academic engineering:

I dress, house, and feed,
but do not sew, build, or plow.
My students I teach.

It was the year of the Watergate scandal, and also that of a notorious fraud that a biomedical researcher painted a white mouse black and claimed the color was that of an accepted skin graft. Guoda called it the year of *a tainted White House and a painted white mouse*. The events seemed to support his recent evolving life philosophy. He felt ever keenly of the significance of the prayer: *Lead us not into temptation*, which he didn't understand when a sophomore at St. John's.

This new life that he had defined for himself was not to be unchallenged. By the end of the year, his department chair asked him whether he was going to apply for a part-time appointment with the Division of Engineering Research. If successful, it would commit himself to the prevailing pattern of writing proposals for external funding. Part of Guoda's written reply went as follows:

"...The present modus operandi aims at 'getting outside dollars.' I am reluctant to commit myself along that line, not so much because of idealism as of the view that, on the average, it is self-defeating and detrimental to the individual and to society.

"External funding is hard to sustain. We all know the rapid rate of technological change. How can one manage to remain in the forefront of whatever is in vogue in order to attract research dollars. There may be a few who can do that. But on the average it is not feasible. To do that kind of research is to specialize. To specialize in some area necessarily means giving up others. As the area that one has been tilling matures, funding shrinks, and the researcher needs to get into a new area that has the money. He should switch his field, says the administrator. But meanwhile the researcher has grown older, if not old. The average researcher could manage some change, but not to the degree, and at the speed, of modern technology. People tried and, more often than not, failed. If one looks around the engineering college buildings in the country, he could see not a few faculty members, researchers, walking the halls drearily with injured psyche. Some were aerospace specialists hired in their heyday; administrators now would only hope that they could trade them for perhaps environmental experts, until the environmental popularity runs its course.

"Brilliant young men, brilliance burned out after a few years, recede to the game of survival, or change of their line to run flower shops or become campus politicians or even administrators. One may say, that is a fact of life, the way it is. Must it be so? What good does it do to society? Is this a system set up to benefit society or a system shaped willy-nilly by the 'rugged individualism' and 'entrepreneurship' mentality? machismo and he-man psychology? Is it masochism?

"The current definition of teaching load in the college is too high. It precludes keeping up with one's area, let alone doing any serious research. Virtually the faculty would have to buy time to keep up with his field with external funding. Part of that money would be used to hire temporary teaching help. Such help, in theory and in fact, is not as effective as the regular faculty. The practice would also imply an insincerity when the school professes to society that their main function is to teach the students.

"The present policy of giving heavy teaching loads for those who have no outside research support would ensure their obsolescence. It penalizes the students they teach. Ironically, the closer one is to obsolescence, the more he is assigned to teach, thus hastening and concreting that obsolescence. Is that good for students or society?..."

CHAPTER 30

There was no immediate response to Guoda's memo in which he hoisted the flag of society's well-being in an attempt to exempt himself from competition that everyone else must face and declined what the chair clearly wanted him to do. He still had his job at the university. The tenure system worked.

His appointment at the university had been thus far on a twelve months basis, which was generally for administrators and certain research faculty. To be consistent with his pronouncement, he felt he should ask for a change of the basis to that of nine months, which applied to the general faculty. The change would reduce his university pay by 25 percent, but then he'd be free in the summer. He brought this up with Jiafeng. "I think I should ask for the change before they initiate it, sooner or later."

"That's all right. I'll take that job if they give it to me." She was a finalist for an accountant position in the largest department store in town. She had applied for the position after a friend who worked for the store told her that one of the three accountants of the store was leaving.

"Michael is going to college next year. Priscilla soon to follow. I can find summer work elsewhere," he said.

"The job I am looking at is not all for family finance. We can get by even if I don't work. But I think it's time I start work again. Paul will be in fifth grade next year."

"You don't have to work. You could go back to school," he said.

"Back to school. For what? To find a job? I may soon have one."

"I understand that. Education is not only for a job. It can help one to enjoy life more, and be a sort of protection against old age when it comes," he said.

"What do you mean?"

"Like literature, fine arts."

"Oh…For that kind of education, I don't need to go to school. Truly, you don't have to find a summer job."

"But I want to," he said. "You don't need to work."

"I want to, for my own sake," she said. That put an end to the circling.

She was indeed offered the job and took it.

The request of changing appointment basis was promptly approved. He was given a full teaching load, four courses, spending all his time preparing lectures, grading homework, making out examinations, etc. Sessions of talking, trying to hold the attention of, or at least not to bore, groups of young intelligent people for one or two hours at a time wore him mentally, and tired him physically, and the discomfort with his varicose veins increased with the time spent on his feet. It dawned on him why so many entertainers were tempted to take drugs. He became low-spirited, irritable, and moody. But the state of a mild depression would begin to end when he received a summer job offer.

Mid-June, he drove to Chicago to work for Sargent Lundy Engineers. For a few days he stayed with a Thai friend, who was a former doctoral student of his, his Danish-American wife and their two year old son, until he found an attic apartment near Lincoln Park in midtown. The neighborhood was clean, quiet, relatively safe—he was told—and yet convenient, close to a grocery, laundry and several restaurants, including a Chinese one and a McDonald's.

The apartment had a bedroom, a living room, kitchen and bathroom. The large slant windows on the side gave the place an atelier air. It was reasonably clean, save the bathtub. When he first turned on the water, a big centipede scampered out from the drain hole. After he took care of that, then it was the compacted hair and grime. Half nauseated, he got the tub to a usable condition with lots of Ajax. Next morning, he complained about it to the landlady, a big middle-aged woman with flaccid chalky cheeks; she said, "Why don't you move out!" he retreated quickly. (At the end of summer, realizing that Guoda had bought a new lamp shade to replace one he had slightly damaged, the same vixen made him blush as she abruptly hugged him, saying, "What a sweet man!")

It was about a ten-minute walk, a good part of it under flowering catalpa, to the L-station, where the train would take him to the Loop. He needed only to cross the Palmer House arcade to get to the high-rise that headquartered Sargent Lundy. He worked on such tasks as stress analysis of nuclear reactor vessels, and safety of buried pipes. The work was interesting and challenging but did not require his attention after hours. Besides working for Sargent Lundy, he tried to bring himself up-to-date. He would read technical journals in the firm's library at breaks. For some journals that it didn't have, he would drive up to the engineering library of Northwestern University in Evanston.

After dinner, he would often take a walk in the neighborhood, among the busy streets, appreciating scenes of big city life. A boy riding a strange bicycle with an enormous front wheel and a tiny rear one, venders of toys, promenading young couples—hands on shoulders, waists or hips—heavily made-up old ladies shaking their way across the street, police cars, sirens.... Sometimes he would amble to Lincoln Park, watching suspended gulls silhouetted against the moon over the waters. He thought that on the WTU campus one might be presented with equally pleasurable views, but wouldn't have the mood to enjoy them.

In the apartment, sitting at the desk below the slanting window, the quiet modulated only by the low cries of the mosquito-hunting night hawks, he would write class-notes on "Civil Engineering Analysis," a course on applied mathematics for undergraduates he would teach next fall.

The peaceful state of mind felt good. Mid-August he returned to Orchid City for a weekend. There in his department office mailbox he found a letter from the chair, advising him that his office had been changed. The new office, he realized, was going to be one about half the size of what he had been using for years. He felt it a deliberate humiliation, a punishment that a reduction of 25 percent in pay did not forestall. (He wouldn't consider the recompense of the freed summer months.) He called the chair and demurred, citing the fact that some other faculty members, who were full time teachers, continued to have their larger offices. The chair rescinded his action. But it made the point.

The point was repeated more pointedly in the fall term. While he had not been doing research himself, he still had graduate students doing theirs. The computer time they would use needed approval of the newly installed Associate Dean for Research, a relatively young hotshot from MIT and successor to the retired amiable Director of Engineering Research. Once, as Guoda made a request for computer time on behalf of a student of his, the new administrator queried him as a bank loan officer does a poor farmer distressed by drought. The student's business settled, he turned to Guoda's activities and commented, "You know, many topflight engineering schools require their faculty to bring in outside funding to pay for half of their salary. Applying that here, you *owe* me...how much? What's your salary?" There was no humor in his tone of voice. Guoda again thought that his change to nine months appointment should have settled this. Apparently not so. Wow! he said to himself. Hallelujah! Thank God for tenure!

He wasn't being singled out. Apparently, the new Associate Dean had been doing that job on a lot of other people in the college too. His stay at the university was relatively brief.

Guoda came to the conclusion that he had to return to moneyed research. Yet experience confirmed that a full teaching load would not allow him time to keep up with the literature, without which no research proposal would likely be successful. In the meantime, it occurred to him that he had not been receiving any request to serve as reviewer of papers or proposals. In fact, his name had been dropped from committees of technical societies that he had served on for years. The reason was simple—he had not been publishing in recent years. Once again, he was behind, now in engineering research, and he needed to catch up before passing the point of no return.

CHAPTER 31

Next year, on his last day of a summer employment with Continental Power, he was asked to comment on a task concerning the cooling towers of a power plant. The modulus of elasticity of its hundreds of redwood columns needed to be determined for an assessment of the structures' safety, and for that purpose, a proposed vibration test of the structures, at an estimated cost of around two hundred thousand dollars, was being considered. He thought that perhaps a much cheaper and direct approach could be used based on the axial wave speed theory: the modulus can be calculated as the mass density times the wave speed squared (uncannily analogous to Einstein's formula of $E = m\,c^2$). If one could create a wave in the column, and mark its arrival times at two points, one could figure the speed as the distance between the points divided by the difference of the arrival times. He was asked to submit a proposal, which he did, and it was accepted.

However, an administrative problem emerged. The research contract would be between the university and the energy company (represented by Continental) that owned the plant. The company would not allow the test data to be made public without its approval, while the university insisted on its right to publish all its research results. Caught amid the hassles among the administrators and lawyers, plus technical uncertainties—after all, his idea was only a theory—Guoda regretted being committed to the work which was causing him anxieties.

It was too late to back out. At bottom, he didn't want to back out; the work could initiate his return to sponsored research. To overcome the impasse of publication rights, two separate contracts were negotiated. One, between Continental and the university, would cover the development of the technique of testing, the results of which would be made available to the public. The other, between Continental and himself, as a registered professional engineer, would be for the field testing of the columns, the results of which would not be published without the permission of the power plant's owner.

In due course, with the assistance of two graduate students, a test procedure was developed and verified in the laboratory. An axial wave would be generated by a mechanical device. The arrivals of the wave at two points of the test column would be determined from the signals of two piezo-accelerometers, photographed on an oscilloscope by a Polaroid. The field test was set on a day when the plant would be down and there would be no water inside the tower.

The plant was located on the south shore of Lake Michigan. On a late afternoon, a week before Thanksgiving, Guoda and two graduate students set out for the site in a rented station wagon. Near their destination, he saw massive black clouds hang in the sky, threatening snow. Damn! But what can you do now? They got to Benton Harbor about seven and checked in at Holiday Inn. His heart sank at dinner time when he overheard the waitress telling the next table that there would be 10 more inches of new snow on the ground tomorrow. He dejectedly returned to his room, thinking I'll cross that bridge when I come to it. The room was very warm and dry. He covered the heater with a wet towel, went to bed and slept fitfully. Up before dawn, he went to the window and moved the curtain a little to see. No snow on the car!

A billboard along the road told a temperature of 28 degrees. They reached the plant office by 8 a.m. There they had to navigate through the plant engineer (who quizzed their test procedure while having his feet on the desk), a representative from the company headquarters (making inane suggestions for choosing the columns to be tested; Guoda told them his team would just do it by throwing dice) and a plant foreman (who watched them like a hawk).

They drove to the South Tower. It was windy on the west side that faced the lake. They tried the stairs up the east side. The steps were covered with ice; the footing was treacherous. They moved the equipment up from the less icy west side onto the fan deck about five stories high from the ground level. Guoda had brought along a good-sized, sturdy baby carriage; it was to carry the electronic equipment and be wheeled around inside the tower to reach the various test columns. All the paraphernalia were to be moved down inside the tower through a hatch, which was so tight that the carriage needed to be partly disassembled first and re-assembled inside the tower.

They began the first test around 10. Everything worked beautifully. They moved to the second test column, the next, etc. An engineer from Continental

Power was their constant companion, following them and recording their every move on a Dictaphone. Around one o'clock, they went to the office and ate sandwiches with hot chocolate.

Later on in the afternoon, having finished 30 columns, they moved every-thing back into the car. They did not call it a day too soon. The lake was satur-nine, darkness settling fast over the desolate road as they left the plant. At dinner, Guoda had seven-up while his two assistants drank wine. He said a prayer of thanks before going to bed.

Shortly after daybreak, they were at the north side of the North Tower over-looking the lake. Gulls glided above heavy waves. To the right, the sun shone on the pines of the sandy hillocks. Since it was a hassle to get the baby carriage in and out of the hatch, and there were only 20 more tests to go, they decided to have the oscilloscope on the fan deck. But it was cold; the wind would snake its way inside the clothing. they moved to the tower's south side, a good part of which was shielded from the wind by the housings of the huge fans. But they still had to watch for icy patches underfoot.

The fieldwork was completed by mid-afternoon. It was getting overcast and colder. After a coffee break, they started to drive back. Snowflakes began to dance in front of them and then dashed madly like kamikazes toward the windshield. Come! Come! Now come as heavy as you want, Guoda shouted silently.

The project met its deadline. The development of the testing technique was written up and published in *the Journal of Structural Engineering*. Subse-quently, two other power plants contacted him to perform similar services. He declined because he would like to return to research in earnest, and testing using a now proven technique would not be research. It would mean some money, sure, but he didn't need that that badly.

Buoyed up by the success of the columns investigation, Guoda prepared and submitted a proposal to the National Science Foundation on the earthquake resistance of underground pipes, based mainly on his experience at Sargent Lundy. In two months, he found a letter in the morning mail from the agency. It was not a good sign—too thin, and too soon, a successful proposal would take more time to process. He read the words, "…We regret to advise you…" and started to break into a sweat. His proposal had never been so declined out-right before. No chance for a rebuttal. He sat numbly in the office for a long while and went out to walk, circling the banks of the Blue Orchid River between two footbridges. He couldn't think straight. I've lost my touch; I've left the game too long. Nearly half a century of age, can I ever recover? How am I supposed to plan the rest of my life? He couldn't sleep, Maalox tablets melting over the tongue.

He didn't tell anyone, not even Jiafeng. I have to cross the bridge myself. No point getting her concerned. Near daybreak he fell asleep for a couple hours. Back at the office, he reread the rejection letter. A footnote, which he had missed before, caught his eye. "…Perhaps it's best to stick to your own field…."—a well-meaning advice from the program director.

He rethought over the situation. It became more clear. It was bad but not that bad. The proposed research involved not only structural mechanics but also soil mechanics in which he was no expert. He had been so anxious to get back to sponsored research—the funding, the money—and forgot about its exacting and competitive nature that he had sent in the half baked proposal with more wish than substance. A correct diagnosis is halfway to a cure. You just have to be more thorough.

The next summer, he got a faculty appointment with the Livermore National Laboratory in California. Priscilla, who had just finished her sophomore year, was also going to San Francisco, where she would try to find summer work. They drove west together. One morning, stopping for food in Nevada, they needed to walk across a gaming hall. Guoda didn't even turn his head to look at any of the tables. Priscilla commented, "Daddy, aren't you at all curious?" He had learned his lesson a long time ago, but he didn't reveal it to his daughter then.

In San Francisco she stayed in a hotel with a friend. He rented a house in Pleasanton. It was near the edge of the city. There were roses in the front- and backyard, which he had to water frequently. Behind the pines in the back of the house, an expanse of grassland swept under the cloudless sky toward the horizon.

It was about a 20-minute drive to the Laboratory. Its grounds had the atmosphere of a college campus. Sometimes at noon, drenched in sunshine while having their lunch, workers could enjoy outdoor live concerts, quartets or duets. His work was also rather campus like, doing a literature review of numerical analysis of nonlinear behavior of shells structures. It provided him an excellent opportunity to improve his knowledge in nonlinear structural mechanics. He would do it even without pay. However, it did require effort. One Sunday afternoon, he writes:

Your Field

I hear a distant horn—
"This is your field. Plow it."
I rise, rub my eyes and take my hoe.
At a patch I strike; nothing gives.
Again and again;
scratches and indents appear.
Again and again;
fissures show like honeycombs.
Again and again until it becomes
fine soil fit for planting.
I lie down to rest until
the distant horn calls me again.

He learned enough to outline a research proposal.

Some weekends he would drive out to San Francisco to see Priscilla. Together they'd visit his mother-in-law, sister-in-law and her family. On his way back at night on Highway I680, away from the big city, the traffic was light, the temperature rising, the car window down, sweet air purring at the ear, and looking down on the valley and the glimmering lights of Pleasanton, he felt as though he were cruising in the clouds of heaven.

Some evenings he'd just sit in the backyard and watch the night fall. He writes:

An Evening in Pleasanton

I

The gold dims across the hillside;
stars emerge above the valley;
distant barking ripples over this sea of quietude.
On the pasture a lone oak, ages one more day,
as dusk falls unawares into the night,
yearns for the yonder lighted window.

The hills exhale the night breeze;
brass chimes and white pines in duet sing.
Scented air brings flashes of faces in,
like little fish gliding in and out
of a coral reef niche,
each face a remembrance, a tune,
a mist and a silent sigh,
or a glow and a bland smile.

II

These hills and valleys will surely outlast
our construct of computers and nuclear technology,
oleander-lined highways and rose gardens,
watered by rains ordained for other lands.
In time, these hills and valleys will likewise
be no more—mere molecules in a gassy whirl.

Be this the truth as well.
I am here and now,
in body, in spirit,
singing my song for this blessed valley,
serene like a starlit bay
harboring a decent people at their rest,
in glimmering lights their boats safely moor'd.
In these lines I'll keep this evening evermore.

Back at the university, he worked on the outlined proposal for three more months and sent it out to the National Science Foundation and waited, as he continued his teaching and guiding graduate students. In April, he received the research grant. In time, he would have technical papers published at more or less regular intervals, doctoral students graduated, others' manuscripts and proposals refereed, as well as his subsequent proposals submitted and funded, some in cooperation with a colleague who was an expert in soil mechanics. He was busy and regarded by others as productive. He thought so too, most of the time. But there were moments when he felt his life had taken on a stationary rotatory quality. It was not making progress, not flowing, except when he looked at his maturing children on the one hand, or communicated with his parents on the other.

CHAPTER 32

✿

Since the late 1960s, Jing Fuli had retired from the China Merchants Steamship Navigation Company in Taiwan with a handsome severance pay and continuing benefits. In mid-June 1972, he came to America on a visitor's visa. Guoda had just resigned from the department chairmanship. When told of this, Fuli frowned slightly and said, "Hum…Yes, administrative jobs are headaches. It's well to avoid them…. I would now just be a scholar, relax, and write, and publish a lot of papers." What cold comfort, Guoda thought, as though technical papers could be written by staring into airy nothing and then with a roll of the eye.

Guoda drove him to see some cities. On the day they arrived in Chicago, it was windy and cool. Seeing his father had brought only light clothing, Guoda bought him a sweater. He also showed him the museums and the Sears Tower. They visited the Henry Ford Museum and the Greenfield Village in Dearborn. After New York City and on their way to Princeton, New Jersey, to visit a friend of his, Fuli told Guoda that this friend "…is a most upright man. He not only expects respect from his children; he demands it…." The remark put Guoda on guard; he pretty much stayed aloof during the whole visit. On their way back to the hotel, Fuli asked Guoda to apply for his immigration to America. The son said, "Let's do one thing at a time." Thinking that Guoda was referring to the fact that he had taken care of the entire trip including the airline tickets, Fuli puckered his brow and said nothing.

At night, in a motel in Washington D.C., they disagreed on the next destination. Fuli wanted to see Boston; Guoda wanted to take him to Niagara Falls. The discussion ended as Fuli said coldly, "Of course, it's up to you." They went to bed. Shortly, Guoda heard his father's snoring, as he lay awake himself, sensing his own breathing and heart beat, and envious of those, like his father, who could turn their mind on and off like with a switch.

They spent a day at Niagara Falls and started for home. During the long hours of driving, their conversations were largely rehashes, over politics—U.S.-China relations in particular—and the Vietnam War. Fuli thought that Americans were too soft on Communists. He branded some leaders such as Senator Fulbright as befuddled and unpatriotic. Guoda would defend the senator as a thoughtful statesman, much in the spirit of a loyal counselor to the emperor in China's dynastic history, who would not withhold his best judgment in the service to his country, even at the risk of having his head chopped off.

"No principled public official would aid the Communists."

"He certainly did not aid the Communists."

"Why would he, and others like him, oppose the American efforts in Vietnam?"

"I suppose he felt that it was not in the best interest of the American people to be so involved in the war."

"It is people like him that uprooted my life in Hunan, you know."

This shift to his personal life confirmed Guoda's suspicion of a basic reason for his father's deep animosity toward Communists. When Fuli further broached the general conspiracy theory involving the Jews, liberals, etc, Guoda figured that he probably have read some extreme right wing literature. When Guoda told him that that kind of views was radical, belonging to only a fringe of American society, he replied that that was precisely the problem, and more Americans ought to have the correct kind—his kind—of perspective. Then when he went on to speak of "Our Forefathers"—not those farmers from Hunan, Jiangxi or northern China, but those gentlemen from Massachusetts, Virginia…Guoda finally figured that Fuli was essentially parroting, and he had perhaps taken him too seriously. He lost interest and disengaged himself from such topics.

At some juncture the talk came much closer to home. "Your mother really loves me, in spite of my dalliances," Fuli admitted.

That was indeed true, Guoda thought.

Fuli went on, "She would get up several times a night to make sure that I was well covered by the blanket."

Indeed, she had told me as much, Guoda recalled. However, he commented clinically: "She had no choice. She couldn't survive without you. In her youth, she simply didn't have the opportunity to get the education to find a job."

"Education—yes, your mother is an intelligent person. No question about that. To find a job?" Fuli sounded confused.

"Yes. Not then. If it were now," Guoda got the needle ready, "she could have earned a degree in computer science, and be out of your life a long time ago."

After a short silence, Fuli complained, "You say such hurtful things."

Guoda felt a slight needle himself for his own malice.

After they returned to Orchid City, Fuli complimented on the supper Jiafeng cooked that evening. "This is great food. I had so many hamburgers on the road."

"You should have told me," Guoda said.

Fuli didn't respond to that. Instead, he said to Jiafeng, "Guoda was solicitous. He was afraid that I might catch a cold. Bought me a sweater in Chicago." Guoda thought the remark was meant not only for her ear.

Before long after Fuli returned to Taiwan, he wrote that he had a new job, one with an investment firm. The tone of the letter, and subsequent ones, indicated considerable contentment and no further mention was made of his wishes to immigrate to America. Rende had recently told his brother, "Our father has had a stroke of so-called old-age's good luck. An old chum got him this cushy job as Vice-General Manager of the investment company. All he needed to do was to keep his eyes open, act discreetly and he would be taken care of. Now he even has a company car that takes him to work."

A couple of years later, Rende asked Guoda's help for his immigration to America. Guoda responded. In due course, Rende came to America, followed by Aili and their son, Frank (used to be called Xiao Pang). They ran a motel first in Barstow, California, and later in Orange City. They labored hard and established themselves relatively quickly. In five years, they became U.S. citizens, owned a house in the suburbs with a swimming pool and a fountain, voted in every election, joined a church (service in Chinese) and went to it every Sunday. But in California the couple still only read Chinese newspapers and watched Chinese TV programs except, for Rende, sports such as NBA games. Rende considered immigrating to the United States his biggest break in life; Aili concurred heartily and told her brother-in-law more than twice. It seemed that she had added reasons.

The summer when Guoda was in Pleasanton, Rende and Aili came up to visit him. Rende told his brother that he had to stick to his guns while preparing to leave Taiwan as their father tried to browbeat him into staying. "Yaya said, 'Who is going to take care of us when we are sick?' Indeed we would be there to help out even when they were going to have a mahjong party, let alone sick."

"I know," Guoda said. He had long felt an indebtedness to his brother and sister-in-law on that account.

"I said, 'If really needed, I could get on a plane and be back in 13 hours.' I have my future, actually, not so much mine, but Frank's, to think about—"

"And mine doesn't count?" Aili interjected.

That surprised Guoda a little. Through the years, he had always known his sister-in-law to be demure, almost self-denying; he had hardly heard a sharp word from her before. However, in this first meeting in America, he had noticed that she had dressed more stylishly and seemed to carry herself with a lot more confidence, if not assertiveness.

"Who's said you don't count? In America, whatever the wife says goes. Right?" Rende smiled. "In Taiwan, I had Yaya to listen to. Now in America…Well, certainly, your sister-in-law was all in favor of leaving Taiwan."

"Guoda," Aili said. "If you like, I'll tell you an episode."

"If it's the one I think, it isn't that necessary," Rende said to his wife.

"I think Guoda would be interested. He is your only brother; there is no need to keep anything from him."

"I am all ears," Guoda was indeed curious.

"Well, once when Frank was still in middle school, he and I were visiting Mama and Yaya. Frank wants to leave by himself first. Yaya asks him why. Frank says—to see a movie with some friends. Yaya says, 'You should do a better job at school, get better grades. Why go to movies day and night.'

"'I don't go to movies *day and night,* only occasionally. I put enough time on my studies. Why do you always criticize me unfairly?' Frank complains.

"'Unfairly?' Yaya slaps him on the face, 'You haven't even graduated from middle school and dare to speak to me like this!'

"I can't help speaking up. 'Yaya, he didn't mean to offend you. He just said what he felt.'

"Yaya turns his anger on me. He accuses me of having insulted him, violated traditional family code of behavior. Mama suggests that I apologize. Before I can consider. Yaya says, 'She must kowtow to apologize.' I am not about to do that. I take Frank's hand, and we two, mother and son, walk out of the apartment.

"Afterwards, Yaya goes around to talk to the relatives, complaining bitterly that he has been insulted by his daughter-in-law. Aunt Qijing and Uncle Dazhan come to talk to me. I wouldn't agree to kowtowing. It is too much in this day and age. Besides, I didn't do anything wrong. They tell your brother and me that Yaya threatens to *Kai Chi Tang*—"

"Do you understand *Kai Chi Tang*," Rende interjected, asking his brother.

"Yes, I do," Guoda said. (It means "to open the family ancestral temple"—an old feudal practice of calling a formal assembly of the clan in the temple, at which the full power of the patriarch could be formally invoked). "But there was no family shrine or temple in Taiwan. In fact, I don't recall I was ever in one in Changsha."

"Yes, there was a little one back in Malin Qiao. Anyway, Uncle Dazhan said the same thing to Yaya. Yaya then talked about going to the government's 'Commission on Restoration of Confucian Virtues'…"

"You are kidding!" Guoda said. He was almost amused. "Was there such a commission?"

"Yes, there was one, or some organization with a name like that. All they did was to have a group of people dressed in colorful costumes stiffly enact certain ancient public rites. I hadn't heard anything about that they would involve themselves in family affairs. Anyway, with Aunt Qijing and Uncle Dazhan coming and going, trying to mediate, finally your sister-in-law agreed just to *make to* kneel and apologize, and then Yaya would stop her, acting as though the apology were given and accepted.

"The act was indeed performed precisely as agreed upon. And the episode ended."

"I wouldn't have done that but for the family at large, particularly Mama, and also for the good intentions of Aunt Qijing and Uncle Dazhan," Aili said.

"Isn't it ironic though? Yaya considers himself so modern, Westernized, yet so old-fashioned, reactionary really," Guoda said to express his total sympathy with his sister-in-law. He also felt sorry for his brother because of the awkward position he must have found himself in.

CHAPTER 33

✿

In December 1978, President Carter announced the establishment of diplomatic relations between the United States and the People's Republic of China, and the simultaneous severance of same with the Republic of China in Taiwan. This time, Fuli did not ask for Guoda's help; he ordered him to go to Chicago or Washington at once to arrange for his and Qisheng's immigration to the United States. Guoda recognized that the issue, at least in his father's mind, was physical safety—the PLA might land. He followed through. After the application was approved, his parents did not come. Taiwan was not as vulnerable as they had first feared. With the immigration papers in hand, they could leave in quick order should the island be threatened.

The next year Guoda went to Taiwan to visit them. He found them generally healthy, particularly Fuli in good feather. He and his father again had ample opportunities to squabble.

They were having tea after lunch. "What a busybody this Kissinger was!" Fuli started.

"And you mean..."

"Mao had locked the door of Mainland. People there live miserably like ants. America is prosperous; her people enjoy comfortable lives. Why should this fellow go about trying to bring them together. What has America gained from that?"

"You know he was not the one mainly responsible for that. It was his boss, President Nixon. You have always admired Nixon," Guoda said.

"Nixon used to understand the Communists. It was Kissinger who talked him into it," Fuli said. "Even a smart person could have momentary lapses."

"Do you really think that a political leader, as experienced as Nixon, would make such a major move because of *momentary lapses*?" Guoda said. "The goodwill of a billion people is a worthy goal."

"Mao and his Communist cohorts are not the people."

"True. But to reach the people you need to open that door."

"It would also legitimize the Communist government."

"You can't punish the people because of their government. Should they stay in their miserable condition for ever? Consider the enormity of the loss of a whole generation during the Cultural Revolution years—no education, falling behind practically in every field of human endeavor, while the rest of the world has been advancing so rapidly. The whole country mired in ignorance in a world so competitive. If that continues, how could they survive! What would happen to them, their children? Should we not care about those souls? Over a billion of them!...." At that moment, Guoda's voice broke and he couldn't help weep for China.

That shook Fuli. His eyes turning red also, "Don't be so emotional, my son," he said.

The words, *my son*, had a special effect on Guoda. For years, only his mother Qisheng had said that to him, and each time they gave him a warm, soothing feeling. He recalled the last time Fuli said that to him was when he was still a little boy. His father had taken him between his knees and taught him the only lesson on Chinese fiddle. He could even remember the prickly stubble of his father's cheek.

"As I said, you two like to argue," Qisheng said. "Guoda, you don't have your father's tough constitution. You are tired from the long trip. Should rest more. Go take a nap."

Guoda stayed in Taiwan for a week and returned to the U.S., joined by Priscilla, who also had stopped in Taiwan to visit her paternal grandparents for a few days. Her maternal grandfather, the ex-minister, had returned to China in the mid-60s and had been teaching at Beijing University. She had come from China, after having spent a year at that university as a guest student from Harvard, a project that her maternal grandfather helped to arrange and her paternal grandfather resented.

In 1980, China had already in earnest engaged herself in the Four Modernizations program. Guoda received an invitation from the Nuclear Society of China to present a short course on earthquake resistant design of structures for nuclear power plants—an area he had worked on at Continental Power Corporation and Sargent Lundy Engineers. He was of course interested. For one thing, it would give him a chance to visit his motherland that he hadn't seen for over three decades. Jiafeng, Michael and Paul accompanied him.

After two weeks of lectures in Beijing, as part of the remuneration, his hosts arranged for the family a tour of cities chosen by the guests. While still in Beijing, they visited the usual sights, including the Imperial Palace, the Great Wall, and Chairman Mao's Mausoleum in Tiananmen Square. Then they traveled to Shanghai, Hangzhou, Wuhan, and Changsha, spending a couple or three days each.

In Shanghai, they visited his Uncle Qizhi and First Aunt. Both were in their 70s now, in good health; he had retired when he was 50. With foresight, very early on they had voluntarily surrendered most of their apartment, keeping only one room for themselves. Thus they had stayed out of trouble. Qizhi's eyes brightened and face flushed some as Guoda presented him with a receipt with which he could take delivery locally of a television set that his grateful nephew had paid for in Hong Kong.

Guoda took Jiafeng and their sons to the old campus of St. John's University. It was being used by two institutions that had no connection with the now defunct school. Most buildings were in disrepair. The green lawn in front of the chapel was replaced by fuliginous cinder. The banks of the Suzhou Creek were lined with a low dike on which unkempt weeds luxuriated.

At the old Albert Road (now Shan Xi Nan Road) compound, gone was its iron gate—as fodder for backyard furnace during the "Great Leap" furor of the late 1950s. Gone was also the beautiful lawn. A crude building now squatted in its middle, replacing yesteryear's park-like view. So had another coarse structure been put up on the earlier wide driveway. The original houses seemed dirty, the walls smudged with dust and grime; they didn't appear any better than the shabby structures added later. Yet, when Guoda looked close and rubbed off the smear, the fine ceramic brick facing of old would appear.

After nightfall, lighting was scarce and low. It was an eerie sight to see in the streets multitudes of heads moving about like herds being guided to corrals at dusk.

The Jings were invited as "foreign guests" to a nightclub (which used to be the Moulin Rouge of Shanghai in the pre-WWII days). An orchestra was playing Western light classical music. Settled in a chair covered by frayed scarlet velvet, Guoda closed his eyes and listened to *The Student Prince: Everyday is a holiday*.... He was back in his St. John's student days. When he opened his eyes, it seemed as though in a wink the musicians and himself had aged almost 30 years. (Apparently, at the time, only older musicians knew those Western numbers.) Oversight by the government of people's lives was tight; he did not get to meet any of his old friends. He couldn't even find out where they were.

On their return they stopped by Taiwan. Fuli was pleased with Guoda's account of the Mainland tour. It confirmed for him the wretchedness under Communism. He pointed to Taiwan's prosperity. And he was right about that. For example, on the Mainland, people still needed coupons to buy food in government-run dim restaurants that opened for a couple of hours only for each of the three daily meals. Conversely, in Taiwan, restaurants stayed busy in bright lights well into the night.

As previously, the visiting Jings were invited to one feast after another by relatives and friends. Fuli seemed happy and contented except on one account. His tall grandsons didn't show him enough respect. They didn't seem appropriately eager to talk with him. Indeed, they seemed to regard him as just another elder relative. He made a comment on the sly to his son, "I have grandsons? I don't." Guoda let it pass. It was a cultural/generational gap. Broadly speaking, he thought, in his father's generation in China, the young were supposed to please the old; in his children's generation in America, the reverse holds. His own generation would seem to get the short end of both (but a right to complain). Before they left Taiwan, Fuli took them to visit the Memorial Hall of President Chiang Kai-shek. He ordered Guoda to photograph the inscriptions on the marble tablet that exhort the classical virtues of fealty to country and parents. Guoda humored him.

Three years later, Priscilla was getting married—to a young lawyer from New York of obvious ability yet mellow temperament. The wedding was to be held in Orchid City. Guoda was in high spirit. Both Fuli and Qisheng were to come from Taiwan. But a few days before they were to leave, Qisheng fell in the bathroom and broke her hip. It broke Guoda's heart. He felt for his mother's pain. Besides, he had looked forward so much to her visit; all these years she had yet to set foot in his house. He recalled a moment last time he and Priscilla were visiting in Taiwan.

"You know you are the first daughter in the Jing family in three generations," Qisheng said, holding Priscilla's hand. They were sitting on the sofa, facing each other smilingly. Qisheng had told her granddaughter that before, through Guoda's translation, when Priscilla was a little girl. This time the granddaughter understood directly as Qisheng continued, "Now you have grown into a beautiful young woman."

"Probably that's because I look a little like you, Aijay (grandma)," Priscilla said.

"Oh! not only beautiful, but how sweet!" Qisheng went on to give her a jade bracelet, and after helping her to put it on, kept slowly patting her upper bare arm.

Guoda had watched them that day with indescribable delight, and now it hurt him to think that his mother couldn't be at Priscilla's wedding. But his father came; so did Rende and his family, and Jiafeng's mother and sisters and their families.

It was a lovely wedding with much exuberance and mirth, particularly those generated by the young at the after-dinner dance. The party over, the couple drove to the Sheridan Hotel on the outskirts of the city. Priscilla called to tell that her suitcase was still in the house. Guoda rushed on the deserted roads of midnight and delivered it at the door of the newlyweds' room.

Generally Fuli was in a good mood. In the few days he stayed over after the wedding, he would wear "cowboy pants" (denim jeans) and shoes with elevated heels—a style Guoda was never attracted to and wondered at the contrast with the plain long gown of an old-time austere Chinese scholar when Fuli was much younger during those dark days in WWII. One morning, Guoda thought he heard rain; then the splattering sounded louder than and unlike rain. He came down and found Fuli jogging in his leather street shoes, back and forth under the roof of the front patio. Later he took him to buy a pair of jogging shoes. Fuli would also do "flexibility exercises" in the backyard, shaking his limbs and body like under some religious spell, which fascinated the kids next door. At 77, he was in excellent health.

While in Orchid City, Fuli had a surprise reunion with his old friend Ni Zhihan. The two hadn't seen each other over 30 years. After the Civil War, sanctioned by the Communist government as a "national capitalist," Ni had stayed on in Shanghai to manage the cotton mill. His wife had died, and his only daughter had come to America, married a U.S. citizen and became one. On the basis of that, Zhihan had gotten his green card, although he lived in Shanghai most of the time. His daughter and her husband had come to WTU for graduate studies, and he would come to visit them every so often. While here, he would occasionally call at the Jing house—mainly to relieve the boredom from being cooped up in the married student housing apartment while the hosts were busy at school.

On one of his visits, Zhihan had asked Guoda to take him to a notary public to sign an affidavit. On their way back, he volunteered the information that the document was to help a female pianist in Shanghai to come to the U.S. by stating that they were married. Thus Guoda understood why Zhihan hadn't asked his daughter or son-in-law to help on this matter. Then as if to induce Guoda's moral support, he spieled what a worthy and talented person the musician was. Guoda gathered she was much younger than he. And then he would wax philosophical, "All my life I have searched for Truth, Goodness and Beauty." Guoda figured that the man felt at least he had found the third.

Zhihan and Fuli had much to catch up. But the cheerful atmosphere between the two old friends didn't last as Fuli wouldn't ease up on his attack on the Communists, while Zhihan would try to defend them at least on some such issues as national independence and social stability.

Fuli stayed in Orchid City for a week and left for Oxford University, England, to take a short course in creative writing. Guoda couldn't help feel the irony of it, remembering how Fuli viewed his son's interest in it years ago. But it didn't surprise Guoda; he had always known that Fuli was partial to the English language. Besides, it would give him an opportunity to see England, arguably the world's most majestic power in his younger days, and to feel some connection, however tenuous, with that prestigious seat of learning.

Nearing the end of that short course, the class, which consisted of participants much younger than Fuli, went on a pleasure trip. To visit a castle, they had to walk across a field of some considerable length from where the bus had parked. Considering the physical exertions involved and his age, his classmates wouldn't let him come along and ask him to wait in the bus. He agreed. After they had gone on about halfway across the field, he commenced to follow them. Then it was too late for them to send him back. Early next morning, some of his still too-tired classmates, awakened by noises down in the yard of their dormitory, looked down and were surprised that it was their senior classmate jogging spiritedly.

Fuli regaled Guoda with the above story in December that year when he stopped by Taiwan again after another visit to China.

CHAPTER 34

❀

The Sichuan Institute of Technology had extended an invitation to Dean Carr and another WTU engineering faculty member, to be suggested by the dean, to visit their school in Chongqing. When the dean came to Guoda's office to ask him to join him, he was surprised, but not very. They had skirmishes, even a few battles, over college matters before, but they had never lost respect for each other. Based on more than two decades of track records of both, there had grown an understanding and trust between them.

After four days in Chongqing of talks on more institutional cooperation and exchanges, of tours and banquets, they flew back to Shanghai, where Guoda would remain for a few days. The evening before his departure, the dean, pleased that the trip had gone well, relaxed and chatted with Guoda in a dim lounge in the Jingjiang Hotel, having after-dinner drinks, brandy for himself and orange juice for Guoda, as the pianist struggled with *Clair de lune*. Guoda had never seen him so easy, almost jovial, before. At one junction, Carr asked Guoda, "You know David Wang?"

"Of course, for over a decade now. Not that well professionally, though. Different departments..."

"That's right. He is in chemical. He'd come to see me recently.... Complaining that he's been stuck at his current rank too long. He is a nice, likable guy."

"Yes, he is that."

"Always scored high on student evaluation forms. Apparently does a first rate job at teaching. But there is nothing I can do. The papers have to start from his chairman."

Guoda wasn't sure why the dean was telling him this. Too much alcohol? Passing the buck? Getting a messenger? He was also a bit surprised at the dean's expression of appreciation for good teaching. No follow-up of David Wang was needed here. "You still teach sometimes?" he tried to do his part on this social occasion, although he'd rather return to his room and call his old college roommate Pengxi, whom he had not seen in decades.

"I used to teach one course a year. Haven't done that for some years now. Administrative work seems to grow faster than the student body. I enjoyed teaching.... I'd like to return to that."

Thinking that the dean sounded almost wistful, Guoda followed with "One course a year?"

Carr took a drink and said, "Yeah.... Actually, returning to full-time teaching isn't such a bad idea either."

Guoda was surprised...hum?

The dean took another drink and continued, "You chaired your department once. You know how it is—administration versus teaching. You have been the only one who had quit administration before the term was over."

"That was because I was incompetent," Guoda said.

"I wouldn't put it exactly that way. I've known you, see...about a quarter of century now. You had your ideas then—sincere, but not realistic. You seemed to think that an engineering college should have the same ethos as a college of liberal arts. Engineers find jobs more easily, get paid better. And there is a price for that. I believe we talked about that before."

"I know. It's not particularly the technical learning needed but the transience of the value of that—"

"The obsolescence threat you used to harp on..." Carr said.

"Nowadays, it might be called the rapid depreciation of the intellectual property. Certainly, the older one gets, the greater that price appears.... Whatever...As chairman, I couldn't do what a competent administrator was supposed to do. And that's incompetence...I did feel the system was masochistic, though, by making the faculty responsible for getting external funding. That wasn't always the case. Right?" Guoda asked.

"Not to the present degree. For one thing, now engineering professors too are paid better. And expectations are higher and different. In that respect, administrative jobs aren't that different. You'd probably be even more incompetent, as you said, at an administration job these days," the dean chuckled. "The taxing part is also about raising money." He chuckled again, pleased with his own wordplay.

"You mean you have to get money too?"

"Yes, to grow, to raise money, or to get money, as you put it."

"How is that?"

"When the president presents a bar chart on the screen at the Deans' Council, showing outside funding, alumni donations, etc. of the different colleges, and highlights a recent College of Business's twenty million dollars gift received for a new building, you know what he was saying to the other deans…. Then you are shown charts of external funds of your college in comparison with corresponding colleges in other universities—first among your peer group, and then, with the top ones in the country…. You can draw your own conclusion," Carr said.

"I thought only research professors have pressure to get money," Guoda said.

"Not true. Our efforts are not directly related to scholarship, often just bricks and mortar. There isn't much glory in that either, unlike research professors…. Some chairmen complained that some big time grantsmanship professors regarded them as super-secretaries. You have to contend with your reviewers and program directors only once in a while. We all the time have to deal with managers, directors of corporations, foundations, alumni, and politicians. Some of them are kind of unctuous, even condescending at times—characters probably harder to deal with than your program directors…. Of course, each of them has their own pressure source."

"Doesn't the college have a new position for assistant dean for development now?"

"Yes. We have hired a guy. He should help. I hope at least he could get enough to pay for his own salary." A chuckle again.

"I suppose everybody is under some kind of pressure."

"Or is accountable to someone else. That's the way it should be; that's what makes America the strongest country in the world," Carr observed.

"How true…. If you were to return to be a full-time faculty member, would you do research?" Guoda couldn't refrain from asking.

"No, I have been out of that a long time ago. But I'd like to complete the basic circuit textbook I had started years ago."

Next morning, Guoda saw the dean off at the airport and started his reunion with his old friends in Shanghai. In his first trip back from America, not only he didn't know where his friends were, even they did not know themselves the whereabouts of most of the others. But since then he had made contacts with Pengxi and Daigu. On this trip, the country—the cities he had visited at least—seemed much more open, the standards of living improved and people more free and happier—no longer giving that impression of being herded. He was also able to move about in Shanghai quite freely by himself.

At the Ni's house, where he had stayed several nights after he had left the St. John's campus over 30 years ago, he met his childhood friend Ni Zhiyu, who had just recently been allowed to return from northern Manchuria where he was exiled because he had criticized the leadership.

Ni Zhihan was there also, to visit his uncle Heye, who was ill and resting upstairs. Out of reach of other ears, Zhihan brought up with Guoda that affidavit affair back in Orchid City. "That woman was the most heartless person I have ever known," he complained to Guoda. Conjuring up a young, beautiful pianist, and eyeing the retired white-whiskered businessman, Guoda wasn't surprised at the word *heartless* in the remark. Curious, nevertheless, he asked, "How so?" "Well, before I got her to America, she'd write me almost every day, saying, I was the person she treasured most in the universe, and that she'd be totally lost without me. After she arrived in America, she wrote me one thank-you letter—more like a note—and ignored me thereafter. Wouldn't even answer my letters." Guoda figured that this aging Don Juan had been making progress in his life's search—after having found Beauty, now he had a glimpse of Truth and Goodness.

On Guoda's behalf Pengxi had arranged a dinner party in a private room at a restaurant, inviting his old college friends and choir members he could locate. At the party they summarized the past years of their own and offered what they knew about others absent.

The old friends did look a lot older, some appeared plain old, with one or more of the attributes: thinning hair, white hair, missing teeth, drooping eyelids, puckered mouth, blotched skin, curved back and the other badges of honor of time. Most were heavier, around the waist, except "bra-strap" Ah Yu, still like a stick—heredity, he said—and Guoda, "beneficiary" of his chronic stomach problems. It was no ordinary social gathering. This was almost a family reunion. Like some rock-bound sea-animals waving their tentacles, they were ready to re-connect, re-form ties. An anecdote reminded would bring it about and click. They'd laugh and suddenly feel and look younger. *One day when we were young, one wonderful morning in May...*someone sang. Their faces flushed—like the geraniums in October—dull eyes suddenly gleaming, movements more flexible.

Pengxi had retired to let his son have a job at his factory, replacing his own quota of a position. Ah Yu's experience almost paralleled that of Ni Zhiyu. He was allowed to return after 22 years of exile in the largely arid province of

Qinghai. In the middle of the party, the door popped open, and in stumbled the center forward of the varsity soccer team, Zhu Daigu, white stubble around the mouth, circles around the eyes. He had just come off an overnight train from Beijing. He was Director of Agriculture Research for the City of Beijing. (The "City" covers an area only slightly smaller than New Jersey.) He and Zhao Qian were married. Her sister, Zhao Xun, the swimmer par excellence, was wife of one of the most famous surgeons in the country; she worked in the Ministry of Agriculture in Beijing.

Of the former male quartet, only Yan Shaohuang was missing at the party. He was now a high official in the Ministry of Foreign Affairs—in fact, he was at one time China's Ambassador to the United Nations. This bit of news was a surprise. When still in school, they had suspected him a leftist, but not a Communist Party member. Apparently he must have been. He had changed his name; otherwise the news about him would have spread earlier and wider.

Mei Helei, now a schoolmarm-look professor of mathematics at the East China University, came with her husband, a professor of chemistry. Shenli Lian, a divorcee, dressed stylishly, taught at a high school. She told Guoda that Juan Zhong had married a former national basketball star (Guoda suspected that he was that long-legged high school student whom Juan had told him once was only an ordinary friend) who was now the athletic director at some college in Xi'an. Juan had worked as an accountant in a cotton mill, but having survived a bout with breast cancer, she had retired.

Guoda also paid a visit to the compound at the old Albert Road. It looked a great deal neater now than it did at his last visit. The buildings added after the Civil War still appeared grotesque, but at least now they were clean. A boy about 11 or 12 years old—Guoda's own age when he first moved in there—in a snazzy red and white warm-up suit was shooting baskets at a net setup on the wall against which Guoda had flailed his jai alai cesta countless times. He said to the boy, "I used to live up there," pointing to the pavilion room on the third floor of his old house, and expected a surprised look to be followed by some warm and feeling exchanges. Expressionless, the boy looked at him with his dark eyes and a slight frown for a second or two, shrugged his shoulders, and resumed his shooting. The lad has no curiosity. What a cold fish! What about He Zhizhang's little poem: "Left here a youngster and now I am home,/ Still having the village tongue, but not my hair./ The children look and are unawares./ Smiling, they ask, "Where are you from?"/

He wandered to the house at the end. The backdoor was open and he stepped in. There were three people dawdling in the kitchen; none paid attention to him. He figured that like most houses in China, this one would have several families in it too, and when a stranger showed up, each would presume he had something to do with the other families.

"Pardon me. Is there a Huang family living here?" he spoke to the person closest to him, but loud enough for all to hear.

"Yes," a white-headed old woman near the window turned to him from a stove.

"I came from out-of-town. I used to live in this compound. Well, a long time, several decades, ago. I remember the Huang family. I am curious whether they are still here."

"What's your business?"

"No business. Just curious…I could recall their eldest miss, by the name Yun Qiu."

"Oh…oh," the old woman now took a harder look at him, along with the other two in the kitchen. "…Sir, what's your name?"

"My name is Jing Guoda."

"Jing…Jing…, I remember the Jings…. They had two boys."

"If you are talking about us, I was the younger one."

It turned out that she had worked for the Huang family all her life.

"Oh, that was so long ago. Before the liberation, Old Gentleman Huang had purchased this house from the original owner. Our Number One Miss was married shortly after the liberation. Now her son's family lives here."

"Does Miss Yun Qiu live here?"

"No. She lives with her sister in Suzhou now."

"You mean Yun Yu."

"You surely know them," she smiled, showing her ravaged teeth.

"I certainly did. I hope they are well."

"They are in pretty good shape. Where now are the Old Gentleman Jing and Madame Jing?"

"They are in Taiwan."

"So you have come from Taiwan?"

"No. I have come from America. I have lived there for many years now. Please give my regards to the sisters when you see them."

"How nice. I certainly will. It's kind of you to remember them after all these years. Grandmother now."

"Miss Yun Qiu a grandmother?"

"Oh yes. In fact her grandson, 12 years old, lives right here."

"Is he playing basketball out there?"

"Yes, he couldn't wait to put on that brand new outfit his grandmother bought for him."

Guoda went on to look for the plot for recreational cultivation and found that it was replaced by a shack.

CHAPTER 35

From Shanghai Guoda flew via Hong Kong to Taiwan. Qisheng had aged considerably, wrinkles deepened on the face. She walked with a slight limp because of the hip surgery. Guoda stayed a couple of days. The morning he was to leave, Qisheng got up early to steam buns and make tea. At breakfast, Fuli chatted about some new Beijing opera talent and complained facetiously how Qisheng had monopolized the evening TV for her soap opera at the expense of his Beijing opera program. She didn't even respond, said little and ate less. Looking absent-minded, her eyes dull and hair disheveled. Guoda was anxious to return to Wisconsin, yet he felt guilty—more so than in previous times when he took leave of his mother.

She reminded him to wear enough lest he'd catch a cold. He assured her he was all right, went out, got a taxi, and returned to the apartment.

"Sorry I wouldn't be able to see you off at the airport. Your yaya will do that for both of us," she said.

"Please take care of yourself," he wanted to hug her but didn't. He couldn't remember he had ever hugged his mother. He might have done that in his childhood, but he couldn't remember. Chinese men normally wouldn't do that.

"Take care and give my regards to Jiafeng and the children. May the winds be behind you."

"I'll call you after I arrive in Orchid City." He left her.

Fuli was already in the taxi, chatting with the driver. Guoda was about to step in. Suddenly he turns around and goes back into the apartment. She is sitting on the sofa, her lowered forehead in a hand, whorls of white hair. Hearing his entry, she lifts her head, "Did you forget something?" her eyes brightens at seeing her son again.

"No…. Yes!" he steps up, bends down and hugs her. "Take care of yourself, Mama."

She pats his back, saying slowly, "Take care…. Take care of yourself well too, Cha-cha, my son."

Several years later, Guoda was on another lecture tour in China, accompanied by Jiafeng. Their last stop was Hunan University in Changsha, their hometown. They went to look for the gravesite of his grandparents, which Rende had visited the year before. The university sent a Professor Zhou to accompany them. A school van took them to the village of Maling Bridge. The driver got directions from some villager to the Fans' Farm and drove the vehicle to the edge of the village town. A great expanse of rice fields lay in front of them, flat except for a few interspersing low mounds and clumps of trees. The clouds hung low, threatening rain. There was no road save the narrow dikes that subdivided the rice paddies. It was decided that Jiafeng and the driver would wait in the van, and Guoda and Professor Zhou would go forward on foot.

They walked in the general direction they were told. In a while, it began to rain. At first Guoda just lowered his head and buttoned his jacket. Soon it poured. He gave up and let himself be totally open to the heavens, as the wide green fields were. Now they were deep in the midst of rice paddies. He had a call to relieve himself, and consulted briefly with his associate. Between heaven and earth with rain beating down he had one of the most refreshing, invigorating reliefs in his life, helping to fertilize his native soil in the meantime. He had an urge to give out a yell, but mindful of his polite companion, he only trudged on, quickly learning to advance on the slippery muddy path. While catching himself in a lurch, he caught sight of a green bullfrog by the gully. It reminded him of the summer days when he was a boy and lived on the farm in order to stay away from Japanese bombs; he and Rende would try to catch big bullfrogs using small ones as bait.

In a while, he and Professor Zhou came upon a peasant wearing a rain-gear made of thatch, the type that one would often see on fisherman in classical Chinese paintings. "Pardon me," he said. "Could you tell me where is the Fans' Farm?"

"Who are you?" The man with a sunburned knitted brow asked.

"My name is Jing. I've come to look for my grandparents' gravesite."

"Are you Jing Guoda? Younger brother of Jing Rende?"

He was surprised. "Yes, I am Jing Guoda."

"Ah!" The peasant's face relaxed and brightened into a grin sans two front teeth. "Your brother was here last year. He had asked me to refurbish the tombstones. Now you can verify that I have done what he had asked him to do. I am Chi Erye. My father used to work for your family. We used to play together when you and your brother came to visit from the city. We were just little boys then," he chortled lightly.

Now Guoda remembered the little boy who bathed the water buffalo in the pond in late afternoon after his father had unyoked it at the end of the day's toil. The lad would pour water on the animal's back while it stood in the pond, flapping an ear and flies darting about. The boy was about his age. Now on a closer look, the man in the thatch gear did not seem as old as at first sight. Although life in the fields had leatherized his face, its features could still recall those of a past familiarity. In fact, now he looked more like his father as Guoda remembered him. Some late afternoons, he would take the two Jing brothers to the village town, each riding on one side of a one-wheeled barrow that he pushed from behind. And how relieved, Guoda recalled, he would feel each time they came out of a darkened, damp stretch of overarching trees, behind which goblins lurked.

His grandparents' gravesite, now marked by two new tombstones, which his brother had paid for a year ago, was on a hillock, close to the farmhouse. The land, which was now owned, like all land in China, by the nation, was still known as the Fans' Farm but was assigned for use by the Chi family. After they—mainly Mr. Chi—cleared the bamboos and brambles around the gravesite, Guoda stood, bowed his head for a while, and then asked his associate to take a couple of pictures of himself, dripping wet, crouching by the tombstones.

On their stop in Taiwan, Guoda had the film developed, printed and showed the pictures to Fuli. He studied the inscription on the tombstones. Besides the names of the buried, it also bore the installers', led by his own and then those of his sons. "You two brothers did a good thing," he said and took off his eyeglasses and wiped his eyes.

He had retired from the investment company, and had just bought an apartment in Banjiao. Guoda wondered about the wisdom of the move, since almost all their friends and relatives, now fast becoming scarce in Taiwan—many having emigrated—lived in Taipei, almost an hour away by car. But then he rarely asked his sons, or even his wife, for their opinion.

A couple of years later, finally, Qisheng made her trip with Fuli to America. They stayed for two weeks in Rende's house in Orange City, California. On a late April evening, Guoda drove to Chicago airport to meet them. Qisheng came out, sitting in a wheelchair. She seems so small now, Guoda thought, do people grow and then shrink? Fuli ambled behind relaxedly.

Guoda went to school only to teach classes in order to spend as much time as he could with them. Jiafeng busied herself to see that they were comfortable. All the children came back: Michael from California where he worked as a chemical engineer for a bio-medical company; and Priscilla, together with her husband Bob, from Boston, where she wrote for the Boston Globe and he was an Assistant U.S. Attorney; and Paul from Madison, a student in the Medical School of the University of Wisconsin. Friends, including the Yans, who had driven from Madison also, called at the house to pay their respects. Qisheng and Fuli were shown the beautiful campus, treated in the better known restaurants. They appreciated it all in the first few days. Yet they said they couldn't stay too long, because they had promised Rende to return soon to California. Besides, they seemed preoccupied. It had to do with their care in the days to come.

Guoda suggested that they consider returning to Mainland China. His reasoning was that for old age care, one needs labor, and labor was cheaper in China. Neither parent liked the idea. Guoda's observation—"Things are different now. People's lives there have very little to do with Communism; it's more like Capitalism"—didn't alter one bit Fuli's aversion to his suggestion. He offered to accompany Fuli for a visit to the Mainland—Qisheng was considered too frail to travel just for that—and see for himself, and to visit Qizhi in Shanghai and get his input also. Fuli wouldn't buy that either.

Instead, he suggested that he would purchase an apartment in California, and the two sons be responsible for the parents' livelihood; i.e., pay all their expenses. Guoda thought his suggestion too risky from the point of view of potential medical expenses in America, since his parents did not have access to Medicare; it was possible such expenses could bankrupt the brothers—a matter the brothers had talked about before. The aged parents stayed in Orchid City for a week and returned to California, where they remained for six more weeks and went back to Taiwan.

Later on, in a phone conversation, Qisheng told Guoda that "Orchid City is too cold for me. I liked your brother's place, particularly its warm climate. But your yaya found it difficult to adjust." Rende, over the phone, had told his brother that he and Aili had offered their parents one of the three bedrooms in their house. Since it was in the suburb, and now that Fuli couldn't drive, Rende would take him out one afternoon a week and his son, Frank, would do that for another afternoon. Presumably some kind of medical insurance could be purchased. Anyhow, the idea of his mobility being prescribed by his son and grandson was not acceptable to Fuli. So the two octogenarians continued to live by themselves in the small apartment in noisy Banjiao, while their children enjoyed American suburban spaciousness and quietude, at least at night. During the day, Rende ran his motel in Orange City, while Guoda plied at his engineering professorship on the Orchid City campus.

CHAPTER 36

Literature and sponsored engineering research seem to be like jealous lovers. A person can choose only one. Next to his bread and butter teaching, Guoda concentrated on sponsored research. In order to stay competitive and motivated—and keep the siren of literature at arm's length—he learned to inculcate himself that his research was most important not only for the advancement of his technical field but also for his own personal satisfaction.

The years passed, like breathing in and breathing out—the breathing would get considerably heavier when working on new research proposals. With successive retirements of older colleagues, involuntarily he took on the role of a senior statesman in the department, even in the college. He would not shy away from speaking "the truth as I see it." When some of his colleagues told him that it had an adverse effect on his salary, he presented them with a formula: real salary = salary + worth of the relief of an itchy tongue.

Instead of a formula, he would cite to some less scientifically minded colleagues a poem by Su Dongpo: "Speech starts from chest and gushes into mouth./ To spit it out would irritate others;/ To swallow it would irritate myself./ I rather irritate others;/ Therefore, I spit it out."

The economy of the state was in the low part of another business cycle. A general freeze in hiring was in effect for the university. The department had to put on hold its search for a tenure track assistant professor, an opening created by a retirement. Then out of the blue at a department meeting, the chair proposed to hire a full professor to fill the vacancy—the provost had made an exception. The chair proceeded to recommend a Dr. Abraham for the position, copies of whose resume were handed out to the faculty. Currently a full professor at Illinois Technical University, he had a doctoral degree from England and a fair number of publications in respectable journals—a reasonably impressive resume. However, according to the current department bylaws, the hiring of a tenure track faculty needed to go through a search committee and advertising in order to find the best person available.

When asked about that, the chair said that the provost's office had intimated that "it's *this person* or none." It surprised practically everybody. While Guoda found the affair distasteful, he thought that the man could surely give the faculty some relief from the recent heavy teaching load. The pragmatic side of him told himself to swallow. But he spit out anyway, and suggested a search committee.

"But Dr. Abraham is qualified for the job," the chair said.

"The issue is not just to have a *qualified* person, but to use the available resource to find the *best* person," he answered with the obvious.

No search committee was formed because none was authorized. But the department had the services of Dr. Abraham after all. He was invited in as a "visiting professor;" the departmental bylaws had not stated that a temporary position needed to go through a search process. It turned out that Dr. Abraham was not only a competent teacher but also a very pleasant, likable person. However, he had not received any outside research funding during his stay and left the university after two years. Word had it that he had a close relative in the provost's office.

The Abraham affair was more of a surprise to Gouda because it ran counter to the growing trend of accountability for everyone, including the administrators. Documentation was the order of the day. Every term, a professor needed to prepare a written evaluation of every graduate student under his guidance. The instructor of a course was asked to report on the progress of every varsity athlete in his or her class. The chair was required to write an annual evaluation of each faculty member in his or her department. When the chair had completed a term, each faculty was supposed to evaluate him. In Guoda's first few years at the university, his "annual report" to Chairman Gordon consisted of one single page, stating the courses taught, number of students advised, and publications. That was all; no research in progress, proposals submitted, proposals in preparation, future plans, and the like. The annual faculty report gradually evolved into a stack of forms of dozens of pages.

A faculty member under consideration for tenure or promotion had to first pass the tenure committee of the department. For the college the candidate would need to supply documentation of merit—causing the scholar embarrassment, caught between modesty and salesmanship and having to negotiate between self-respect and self-interest. The documentation would include evidence or testimonials in the three categories of teaching, research and public service. Each category would be reviewed and graded by a separate college committee, before the files went to the College Administrative Committee. The files of all candidates piled almost half a foot high over the conference room table to be read by members of the sundry committees. Considering all the hours and energy spent, one couldn't help wondering how much of them was entropy, since overall, such actions as promotions, like salaries, are often determined, by "market," and occasionally politics, which would override refined, formalistic, internal tuning.

A department chair's job was not really the most pleasant kind. For example, the ten decisions he made that would favor a faculty member the latter would soon forget; yet he would dwell on any single one not to his liking. Nevertheless, seduction of name and fame often leads people to vie for the job. Such an opening occurred in Guoda's department once again. The Search Committee invited three finalists to visit.

One candidate was particularly impressive; he *promised* growth—to double everything: research dollars, number of faculty, and enrollment. A tall, swaggering individual, impeccably dressed by even non-engineer standards, he wanted to talk separately with each of the faculty groups of the different specialties within the department. With the structures group, leaning back in a chair at the head of the table and crossing his feet on it, he went around and asked each member in turn: "Why are you interested in civil engineering?" (The question suddenly made the faculty feel young again.)

Answers would come like, "We deal with the fundamental needs of society." Or, "We build the infrastructure of society," etc.

The candidate would nod his cocked head in agreement with a little twitch of his lip and rotate his wrist to point at the next person and return it to his chin, "And you?"

Guoda's turn. "Just to make an honest living," he answered.

The interviewee, who had turned interviewer, retracted his feet to the floor, raised and straightened his back, smiled and mumbled "Interesting," and went to the next colleague.

A good number in the department were taken by the self-confidence the man exuded. "The guy is a leader. We need such kind to fight for our share of resources in the college...." Indeed, the man garnered a plurality of votes, though only barely. However, the dean—concerned that more than one senior member of the faculty had serious reservations about the person—did not offer the job to him and ordered a new search. Eventually a more mature, experienced academic administrator filled the position.

Shortly afterwards, one of Guoda's closest, respected colleagues, James Mitchell died in his office of a massive stroke, slumping behind the desk with stacks of students' papers. On the last workday of that year, Guoda wrote to the new department chairman that he would like to retire after a year of terminal leave.

Returning home that afternoon, he found a letter from Beijing. He and Zhu Daigu had written to each other two or three times a year. In this letter Daigu told of the death of his sister-in-law, Zhao Xun—of a heart attack. He had ordered a wreath for her funeral on behalf of several old choir members in Shanghai and had also included Guoda's name on the cloth band listing the offerers. "...I presumed you wouldn't mind...."

She was one of the healthiest person I knew then, Guoda brooded. Also talented, handsome, decent.... Heart attack—it probably meant less suffering than most other kinds of the checking out process. That is life in this world, this transient, unpredictable world. *Oh God our help in ages past...our eternal home....*

CHAPTER 37

❀

The baby is sleeping prone in the bassinet, legs drawn under the diaper-covered belly, little hands up on each side above the head that lay on one side, a rosebud pink nose, cherry-like red mouth, eyelids closed like flower petals on chicks, and the hardly perceptible pulsation of the back. So very quiet.

He returns to his book.

A hint of a snort and a gag. One tiny leg draws up as the other scrapes down. The head turns, and returns as the nose gets in the way. A throaty, muffled cry. One hand stretches upward in jerks and then the other. HGNA, HGNA…HGNA (not WAH).

He picks her up, one hand under her belly, another supporting the head. So soft, almost limp, except for one curling leg. He props the little bundle up, let her head rest on his shoulder, and pats her back.

She gives out little grunts as he is doing all the arranging.

He paces around the dining table, singing "Rock-a-bye baby on the tree top…" It doesn't work—HGNA HGNA…They get over to the kitchen. He shakes the water bottle, which has been sterilized by her mother, to deposit a few drops on his wrist. A little hot. He sets it aside to cool. He sits down on the sofa, and bending his left leg horizontally over the right, he rests her head on the side of his knee, the body snug over the thigh. The crying stops. Eyes open, black as midnight; mouth working, as if about to talk. As he is enjoying this, a small burst is heard.

He carries her to her room to change. The flowery side of the diaper should go in the front with the sticky tape, he has been told, (no more delicate operations with safety pins and sudden screams), and he figures out the use of wipers. She has started to cry (WAH now) the instant he lays her on the stand.

After he takes off the soiled diaper, the crying becomes yelling. So vehement, he is almost scared. Lifting her up, making sure she is not choking or anything. Putting her down again, he cleans her tush; the protesting softens. He hurries to put on the new diaper. It is too loose; haste makes waste. He redoes it and holds her up against his chest again.

He waddles over to the sofa. The cradle of his left leg doesn't work this time. She continues with her HGNA HGNA…"Let's see that water bottle has cooled enough, O.K.?"

He coaxes her into taking the rubber nipple. She sucks it for a while. Then he hears a short murmur. She begins to squirm. They go over the diaper changing routine again. Only this time she seems to be more tolerating, only relatively, though, still fusses all through the process, more like a perfunctory protest. As long as she doesn't seem to be hurting, it's all right.

She has more water, almost finished the 2-1/2 ounces. He pats her back again, enticing a major league burp. He sets her in his left thigh lair. She is calm now. Looking at him with her large eyes, quizzical, Who are you? I am your Wai-gong, your mother's dad. And welcome to this world. She responds with pouting and pursing her little red lips in succession, an eye opening and closing and half-opening and half-closing. She waves her long legs and long hands (long fingers too) up and down, left and right, in a slow rhythm, like a pink, translucent octopus.

He chants in Hunan dialect:
"Dian dian zhong zhong fei; (Pointing, pointing, bugs fly;)
Zhong zhong zho yi dei. (Bugs caught by a pair.)
Zho guo xi mao zhong; (Catch a tiny hairy bug;)
Yao dao mei zhe dei guo bei bei! (That bites the little lass's doggy back!)

Her limbs begin to settle. He keeps repeating the rhyme, rocking his leg gently. Her eyelids lower. She falls asleep.

He looks at her for a long time as though she is the only thing in the world. Then he puts her back in the bassinet.

Stephanie, Priscilla's first daughter, was born a few months after her parents had returned to Boston from Orchid City to see her great grandparents. Guoda had offered her mother and grandmother a break to visit the CambridgeSide Galleria shopping center.

CHAPTER 38

For decades, Guoda would write to his parents at least once a month. As over-seas telephone calls became less expensive, he used them more frequently, on Mother's Day, Father's Day, their birthdays, Chinese New Year, etc. On rarer occasions, there were phone calls for him crossing the Pacific the other way round, such as that one from his mother. After short preliminaries, she said, "…You should know, after I am gone, you two brothers ought to treat your yaya nicely."

"What brought this up, Mama?"

"Nothing, I just thought of it and wanted to call you two. Take good care of yourself." (Both of his parents were very brief in long distance phones, because they considered them too costly.)

What a strange call! he thought.

Shortly afterwards, one midnight in November, the phone rang. It was from his Uncle Xian in Taipei, saying that his mother was quite ill at the Central Hospital of Taipei, and his father had a sore foot; although his condition was not serious, he was also hospitalized—in Banjiao Hospital. For years, consider-ing their advanced age, Guoda had anticipated and dreaded this sort of late night phone call.

He got in touch with Rende, whom Xian had failed to reach. Rende said he would have someone go to the Central Hospital to find out more about their mother's case. Later, he called back saying that a cousin of his daughter-in-law, Joyce, had visited Qisheng and reported that her condition was not considered critical. However, Joyce would be leaving for Taipei to see her grandmother-in-law. Apparently, it was the outcome of a powwow of the California Jing family.

Afterwards, Guoda managed to reach Qisheng by phone. She said, "I feel tired and weak; otherwise, I am all right.... The doctor said my bladder is getting old, degenerated some.... Yes, he's prescribed some medicine that I have been taking.... I have no appetite. I know I have to eat.... I know nourishment is important.... They are feeding me intravenously.... I know it's not enough...."

Guoda was trying to make a decision whether to go over to Taiwan right away. He had a notion to put the decision to his mother, but decided against it. "I am glad your voice sounds strong enough. I am sure you'll feel better before long. I'll call you again. But as I told you, you must try to eat more," he again admonished his mother. After hanging up the phone, he checked his passport and proceeded to apply for a visa to Taiwan so that he could set off right away if needed.

He continued to call her every couple of days. She sounded stronger and said that she had been eating more. The week before Christmas she told him that the doctor had said she could soon go home to recuperate. Fuli had also recovered from his foot ailment and had been visiting her every other day or so.

There was a break of one week between terms. Guoda told his mother, "I would like to come to see you now. But then I'd have to hurry back to start the next term. By May the academic year will have ended, and I can come and stay longer. I'll be on terminal leave, virtually retired." Saying this, he envisioned that, while in Taiwan, every morning he would go out for breakfast and bring back his parents' and make tea for them. He would stay with them for two or three months.

"May, er," her voice had a hint of hesitation—disappointment, he suspected. "That'll be fine. Travel is tiring. Chacha, my son, you get tired so easily from traveling." He did dread the fatigue of the cross-ocean flight. On the plane he couldn't sleep and his leg with the varicose veins felt heavy. Now, he could look forward to spending Christmas with his own children and grandchildren, all coming to Orchid City for the holidays.

Indeed the Wisconsin Jings had a very merry Christmas, anchored by the traditional holiday dinner and the following candle-light church service on the Eve. The next morning, oohs and aahs filled the living room in the hour-long session of presenting and opening gifts with camcorder rolling and firewood crackling. A couple of days later, as Guoda had offered to baby-sit Stephanie and her four-month old sister Katie, and the others were discussing which movie to see, Rende telephoned to say that their mother's condition had suffered a relapse and was getting worse.

Guoda left the next day for Orange City, stayed overnight there, waiting for Rende to get his visa. The following afternoon, they boarded an EVA Airline plane in its oxymoronic "economic deluxe" class. After they checked in a hotel in Taipei, it was already midnight. Rende called their Uncle Xian and let the phone ring twice and hung up, fearing he might be asleep already.

Next morning, he dialed again. "Uncle Xian…This is Rende. Guoda and I have arrived…. What!…Left!…"

Guoda felt his body turned to lead, then a flash of heat followed by a flash of chill.

"Mother had passed away," Rende said calmly.

"I got that." They were silent for a while. "I thought she was getting better."

"Actually I was worried when I heard the other day that she looked better than expected," Rende said, "You know, there is this saying about 'Hui Guang Fan Zhao' (reflection of the retreating light)."

The taxi crossed the Dan River Bridge heading for Banjiao. The driver found the lane. The buildings on both sides of the lane were almost identical, four stories high, with metal grids caging the ground floor windows. Banners advertising merchandise and services hung on some upper story walls. Picking his way through parked motorcycles, Rende pushed a button on a panel on the wall, and they were let inside and walked up the concrete stairs. One story up, Xian was holding the door open, watching the brothers ascending. They greeted one another on the veranda overlooking the street and in front of the living room. As Guoda was taking off his shoes (customary in Taiwan, to keep the inside dwelling clean), he heard a dry wail. Lifting his head, he saw Fuli standing behind Xian. Rende went in and hugged him. Guoda followed. Their father looked older and shorter, shrunken, and slovenly in a rumpled plaid sports shirt and gray trousers, his face waxen and eyes listless.

"There is no need to cry," Rende said. "Her journey in this world was completed; she just went home." He appears rather cool about the whole thing, Guoda thought.

First thing first. Shortly, the brothers were back in Taipei in the office of Yi De Company on Ming Chuan East Road, almost directly across from the First Municipal Funeral Parlor (FMFP). There, Guoda watched Rende negotiate the arrangement of the funeral with a Mr. Cai.

Afterwards, accompanied by Mr. Cai, they went across the boulevard to FMFP. Inside the parlor compound, Cai led them into a windowless room and introduced them to a man sitting at a small desk. Rende handed him NT$150, as suggested by Cai earlier. The man rose and led them into the chilly mortuary. They passed banks of large drawers. He stopped at one spot, waited for a few seconds, and pulled out a drawer near the floor.

Guoda saw his mother in the pale florescent ceiling light. Her white hair in whorls floated about her head. The face pallid, eyes closed, mouth also. He thought she looked serene enough, better than he had anticipated. In her younger days she was known to be a beautiful woman. She looks beautiful now—like a faded flower, like the frozen geranium in the front yard the morning after the first hard freeze. But she is not really here. Is she? She does look peaceful, though.

Rende dropped down on his knees and kowtowed three times to his mother in repose.

The next day was New Year's Day. Most merchants in Taiwan did not observe it as a holiday, as they did the Chinese New Year. The brothers ordered flowers for the obsequies for their own families and on behalf of other close relatives and friends in America. Rende also bought such paraphernalia as paper "gold ingots." They reserved a parlor at the FMFP for the obsequies on the fifth of the month, since the second and third fell on Saturday and Sunday of which the time slots for all parlors had been booked, and the fourth was not a propitious day according to the Chinese almanac.

By the time they returned to the Banjiao apartment it was already dark. "How come you two 'young masters' are so late?" Their father, who didn't look so distressed now, would sometimes use the 'young masters' epithet as a sarcasm on them for what he asserted to be their presumptuous, arbitrary behavior. More interested in the smell of cooked food in the apartment, Rende contracted his lips to sniff the air first and offered a half-hearted defense, "It takes time to get things done." Guoda ignored the barb. A woman came out from the kitchen behind the living room. Fuli introduced her as Mrs. Ju, his part-time housekeeper. She appeared to be in her late thirties, swarthy and muscular. She would work three hours a day, to cook dinner, usually with a little extra to cover Fuli's next day lunch, wash the dishes and clothes, sweep the floor, etc.

The brothers decided to sleep in their mother's room. Besides the bed, it had two stacked trunks covered with a tablecloth and a dresser. Close by the door, a large picture of Kuan-ying, the goddess of mercy, hung on the wall above a small table. On it a three-legged bronze censer squatted, from which protruded several half-burnt joss sticks with ashy tops.

Rende would sleep on the bed, and Guoda on the floor, on which Mrs. Ju had laid a comforter as a mattress. As they were getting ready for bed, their father shuffled by, standing outside the door and asked, "Aren't you afraid?"

"Of what?…Why should we be?" Rende said, "If Mama showed up, wouldn't it be just wonderful?"

Lying on the comforter, in the silence Guoda gazed into the darkness under the bed. The darkness grew to envelop the world. A sea of blackness. He knows grief now. It grips his chest, squeezes, again and again. Warm tears flowing from his eyes. If I had come directly from Chicago, I might be with her before she left this world. How lonesome she must have been! Too late, too late! Ai! Ai!…

The next morning, Xian came. They jabbered about politics, each having an opinion on Taiwan and other affairs of the world as well. Then Rende said, "O.K. I have more important things to do today."

"What's to be done?" Fuli asked. Whatever it is, Guoda thought, you wouldn't be the one to do it.

"First, Uncle Xian is going to take me to the Temple of Ten Shoals to make the final arrangement for the requiem. Then as you know, the Cai guy wanted to be paid today half for the contract."

"Brother Fuli," Xian said offhandedly, "you can give the money to Rende now so that we can be on our way."

Fuli seemed surprised by the prompt. "Umm…Oh," he hesitated for a second and went into his room.

"Before you two came, he told me that he had all the cash for the funeral ready," Xian commented.

Fuli came out and handed a thick envelope to Rende.

After Xian and Rende left, Fuli went into his bedroom. Guoda noticed that Fuli's countenance seemed solemn, but he did not think much of it. He sat at the dinner table by the wall and started to read a Taiwan magazine. The current issue featured an article on the life of Sun Ke, son of Dr. Sun Yat-sen, and another piece on the outdated Chinese custom of foot binding. Fuli came out and sat across the table. Guoda looked up to see if he had something to say.

"I don't know what's gotten into Xian, barging into other people's family business," Fuli said.

"What do you mean?"

"He needed not tell me to hand over the money to your brother. I'd repay your brother whatever he spends for the funeral."

Guoda thought that Xian had unstintingly helped his parents on household chores ever since Rende and his family moved to America; in that hour, Xian could well be considered a member of the family. Trying to put the light issue in perspective, he said, "Uncle Xian did not mean anything. Just a reminder for you, as from a sidekick, you know."

Fuli did not respond. Guoda resumed reading the magazine. But he sensed some tension in the air. In a moment Fuli said,

"You know, Guoda, the letter you wrote two months ago seemed to me a little too direct."

Suddenly Guoda feels like a target. He dislikes it, but what can he do? "Um?…Oh, that letter about my suggestion that we go visit First Uncle in Shanghai? I meant no disrespect. It's just being realistic. Not only your generation is in old age; mine is almost there. We need to make plans to take care of ourselves. If one lives long enough, eventually he needs to be cared for by someone else. I have brought this up with you several times. You have not taken it seriously."

"You have always been direct toward your elders. You consider yourself someone extraordinary. Not really! You ought to remember all the help I had given you. That you have done relatively well in America is mainly because you had gone to St. John's and gotten all that training in English. Remember it was I who steered you to that direction. In your first year at St. John's Middle School, you failed in almost every subject. I helped your English lessons, and you survived. Remember?"

A frontal assault, or opening up a can of worms, or of wasps. Guoda is surprised at his father's interpretation of the facts. Yet what he said are facts, at least from his vantage. How about from my vantage? Guoda looks across the table at his father. An old man of 85, but at that moment, in the bright morning light, transmitted through the veranda and reflecting against the white walls of the living room, the face is stern, deep-set eyes shiny, sharp and penetrating, reminiscent of those that so intimidated him when he was young. They are so different from the grayish, listless ones when he saw him, standing behind Xian, only a couple of days ago. Guoda wants to fight back by retorting, for example, that, had he not been forced to skip grades so many times, he would not need help from anybody. But he keeps his peace.

Meanwhile, Fuli continues, "I remember that time in Hong Kong. You had just finished college and had the gall to slam the table in my presence." Either to illustrate the action being alluded to or to demonstrate his emotion, he bangs the table with his fist. The wooden top reverberates like a drum. "Then I ordered you to get the hell out of the apartment. Later I got your brother to find you and took you back."

Guoda is certain that Fuli is confusing the incident involving Frank, a toddler then, that led to his leaving home in Hong Kong, with that time, when he was still in high school in Shanghai, he tried to run away from home after being unjustly punished. Furthermore, he has never slammed the table at anybody before. How the old man gets the facts mixed up! Counter-attack, I can't lose! Or I can simply get up and walk out of here. He stands up, finger tips on the table. Fuli startles, recovers quickly, and says, "What are you going to do? You want to leave?...Leave! Leave then! I don't care! I am not afraid!"

Guoda clamps his mouth. The phone rings. Fuli doesn't make a move. Guoda goes over to the end table by the sofa to pick it up. It is Mrs. Ju; she is going to the market, wanting to know whether they would prefer chicken or duck for dinner.

"Whatever is more convenient for you," Guoda says. He isn't about to ask Fuli.

"All right then. You brothers take care of yourselves and the old gentleman," Mrs. Ju hangs up.

He hears his mother, "After I am gone you two brothers ought to treat your yaya nicely." He returns to his seat at the table.

"That was Mrs. Ju. Wasn't it?" Fuli asks.

Guoda clamps his mouth.

After a moment of silence, Fuli resumes, "You know the monthly remittance you sent me actually isn't that much either."

Guoda keeps mute. I don't deserve this.

"Your children, my grandchildren...I have no grandchildren. They don't pay any attention to me. They don't apply themselves...."

Guoda maintains his silence. He starts to recite in his head, "Our Father, which art in Heaven....Forgive our trespasses...." and he feels his body beginning to relax some, his stare softens, and suddenly the thought occurs to him that his father may be getting senile. But no!...Not having those fierce eyes and stern jaws.

Fuli does not challenge his silence. Seemingly running out of steam, he sits there with averted eyes. In a while, he gets up and goes to his room. Guoda returns to the magazine, looking at it blankly.

Around noon, Fuli comes out, hesitates a second and asks "Are you hungry?"

"I can have lunch now if you want it," Guoda says.

Fuli walks to the kitchen, saying, "We need only to warm up some left over food. I can do it. I have been an 'old maidservant' all these years."

For him, any house chore means a humiliation. Ignoring the gripe, Guoda says, "I'll do it," and proceeds with the kitchen job.

CHAPTER 39

On the morning of the requiem, the Jings set off to the city. Rende took his father's cane and walked down the stairs first. After Fuli locked the front door, Guoda tried to help him negotiate the stairs by holding his forearm. He jerked it away, complaining that, in that manner he was being hindered rather than helped. He showed Guoda how to put his hand under his armpit to properly provide the support. Outside the building, Rende handed him the cane; slowly they walked along the alley to the street, Guoda shielding him from the traffic, and hailed a taxi.

It took them to Cai Yuan Xing, a restaurant in the city featuring Shanghai food. Xian was waiting for them there. After lunch, Fuli shuffled slowly across the crowded dining room with the cane and Guoda by his side. A tall and trim waitress stopped and stood aside by the door waiting for them to pass. Fuli suddenly stopped, turned and moved closer to look at her face steadily and calmly through his eyeglasses, like a museum visitor appreciating a painting. Mortified, Guoda gave him a nudge and they continued their exit.

The temple was unlike any other Guoda had seen before—none of the massive gates and magenta walls and halls with prominent flying eaves. Outside it was like a modern institutional building, all concrete and glass. The lobby inside gave a similar impression. They announced the purpose of their visit to a worker in street clothes in an office and were directed to go upstairs.

The hall on the second floor was bright with natural window light. At the far end, a giant gold colored statue of Buddha glowed on a platform. A large vertical scroll hung on each side of the statue. On the right, "*Fo Guang Pu Zhao* (The light of Buddha shines on all)"; on the left, "*Hua Kai Xian Fo* (The flower opens to reveal Buddha)." In front of the platform a row of thick red candles lighted an altar, below which several cushions lay on the floor. In the middle of the hall was a long table. By the right side wall near the hall entrance, where the visitors were standing, was a shrine in which was set a paper plaque with the inscription: "The Seat of Grand Madame Mother Jing," illuminated by red candles. A middle-aged man in a black Chinese jacket and trousers was sweeping the floor near the Buddha. He paid no attention to the visitors. They sat down at a round table between the shrine and the door, and waited.

Shortly a fortyish man in a gray tunic, black trousers and puttee, walked briskly to them. Putting his palms together, he bowed slightly. A monk—he had nine burnt bald spots on his scalp. He told them that the chanting would be from the *Diamond Sutra*. They knew it was the name of a Buddhist Scripture, but not any more about it. The rite was for the deceased.

After he left, in a while, they heard the sound of drumbeat, followed by light clanging of cymbals and ringing of bells, then a male chorus. A team of monks in black robes debouched from the far end of the hall in a procession, chanting harmoniously. Six in all, led by the one who had met with them, each holding a musical instrument: a "wood fish"—a hollowed-out wood block shaped like a fish head producing a deep, hollow sound when struck—a pair of small cymbals, a small gong, a cup-shaped bell attached to the end of a rod, a bowl-shaped bell, and a small drum. Deliberately the monks moved in file to the altar, turned and stood in front of the Buddha for a while, bowed, and walked around the long table, their continuing chanting energizing the cavernous hall. After they lined into threes across the table, the chorus ceased. They sat down, and each opened a large book in front of him.

The chanting resumed, slowly, starting low, in unison, purling like a valley stream. Then one could hear tenor voices floating in counterpoint on top of the bassos, all in corrupt Sanskrit that none of the visitors understood. The pitch went low and it went high. It was pianissimo and then fortissimo. It was like morning lights dancing on wavelets in a pond. It was an ocean swell breaking on a rocky shore. The tempo was kept by the beat of the wood fish. When low, the chanting was punctuated by the crystal-like ringing of the bowl-bell. One segment featured a droning chorus—the sound seemed to come out from the tops of the hairless heads, resonating everything around, like a steady wind blowing through a deep canyon, and then like a thousand beehives warmed by the sun. At intervals, a change of rhythm would be signaled by the drum, and all instruments would join to rise in a mild crescendo and subside to an undulating murmur.

After the first crescendo, the middle-aged man in street clothes, who had swept the floor, came over and led Rende to the main altar. Rende knelt down in front of the Buddha. In a moment, they moved to the small shrine. Rende took several incense sticks, lighted them in a candle flame, and arranged himself in front of his mother's "seat." Like a drill sergeant, the man commanded him to kneel again, and then chanted, "Once...twice...thrice." In rhythm with the chanting, Rende kowtowed, rotating his trunk until his head touched the floor and moved back upright again.

After that, the monks rose and filed out of the hall. It was the first session. There would be a twenty-minute break and two more sessions to follow.

Rende was not asked to participate again until the middle of the third and final session. The sergeant led him to repeat the kowtow ritual. After he returned to the family's table, the monks ranged themselves in front of the small shrine. Their leader pulled up the paper plaque—"the Seat of Grand Madame Mother Jing"—accompanied by a sudden volume increase of the chanting. Then they returned to their long table and remained standing. The chorus lowered to a murmur, and the leader began to intone in a baritone. It was in Chinese, giving the name and address of the beneficiary of the requiem, and the chanters' supplication to Buddha to let her enter heaven. The leader handed the plaque to Rende. The monks moved to the main altar, kowtowed and then marched around the long table once more. "Dang—Dang—Qiang," two strikes of the gong followed by a crashing of the cymbals, "Dang—Dang—Qiang...Dang-Dang-Qiang—Dang—Qiang—Dang—Qiang...." the chanters in broad strides recessed through the door they came in.

Guoda knew that Rende went to church in California every Sunday with his family. But he was not surprised that Rende participated in the Buddhist ritual. They did not discuss the religious aspects of the event at all. In fact, they seldom discussed religion before or after, avoiding it as a pedantic, pretentious or even hypocritical subject, implicitly agreeing that it is essentially a private matter.

CHAPTER 40

❀

Mrs. Ju had done her work and left. They watched a variety show on television for a while, each making cursory comments on the performances. In a while, Rende was dozing on the sofa. The television was turned off. Guoda went to the magazine that had been his time filler in the last few days.

"Have you read that article about women's foot binding?" Fuli asked him.

"No, I have not. I know all I want to know about that heinous practice," Guoda said. He had not read the article but had glanced at a couple of sketches. One showed a young woman sitting on the edge of a bed with one leg bent over the other, unwinding the bandage. Another gave the dimensions of the disfigured foot as some objet d'art.

"You know these feet were considered to be quite erotic objects," Fuli said.

Objects? Erotic? Guoda was revulsed. Such talk is not only insulting to women in ordinary times, but at this hour? He wouldn't respond.

Fuli suddenly said to Rende, whose just-awake eyes were wide open staring at the dark television, "Xian was talking to me about the cost of the funeral. He said that that line of business is fraught with underhand practices. Do you have a list of the cost of the funeral, item by item?"

Guoda could not believe his ears.

"No. What's the point, list or no list? We have already signed an agreement. We are committed," Rende said matter-of-factly.

"Yaya, I think you are not being fair here," Guoda interjected. "Actually I think I have the costs of the items to make out the list you are talking about. But what's the use? I saw how Rende tried his hardest to get the best price he could. We walked up and down Ming Chuan East Road to get the job done properly. In actual dollars, I am not sure it was worth the time and effort. But we did it in order to save you money and have a respectable funeral for Mama." The brothers had felt that the more time they put in the task, the greater respect and love they were showing their mother, like a kind of atonement. "Rende has given you a statement from Yi De Company. Why would you not trust him?"

"You two are jumping to conclusions. It is not that I don't trust you brothers. But I don't trust that Cai."

"What good would do it now?" Rende reiterated, "We are committed."

Guoda could not understand why his brother was not as miffed as he. "You asked us to do a job," he said to his father, "and even if you don't question our integrity, are you questioning our judgment?"

"You are making too much out of this. All I want to make sure is that we are not cheated."

"How can you tell? Do you think you have a better idea on the proper pricing than we do?"

"You two brothers surely have a short temper," Fuli said.

"I don't think he does. I might have," Guoda said. "I have all the records. If you really want a list, I can sort the items out."

"OK, OK. Let's go to bed." Fuli went to his room.

Lying on the floor over his mother's comforter, Guoda said, "I really don't understand Yaya. How can he be so insensitive? Is he getting senile or something?"

"Either he is or we are, or all of us," Rende said. "Seriously, no, I don't think so. He couldn't possibly mean that his sons would be cheating him in managing their mother's funeral. That's absurd. He just wanted to talk. Old age—loneliness, you know. We are getting there ourselves. But he is kind of peculiar about money matters. Always has been, I know. I have lived with him much longer than you have. That's why I didn't get excited about it as you did…. But you did sound a bit touchy tonight…. We are all upset that Mama is gone."

On the morning of the obsequies, they arrived at the FMFP around half past seven. Mr. Cai was already there to supervise his workers at decorating the parlor. Outside the parlor, under the classical upturning eaves was hung a horizontal, yellow flower-fringed panel on which were attached large characters: "Hall of the Spirit of Venerated Mother Madame Jing Qisheng" above the garlanded columns of the portico.

The parlor—one of several within the FMFP—was some 10 yards wide and twice as deep. At the far end was an altar, in the middle of which was set a wreathed portrait of Qisheng. On each side of the altar stood a large floor lamp with a cluster of spherical lights. The altar was fronted by a long platform covered with white and red flowers. Behind the altar hung a curtain in the middle of which was attached a frame displaying a single large character: "Dien," (oblation). On each side of the frame draped strips of white cloths on which were written couplets extolling the virtues of the deceased in the voices of her spouse, children, grandchildren, relatives or friends. (The couplets were copied from standard compendiums by Yi De Company staff.) Along the walls close to the platform were gathered all the paper articles—a miniature house, an automobile, chests of gold and silver ingots, bags of money, etc. Beside the rows of chairs there were more flower baskets and panels along the side walls. As the room could not hold them all, many had to be placed outside the hall, on the portico and overflowing to the courtyard of the compound.

A friend of Rende's manned a booth in front of the parlor for people to sign in and deposit their condolatory messages in envelopes that usually contained cash gifts also. Several had come early and sat in the front row. One of them, an old friend of Qisheng, examined the paper items. Suddenly, she exclaimed, "Where are the servants?" Rende came over and said he was sure they were ordered. He looked around and about the agglomeration of paper articles and located a miniature paper male servant and female servant. The lady ordered Rende to place them near the paper mahjong table.

More people came. Xian told Guoda that he was wanted behind the parlor. All the individual parlors were connected at the rear to a corridor, on the other side of which was the mortuary. In the dim lighting, Guoda saw, standing by the mortuary door, a tall figure in a long flowing gown and wearing a tall flat-top hat—a Toaist priest. The ecumenicalism of the funeral rather aptly represented his mother's religious beliefs, he thought. Two workers rolled out the coffin on a gurney. The priest started to chant, leading the gurney toward the back of the parlor. The chanting was accompanied only by the pure ringing of a small bell he held in his hand almost hidden from view by the spacious sleeve like a huge pelican's pouch. Guoda and Rende followed, holding sticks of burning incense.

Inside the parlor, the coffin lay behind the curtain. Mr. Cai opened the casket for a final view. Guoda moved close. Mama is wearing a black gown embroidered with small carmine and white chrysanthemum patterns, and trimmed with edgings of pearls. Mrs. Ju has said that the gown was her favorite. The face is rouged and hair too neatly coifed. I liked it better last time with the flowing, more natural state. What difference does it make? She is not here.

Mr. Cai asked whether he could close the casket now. The brothers nodded and came out from behind the curtain to meet the early arrivals. Guoda heard chanting and ringing inside. And then the sound of pounding. Nails are being driven.

Pound! Pound! Pound! She is not there. Ai!…Ai!

Around nine o'clock, people began to come in a stream. Guoda knew less than half of them. Some would introduce themselves, saying that they had met years ago—ten, fifteen, twenty, or maybe even thirty. It did not matter. Guoda could not tell from the distorted faces anyway. He simply stood there and bowed to them ritually and repeated that the family was grateful for their presence.

Each visitor would come in front of the platform and bow three times. Rende, standing by at a slant to the altar, would bow to them in response. It was a relatively quiet ceremony except for the soft weeping of some lady friends and relatives. An hour or so later, the workers of Yi De Company began to carry the paper articles to a burner in the courtyard—a big perforated metal can. The paper house, automobile, refrigerator, TV, mahjong, etc. were all deposited inside it and lit by red candles to a burst of roaring flame.

The brothers rode in the hearse to the Second Municipal Funeral Parlor on Shin He Road at a foothill near the edge of the city. Fuli arrived by taxi. In front of Unit One, in which the body would be incinerated, was a small altar on which the same wreathed portrait of Qisheng stood with chrysanthemums, a plate of assorted fruits and a censer. Red candles burned in the open air with shivering flames, shedding blood-like tears.

Mr. Cai told the family that the incineration would begin in about an hour, and after the sons paid their respects, there would be no point to stand around; all could relax and wait in a café in the compound. Fuli said that he would like to pay his respects too.

"Customarily husbands are not supposed to do that," Mr. Cai said.

"Then I would insist on changing the custom," Fuli said. Aided by his cane, he walked slowly to the altar. Standing erect, he bowed three times, slowly and in apparent reverence—a few strands of white hair trembled in the air.

Guoda looks at his mother and sees a hint of a smile. Those fights when both had a full head of jet black hair. She would go along with him on almost everything except his girlfriends. Then again, the man had been there for her and supported her all those years, taking care of her responsibly, in sickness and health, cherished her in his own imperfect way. He took her mother under his wing over eight long war years, not one word of disrespect or gesture of displeasure to the old lady personally, nor about her to others. That was decency.

Rende bowed three times.

It was Guoda's turn. He wanted to say a prayer, but he didn't know what to say. He felt half of his cylinders were not firing. He managed, "Dear God, have mercy on this gentle and good woman, my Mama."

Following Rende, he also put some paper money into one of the stone burners around the courtyard. He felt like a boy playing at it. Like everything else since he arrived in Taiwan a few days ago, at age 63, he was just following his elder brother's lead.

Fuli left in a taxi. The brothers waited in the café. In about half an hour, a worker called them to the altar.

The door of Unit One opens with a clang, and a gurney is rolled out. On a large metal tray lie the ashes in the pattern of a human form. Like a tooth given a shot of novocaine, Guoda has been for some time numbed. The powdery outline still gives him a jolt, as when the dentist's drill gets too close to an incompletely drugged nerve. The worker hands Rende a pair of tongs. He picks up some of the larger bones to deposit them into an urn. Guoda follows, reciting in his mind, "Ashes to ashes; dust to dust…"

CHAPTER 41

❀

Guoda looked blankly outside the taxi window. People were hustling, and cars stopping and going in the Taipei traffic. He said to Rende, "You are leaving on the 14th, right?"

"Yes. I have to set a definite date. Otherwise, he'd take the initiative and have me wrapped up, waiting for his decision. Lots of business are waiting for me back at the motel."

"He is going to stay with you?"

"If he wants to…What can I say? He is my father. I have called Aili. She is psychologically prepared for that."

"I must say you are a filial son, a better son than I am."

"I don't know about that. As I said, he is my father," Rende said.

"It seems that I could not help getting into an argument with him every time I open my mouth. There are just too many things that I disagree with him philosophically."

"Do you still resent the pressure he put on you when you were young?"

"It was not simple pressure. Sometimes I thought it was more like a child being thrown into the river—you swim or sink."

"Perhaps into a swimming pool and being watched."

"I could have drowned."

"You didn't."

"But still, today, I don't know why he would want me to skip those grades. You know I was not that superior a student. I was a fairly good student, if I worked hard, at best a B-minus material."

"C-plus," Rende said.

Guoda felt deflated, but good and relaxed.

At the airport, Rende went ahead to get the export permit for the ashes as Guoda stood in line for checking in. Both done, they waited in a coffee shop to escape the heavy cigarette smoke in the lobby. Nearing boarding time, at the passenger check-in station, Guoda shook his brother's hand, "Thank you for everything."

"What have I done?"

"You know what I mean—for taking care of everything."

"Bon voyage."

"Take care," Guoda said. As he picked up his travel bag from the rack past the X-ray machine, he turned and saw his thickset brother, moving with a straddling gait disappearing into the crowd. He thought of all the work ahead of his good-hearted brother in the next couple of weeks, and beyond—particularly the part in having to deal with their father.

Guoda had thought he would rest after getting on the plane. But he found himself chained in a conversation with a handsome woman passenger until he took out his wallet and showed her the pictures of his granddaughters. The woman never spoke to him again in sentences longer than two words. He alternated between reading a history book and closing his eyes trying to sleep; but scenes of childhood and his mother kept coming on. He heard a bell, followed by a PA announcement to ask that seat belts be fastened as the plane was to go through a jet stream. Shortly he felt the seat belt pressed against the belly. The plane was dropping. It did so fitfully, over no more than a minute. It was a frightening sensation—of having lost support. "Without mother, one loses prop," as said in the *Book of Songs*.

When Jiafeng met him in the airport, she said, "You have lost some weight."

"I have lost more than that."

Fuli lived in Orange City, California, for about two months before he returned to his apartment in Taiwan. Later on, in a letter to Guoda, he wrote, "...Your sister-in-law overly cares about cleanliness in the house...."

That October, Guoda and Jiafeng went to Orange City. Aili told them, "I picked up and cleaned after him often. He wouldn't bother to lift up the toilet seat. In the beginning I dared not to speak to him about it. Finally, I suggested to him, as softly as I could, to be a bit more mindful with the bathroom; apparently he was displeased."

The brothers and their wives rode to the Rose Hill Memorial Park in Whittier. Their mother's black marble plaque was planted on a grassy hillside facing west and overlooking the city of Monterey. Rende fumbled in front of the plaque, located a buried water receptacle, and filled it from a drinking fountain nearby. They inserted into it the carnations they had brought along. In silence they bowed their heads in the sun. After a while, Rende said, "Looking down the slope, she could see the Chinese characters on the shop fronts in Monterey. She was always afraid of cold. She would enjoy this California sun."

CHAPTER 42

At first Guoda wasn't sure what he was going to do after retirement. But he was sure of what he was not going to do, namely, to remain in engineering, or sit in some rocking chair with a cup of tea in hand. He had thought of studying history, even formally enrolling as a student, or of editing the poems he had written with the hope to assemble them into a little volume. The former he thought too bookish, too little creative challenges. Of the latter he had doubts about the poems' worthiness. So he returned to what he had considered for some time—fiction writing. He tried his hand at a short story, weaving one about the malfeasance of a Communist cadre in a Chinese village. The exercise gave him some confidence.

Not long after he had sent a copy to his father, he was called to Taiwan; the trip ended with his mother's funeral. Returning to the U.S., he had problems with sleeping, suffered nausea and a general malaise, and lost weight and hair. He underwent another incident of stomach bleeding, fainted on the floor, and after regaining consciousness, spewing mouthfuls of fresh blood.

But he recovered. By April, two years later, when his colleagues gave him his retirement party, he pretty much knew what he was going to do. He was going to write.

In July he went to Taiwan to visit his father in the hospital. After he had made arrangements to have Fuli move to a nursing home upon the completion of the first stage of treatment for tuberculosis, he returned to America.

Subsequently, Rende went over there. Their father seemed to be on the mend, adjusting to the nursing home, although he still complained that the helper was too strict, as he had done to Guoda about the caretaker in the hospital. In the latest update to Guoda, Rende said, "…Yaya has been doing fine. He should feel even better now; I just bought a pneumatic mattress for him today to prevent bed sores…."

But a few days later, Mrs. Ju phoned, "The old gentleman was gone!" It was soon confirmed by Rende's call. Their father had died of pneumonia. "When are you coming?"

"Right away," Guoda answered the peremptory question.

On the day of Fuli's funeral, before the body was placed into the casket, Guoda went over to the gurney, had a last viewing. His father seemed little changed, with his strong nose and thin lips. The rouge on the face softened the stern cast some. Guoda laid his hand on his father's wrist. Last chance. The initial shock of the iciness was soon overcome. He grasped it and felt warmth in the bodily contact. In fairness, I owe him more than he did me. In spite of the sufferings he caused me in my youth, while he could well be himself without me, I couldn't be what I am without him, not only biologically. Guoda bowed his head.

In the apartment, the brothers looked at all the books on the shelves, the wardrobe, full of clothes, including several new suits and a overcoat, which were, as Fuli had proudly told them, tailor-made in Regent Street, London—on that trip he took after Priscilla's wedding. They decided that they would leave those as well as such items as the refrigerator and the air-conditioner to Mrs. Ju. They'd try to sell the apartment later.

Guoda returned to America, leaving Rende to take care of the rest. Two weeks later, Rende called saying that he had arranged another memorial service—a Christian one this time—at the Rose Hill Memorial Park in Whittier, where Fuli's ashes and marble plaque would be placed beside their mothers'. Guoda was weary of travelling and asked Michael, who now lived in Foster City, California, to represent his side of the family at the ceremony, which Michael did gladly.

Guoda had the use of his office at the university for a few months before the chair told him to move to one of the cubicles in a large room—the green pastures for retired professors. He had sent most of his books and journals to Hunan University. With the rest of the books and his notes, etc., he invited his graduate students to help themselves. Then he told the department secretary that whatever was left in the office should be disposed of by the building custodian. Later she called Guoda to reconfirm the request, saying, "Are you sure you want to get rid of them all? There is still so much in the room. After all, those are your decades of work," she sounded admonitory and commiserating.

One afternoon, he stepped out of the office for the last time, pulled the door behind him, and hearing the clicking of the tongue of the lock, walked on. He was going to the Main Library. As he came to the Blue Orchid River footbridge, the quivering light over the stream slowed him. He went over to the railing. Everything looked and sounded just as 35 years ago, the redbud branches overhanging from the banks, the ducks, the singing of the weir, laughter of the young ambling past. A fallen spray flowed by, the leaves, golden in the sun, a couple of pods trailing. He gazed at them for a while and moved on, to get the book they were holding for him.

0-595-27709-8